# SERPENT IN MY CORNER

# SERPENT IN MY CORNER

## JDaniels

**BET Publications, LLC**
http://www.bet.com

SEPIA BOOKS are published by

BET Publications, LLC
c/o BET BOOKS
One BET Plaza
1900 W Place NE
Washington, DC 20018-1211

All Kensington Titles, Imprints, and Distributed Lines are available at special quantity discounts for bulk purchases for sales promotions, premiums, fund-raising, and educational or institutional use. Special book excerpts or customized printings can also be created to fit specific needs. For details, write or phone the office of the Kensington special sales manager: Kensington Publishing Corp., 850 Third Avenue, New York, NY 10022, attn: Special Sales Department, Phone: 1-800-221-2647.

BET Books is a trademark of Black Entertainment Television, Inc. SEPIA and the SEPIA logo are trademarks of BET Books and the BET BOOKS logo is a registered trademark.

ISBN 1-58314-375-0

First Printing: July 2003
10 9 8 7 6 5 4 3 2 1

Printed in the United States of America

# 1

Los Angeles, California . . . Tristan

"T.J.! I can't go any farther. I just can't!" Natalie cried. She looked at me with a pained, aching expression. Sweat beads streamed down her face. I knew she was tired. I knew this whole thing had been too much for her, but she had insisted on coming along. Both of us could hear Hawk honking loudly for us to come on after we had snatched up the Renaissance Jewels. I was fighting hard to get Nat to hurry; police cars were roaring out, their sirens blaring, in search of the culprits, namely me, Natalie, Reynolds, and Hawk.

"Come on, baby, it's not much farther," I said, encouraging her. She ran behind me at a quick pace. Having been reassured of her presence, I quickened my own pace, racing steadily toward the slow-moving vehicle. I could still hear Nat running swiftly behind me as I got to the tinted minivan. Reynolds slid the side door open quickly.

"Man, what took you two so long?" Hawk spat from the driver's seat. I looked at him incredulously and handed Reynolds the thick vinyl case that housed the Renaissance Jewels. Somewhere in the deep recesses of my mind I thought of Nat, who had been right behind me. I looked around to see *her still running toward the van frantically, her auburn hair swinging wildly in her face. I sensed, rather than heard, the gunshots. Nat's eyes meshed with mine as bullets shattered through her slim, beautiful frame. She swung around as if to block them, as more iron pellets coursed through her. My mouth opened and closed in a silent scream; my body went on auto-pilot as I fought to make my way out of the van, only to have Reynolds fighting to keep me inside while Hawk quickly sped away from the bloody scene. All I could see was the look of be-trayal and pain in her eyes. I had left her, and she was dead.*

*Natalie! Natalie! Natalie!*

"No!" I screamed. I sat up with a start. My nightmare of Natalie's death was never ending, neither was my guilt. I ran my hands over my sweat-covered face, taking a deep breath. I got up and walked over to my bedroom window, looking out to the ocean with its sudsy waters washing up against the hot sands. Sleep was not my friend and hadn't been since that fate-ful night one year ago when my actions had finally come to roost. When the god of good luck had laughed at me, finally asking for payback for my sins. Payback, which had cost me the woman I loved. After her death, I took a break from my *ca-reer*, trying to find meaning in everything that had happened, and in what my actions had done to a beautiful, innocent angel named Natalie.

I looked at her portrait that still sat on my nightstand. The same look appeared to be in her eyes, the same accusing stare I had seen that last moment she had looked into mine. I closed my eyes as the intense pain washed over me anew.

"One more job, baby," I whispered to myself hauntingly. "Then I'll give this up; I promise, I promise. . . ."

My promise was more for me than her. She couldn't hear me, I knew that much. I didn't believe, as most people do, that the dead were in some spiritual realm watching over us and lis-tening to our prayers. Natalie was gone; her thoughts had per-ished and she was now sleeping in a forever death.

But no matter what, I would keep my promise to her. This would be my last robbery. . . .

*Washington, DC . . . Hennessy*

My breath heaved as I ran up the six flights of stairs that I opted to take instead of waiting for the elevator. I knew I was late, but I was *always* late. And I didn't feel like hearing Sebastian's mouth again about irresponsibility, nor hear him joke about how women and the FBI did not mix. You see, Sebastian was old school, he believed in the man take charge, woman cook that chicken and stir them peas deal. And what was even more amazing? He believed that men were actually doing women a *favor* by ruling the roost so to speak. It was men like him that served always to remind me that I could do bad all by myself, and be good at it, *without* a man.

I didn't have time to stop for a quick look in the mirror before running to his office, even though I could only imagine what my hair must have looked like after my whipping out of the cab and up those stairs like I did. So I stopped at the door, took a deep, needed breath, fixed a confident smile on my face, and waltzed in to face Special Agent Sebastian Rogers.

"You're late."

"I'm sorry; I had a hard time getting a cab," I breathed.

"You always have a hard time getting a cab, Hennessy. This isn't Manhattan or Brooklyn; you make enough money to afford a vehicle. You just have not gotten that dirty city out of your mind." Sebastian lit a cigar as he spoke, blowing on the lit end to watch the flames flicker.

"Oh, and DC is supposed to be a *clean* city?" I asked sarcastically. "Last time I checked, whether or not I had a car was not a requirement. Besides, I use the metal heaps here." I smiled.

Sebastian smiled back. "You walk everywhere, whether we supply you with a car or not. But I guess it doesn't matter. The job I have for you now won't call for one."

"Why have you been so secretive about it?" I asked. I had known that he had a special case for me, but he hesitated to tell me exactly what it was. Knowing Sebastian, it was probably some off-the-wall excursion that he knew I wouldn't want to get involved m.

"This man." He handed me an eight-by-ten, black-and-white photo. It was a black man, handsome devil, too, with a face that looked almost sculptured in its perfection.

"Ohh, who is this sexy papi?" I crooned, smiling up mis-chievously at Sebastian.

"Put your tongue back in your mouth; that face you're swoon-ing over is the one and only T.J. Jackson, one of the biggest crim-inals in the country, a big-time tycoon. He's into everything, jewel theft, illegal gambling, and for a while there, he was into overseas drug trafficking. You name it, he's top dog at it. And I want him." Sebastian had a cool, determined look on his face. He was a six-four giant of a man, with cool blue eyes and brown hair peppered with gray that betrayed the forty-five years he had lived. Even his body was one of a man fifteen years his junior. Regardless of his caveman attitude and ideas, I knew that I couldn't ask for a better ASAC, Assistant Special Agent in Charge. And even though he had many special agents under him, he would take care of a lot of situations by himself, show-ing his dedication to the job. I would always jokingly tell Sebastian that when I grew up I wanted to be just like him.

"Figures, with a face like that he would have to be the devil's seed." I sighed, looking at his photo wistfully. "So, he's a thief, one of millions if I may add. What's so special about him that they would go federal on him?"

"He's not just a thief, Hennessy. Here, read his profile." He handed me a manila folder.

I have to admit I was impressed. T.J. Jackson was infamous. And he had been involved in many high-profile robberies, or at least, suspected of being the head honcho in charge. I flipped through more pages in his profile. Suspicion of his involvement was just about it, they had absolutely nothing on him.

"Sebastian, you have nothing on this guy. What's the point of pushing things if you can't get him?"

"Who can't get him?" Sebastian huffed. "That's the god-damn problem right there. He thinks he is so smart, so un-touchable, that he can do whatever the hell he wants. Look at his profile again, Hennessy. A couple of the robberies that he is suspected of were in federal museums. We're talking millions of dollars here, millions of federal dollars!"

"Were there any murders at any of these heists?"

Sebastian paused before he spoke.

"Well, were there?" I pressed.

"No," Sebastian said, blinking rapidly as he spoke. He cleared his throat. "No, there were no murders. He's too smart for that. He's also too smart to leave anything behind that would point the finger at himself, or anyone in his entourage."

"Okay, then how do you plan to get him when . . ." I flipped through the pages in the profile folder Sebastian had given me. "When from appearances, most of these cases have been closed as unsolvable?"

Getting up slowly, then leaning on his desk with both arms, Sebastian said gruffly, "There are *no* unsolvable cases. Only the ones weak agents, or those too lazy to put forth the effort, simply give up on. You know me, Hennessy. I don't give up on any-thing. But now," Sebastian said, as he grabbed the manila folder from my hands and threw it on his desk, "none of those past robberies are my concern right now. We have an informant that has given us pertinent information about Jackson's next job. It's scheduled for one month from now."

"O . . . kay, and you need me to do what?" I asked, although I could almost guess what Sebastian's next words were going to be.

Sebastian hesitated a moment, then coughed out, "Deep cover."

"Sebastian! You know I told you I didn't want to go deep cover anymore; come on now, you know what I went through before!" I exclaimed. Sebastian of all people knew that I wanted to keep my head above water; no more deep undercover work for me, and now he had the gall to come at me with this!

"Hennessy, we cannot go into this walking blind. We need an agent who can watch step by step and be a star eyewitness once we get his ass. There will be some ancient Egyptian artifacts transferred to the Metropolitan Museum of Art in a month. We are almost certain that T.J. Jackson plans to steal these artifacts." Sebastian smiled and then paused briefly as he walked over to his coffeemaker to pour himself a cup. He nodded toward it, asking if I wanted some, which I politely declined. "You see, we *want* him to steal these pieces," he finally said. "He thinks he's going to get away with it, as he always has. He thinks he's smarter than our agency. But he won't get away, not this time. It would insult my intelligence if he did, and I can't have that," Sebastian hissed angrily. "This time, I'm one step ahead of him."

"You're right, nobody is smarter than you, darling," I said flatly. I was still seething over his announcement. "But why me? Why am I the pick of the litter for Jackson?"

"Well, after going over all of the agents we have available, I came to one conclusion. You have four things going for you: you're smart, beautiful, female, and you're a native New Yorker. According to our informant—"

"Just who the hell is this informant?"

"Don't worry about that right now, Hennessy, I'll fill you in on it later," Sebastian said impatiently. "Just trust me that he's reliable, okay? But like I was saying, Jackson is looking for a female accomplice to join his team, and he will be less suspicious of you. So you see you're the perfect agent to snag this fancy cat." Sebastian tapped me softly on the edge of my chin. "Look, I know you've had your reservations about deep cover work again, but you are also a dedicated FBI agent. And this time things will be different, I promise you. It's a very short assignment, and if you take the case, I will recommend you for that ASAC promotion that you've been dying to get."

"You mean you would recommend me to become your equal?"

Sebastian laughed. "Oh, never that."

"You really think you're slick, don't you, Sebastian?" I said, smirking at him.

"Are you prepared to tell me you don't want this job?"

I sighed. The asshole knew me too well. Sebastian grinned at my expression.

"Your plane leaves for LA at six P.M., so I guess you better get home and get to packing."

## Malibu Beach . . . Tristan

It was quiet over the beach waters; only the soft, soulful sounds of my stereo system could be heard, flowing from the wide picture windows of my elegantly decorated beachfront home. It was odd to those who knew me from way back in my Compton days that now I had become somewhat of a recluse. Back then I was loudness itself. But what a lot of people don't understand is that most people aren't in the projects, hood, ghetto, or whatever term is politically correct, because they want to be; most are there because they have no choice.

I was raised the only son of Jillian Jackson, reformed crack fiend mama and streetwalker. I thought about my mother whenever I heard the "Dear Mama" cut off one of Tupac Shakur's CDs. That was my mama for sure. I never knew my dad. I do know that he was some dude she had met at a block party, kicked it with him one night, and now could hardly remember his face. That is unless she was looking into mine. One thing that my mom has always said is that my father had light brown eyes with green circles around the irises, just like mine. And he was tall, like me. And I even once heard her tell one of her girlfriends that basically the bootie was so good with her that night, it was like he took a good shit and out came me. Now that's a good way to describe your kid, right? Like I'm a good piece of shit.

I grew up in the mix, the way most kids in the hood did. Wore my blue colors proudly, and could be counted on as trigger finger, somebody who would put a cap in a nigga with no second thought. That attitude and the carjacking and drugs landed me in a boys' home more times than I could count, which eventually led me into the big house at age eighteen. I was one scared brotha. Just knew one of those big, tattooed niggas or spics was waiting for a young dude like me to make a woman out of me. And for a while, I spent so much time fighting off sissies I didn't have time to think about anything else, like trying to do my time and get my life together so that I wouldn't ever have to come back in the hole. I got lucky though; I got a connection with a professional. I mean a *real* serious pro. Earl Walhman was his name. This dude knew his shit, a McGyver imitator. Earl had to have been one of the smoothest of smooth when it came to slipping in and out costly artifacts from the most prestigious museums both abroad and in the United States. His last job, he had told me, could have set him moneywise for life if he had been able to pull it off. Unknown to himself, he had a rat in his corner. A rat who spilled everything to the FBI. Once he realized that he had been betrayed, it was too late. With federal agents and police surrounding him, his infamous career as a master jewel thief was over. Couldn't help but wonder how someone as smart as he was could have let himself get caught. I never did get a straight answer to that, but what I did get was the best training in high-tech robbery since Bonnie and Clyde. I spent nine years in training, learning from Earl and pumping the iron so that I wouldn't have to keep worrying about getting caught, shackled, and womanized.

Earl also taught me some other things. Like dropping the homeboy image and hood lingo. Earl's strategy was, a good thief doesn't look the part, and a good thief is the ultimate actor. So Earl trained me also to be cultured, polite, and well mannered. He taught me everything he knew.

Once I was released at age twenty-six, I didn't look or act anything like the cocky eighteen-year-old Compton crip I had been when first coming in. I was T.J. Jackson, stylish, handsome, mature, ripe, and ready for the world. Six years later, at the age of thirty-two, I'm rich, stylish, mature, smart, hand-some, and still reaching for the gusto.

I stretched, jumping as my pager went off, and quickly ran up to my house to grab my phone. "Damn, I should have brought my cordless with me," I said out loud to myself.

"Hello," I said, breathing heavy.

"Is this T.J. Jackson?" came a soft feminine voice.

"And who wants to know?"

She cleared her throat, before saying, "Well, I'm Hennessy Lewis, and I had a meeting scheduled with you for eleven A.M. I was just doing a double check to make sure that we're still on."

The name didn't push a button. "Hennessy Lewis . . . how come I don't recall setting up any meeting with you?" I asked, cocking an eyebrow slightly.

"Look, Mr. Jackson, don't waste my time. I've come a long way to see you."

Who the hell was this woman? "Look, lady, who did you talk with?"

"I talked with a man who said he knew you, and that you were looking for someone like me, in my field. Listen," she said, in a whispery voice, "I really don't feel like discussing this over the phone. I don't trust Verizon, if you get my meaning. Can I just come by and we talk about it?"

I looked at my watch. It was 10:15 A.M. "Okay, look, come by my place in about forty-five minutes. We can talk for a minute. After that, I got shit to do. And whoever you are, woman, don't play with me, I'm not a man you'd want to toy with, you understand?"

"Neither am I, T.J. Jackson. See you at eleven. . . ."

*Hennessy*

Wow, didn't know if I had played the tough girl act too much; didn't want to run Jackson away. But something told me that if I played the dumb female, it wouldn't roll over too well with a guy like him. I had been practicing saying my new name all morning, trying to be sure that I didn't slip up. Undercover work took acting skills to the limit, at least *my* acting skills. I had had so many aliases I'd lost count, but the name Lewis rolled pretty easily off my tongue; so I knew I'd get used to it sooner or later.

I dressed carefully in my Beverly Hills hotel room. Sebastian had spared no expense in making me look the part of a sharp, East Coast–born cat thief. I looked in the mirror and a tall, caramel-complexioned woman with big brown eyes and thick but well-groomed eyebrows looked back at me. I smiled, causing the deep dimpled grooves in each cheek to stand out. "It's gonna be fun playing cat and mouse with this crook," I said aloud to myself, thinking about the handsome face I had seen in the picture. Of course, I was totally professional. But foine was foine, and if the real thing was any close resemblance to the photo, well . . .

I was to get in tight with him, make him trust me, flirt a little, Sebastian had said. *Work that feminine charm like only you can, Hennessy.* I giggled to myself. "Let's go work it, girl! Some jobs are so much more fun than others."

I went out to my waiting taxi to finally go meet the one and only T.J. Jackson.


"Good Lord," I said, "somebody's got bank!"

Jackson lived on the beach, actually like a private beach house, but not small at all. He had *good* taste; his house was all windows, raised high upon a hilly bed of red sand. The same colored sand that surrounded the whole beach. I had never seen sand this red before. And this was not the first time that the bureau had sent me to the West Coast undercover. While I stood admiring the beauty around me, the front door opened.

"Hennessy Lewis, I take it?"

"T.J. Jackson?" I responded, although I didn't need to ask. He looked *exactly* like his picture, if not better. The black-and-white photo hadn't done justice to his coppery brown complexion, and especially hadn't done justice to his eyes. I smiled softly, remembering that I was to be strong, firm, yet sensual, qualities that Jackson was supposed to like in women.

He gave me an up-and-down look, slowly if you will, finally resting on my lips and eyes. "So, Ms. Lewis, what can I do for you?" he asked, walking away from the door with his back to me. I guess that was my invitation to come in, so I did.

"I was admiring your red sands; they're beautiful," I said sweetly.

"I think so, too. Okay, when do you plan on telling me what's up?"

Dang, he didn't waste any time, did he? I could see that I was going to have to resize Mr. Jackson. Sebastian may have had him, and his taste in women, off a bit.

"I was told you are looking for associates to help you on a job."

"And what job is that?" he asked suspiciously.

"Is this a joke?" I asked hotly. "I came to LA because I was told you were looking for the best, and I know that *I'm* the best. Now are you telling me that it's all a hoax? That you are not looking for a professional?" I walked over to his black leather couch and sat down. "Leo Jenson contacted me, told me that you were looking for a female who could *help* you with something. Ring a bell?" I asked, crossing my legs and staring him down.

"Okay, now you're talking," he said, sitting down on the glass table in front of me. I breathed a silent sigh of relief; I was starting to feel like he was going to ask so many questions it would give me away. Of course, Leo Jenson hadn't called me, we had contacted him, at least Sebastian had. With our having him on four counts of robbery, he was only too happy to cooperate and be the informant for Jackson.

"I haven't heard from Leo in a while, so I didn't know what had happened to him. He did tell me he would have someone calling me soon." Jackson looked me over again. "You're a little bigger than what I had expressed to him though; I told him I needed a petite woman."

"Excuse me?" My face got hot. "I am not big!" The nerve of him! I was not a tiny woman, but I was definitely not fat. I hadn't an inch of excess on my body, and worked out religiously. I was just a strong, muscular woman. Hmph!

"Hey, chill out." He laughed. "I wasn't calling you fat; I'm just saying I needed a small-framed woman, which you're not. You're more on the muscular side." He looked me up and down. "It looks good on you though; you're still very feminine." He winked.

*And now he's trying to kiss up,* I thought with a smirk. "Well, petite or not, Mr. Jackson, there is no hole I cannot slip through." I looked him over again. He wasn't small either; not necessarily a big man, but tall, with abs that other men would kill for. I looked down at his tight stomach, and then my eyes rested lower, on the bulge in his pants. I swallowed, looking away quickly. When I looked back up at his eyes, they had a teasing, amused look in them. Damn it, he had watched me watching him. T.J. Jackson knew exactly the effect he had on women.

"Listen, why don't we go have lunch? I know a nice quiet place in Beverly Hills; we can get comfortable and see whether or not we really do have a mutual interest. How about that?" he asked.

"Sounds good; I missed breakfast, and I'm a bit hungry, although not to the point of *gluttony,*" I said pointedly.

T.J. Jackson looked at me, laughing a deep sexy laugh as we headed out the door. The man had warmth and a sense of humor. Hmm. . . .

*Sebastian . . . what have you gotten me into?*

# 2

Beverly Hills, California . . . Tristan

I picked Shelly's for lunch, being that it was not only quiet and had a fantastic view, but if you were lucky enough to get one of the tables on the second floor, you could almost see past the city smog to the beautiful hilly view that was Beverly Hills. Also the service was superb.

It was hard to say what kind of impression I was getting of Hennessy Lewis. I am, and have always been, a very cautious person, with good reason. But one thing I could say was that she was extremely beautiful. I had to snicker as we walked into Shelly's. Looking at her from behind, I found her "I'm not fat" comment hilarious; she was a feisty one, and no, she wasn't fat by *any* means.

We were seated at my regular table, me being in pretty good with the manager. Hennessy had a serene look on her face, as if the warm California air agreed with her.

"So, tell me about you."

"What would you like to know?" she asked softly.

A smiling blond waitress walked up to our table, briefly halting our conversation. We ordered, me opting for crab cakes over seasoned scalloped potatoes, and a salad, with Hennessy following suit by ordering the same.

"But I'd like Caesar in place of tossed please, with dressing on the side. Oh! And could you please be sure that my crab cakes are well done? I hate mushy fish." I was amused; the lady was picky.

"Okay," she said, looking up at me. I straightened my face, trying not to let my amusement with her show. "You wanted to know more about me. For one, I'm a native New Yorker, born and bred in Yonkers, but right now I'm living in Manhattan, with definite goals of resettling elsewhere. But of course that takes money."

I made some mental notes of what she was saying; for sure I was going to check her history out, even down to who her last lover was.

"You do have that slight Yonkers drawl." I laughed. "So, you said that you were the best; tell me exactly what you are the best *in*," I said.

"Well, what do you think, Mr. Jackson?" She inched closer, moving her lips slowly. "I'm a thief, and a damn good one; now what about you?"

"Well, I wouldn't define myself as a thief, as you are so free to do, but let's just say I take advantage of opportunities. I do whatever I *need* to do," I said calmly.

The waitress returned with our drinks and salads, Hennessy thanking her politely. "I've heard about your reputation, Mr. Jackson. Leo sang your praises."

"How did you meet Leo?"

"Oh, we've worked together before, in DC. I lived there briefly after college."

"Leo is from DC, but I can't remember him ever having mentioned anyone by your name. You do have a very unusual name. Hennessy," I stated, feeling it roll off my tongue. "How'd you come about it?"

"How do you think I came about it? The same way that everyone gets their name. My mama named me," she said, grinning. This lady had it going on with her dimpled smile.

"Well, I was just wondering if your mom was maybe getting

her drink on with some Hennessy the night you were born or something."

"Afraid not," she said, laughing out loud. It was interesting how she covered her mouth when she laughed. She must have worn braces as a teen, I thought, but I'd find that out, too. I made another mental note in my head. We ate quietly for a while, both obviously trying to feel each other out.

"What about you, smarty-pants? What does T.J. stand for?" she asked, after having polished off a crab cake.

"Tristan James Jackson."

"Tristan? Wow, the Knights of the Round Table, hmm?"

"If you say so." I smirked. "So are you a lady-in-waiting?"

"Well, I am a lady who is *waiting* to know what you think of her so that she can know when to expect to get paid. And I would also like to know the complete ins and outs of this job."

"And you should also know that I won't tell you anything until I have thoroughly checked you out. You do know that, right?" I was hoping that this woman didn't take me for a fool, or think that I got where I am by falling for every pretty-face and tight-ass woman that smiled my way.

"You'd be a fool not to, Tristan Jackson," she said, as if reading my mind. "And I would never work with a fool. I expected a background check."

"Good, then we understand each other. So tell me . . ." I waited for her to look at me directly, wanting to be sure to look into her eyes. "Are you a federal agent?" A few seconds went by, with us looking eye to eye. She didn't flinch.

"Do I look like a federal agent, Tristan?"

"Looks can be deceiving, Hennessy. . . ."

"Point well taken," she said. With the elegance of a swan, she wiped her mouth with a white napkin and smiled.


*Hennessy*

I would call my lunch with Tristan Jackson interesting to say the least. It's funny; he speaks very well and without street slang. I found that a bit odd, seeing that Sebastian had said he was an ex-gang member and originally from Compton, a place notorious for street and gang violence. There was also the fact that he spent nine years in the penitentiary. I couldn't help but wonder just how a street thug evolved into the polite, cultured man I had lunch with.

As I sat relaxing in my warm bubble bath, the musical sounds of my cell phone jarred me. "Hello?" It was Sebastian. "I should have guessed it would be you." I smiled.

"Okay, then you must know what I want to know," he said.

"Well, we met. And had lunch."

"So, what happened during lunch?"

"He really didn't tell me anything; but he's a very intelligent man, Sebastian. He did say, a couple of times actually, that he was going to have me checked out. As long as there are no loops in my cover, everything should be fine."

"Loops? Hennessy, come on, just who do you think you're dealing with? Your whole life history is fixed. Jackson will only see exactly what we want him to." Sebastian sounded confident.

A picture of T.J. Jackson's face came to my mind. "Okay, if you say so. I'm just saying that we may have underestimated him a bit, but you're the boss, so . . . ."

"That's right, I'm the boss," Sebastian said smugly. "So, does he like you?"

"I guess he likes me all right."

"No, does he seem attracted to you, like you could get in close with him, find out things?"

I laughed a little, wiping some of the soap bubbles from the end of the tub with my painted toes. "Sebastian, what makes you think he would like me anyhow? Just because I'm black, then a black man would, of course, be interested?"

"No, because you are also very beautiful, and I'm betting on Jackson to notice it, and to take heed; that is, if you play your cards right."

"And if he does become interested, then what?"

"Well, I'm not telling you to sleep with him or anything.

After all, you're an agent, not some whore." Sebastian had the nerve to sound embarrassed. I giggled a bit at his tone. "But definitely play him like a fine guitar. I want his ass, I told you, and you can get him if you're smart about it, Hennessy, and then of course, safe about it also."

"I'm always safe, darling."

"Not always," he said, obviously talking about the job I had done a year ago, trapping a child pornography king, which had almost gotten me killed. I was a risk taker, especially when I was feeling something deeply.

"Listen, Sebastian, if that's it, then I'm gonna go now, okay? My skin is starting to do the shrivel thing."

"Later, beautiful."

"Whatever, you faker!" I laughed, hanging up quickly. I had to think of my next move. As it was, Tristan had left me hanging, where I really didn't *have* a move until he got in touch with me. Smart *move* on his part, I thought, smiling.

*Compton, south central LA . . . Tristan*

It's odd how differently one can see things, once you've grown up, or rather grown past it. I got out of my car slowly, with the sun beaming down on me in south central LA. Kids on their roller blades gliding past me; round-the-way girls braiding hair on the front porch. And the typical homeboys chillin', still chillin', like always, on the corners. I sighed, shaking my head as I made my way up the stairs to my mom's front door. I knocked softly, and then looked around again at the street where I had grown up. I sure as hell didn't miss it. When I thought about my childhood, I had no fond memories. Only memories of a struggle just to survive on these vicious streets.

"Come on in!" my mom screamed. I opened the screen door slowly. My mom had also lived in this neighborhood all of her life, yet she would still leave the door unlocked as if she didn't know the danger of it.

"You really should keep this door locked, Mom," I said.

"Oh, ain't nobody gonna mess with me. I'm glad you're here though. I need money, baby, really bad."

"For what, Mom?" I asked, irritated. "Is this the emergency that you were talking about you had?"

"It is an emergency. I wouldn't ask you if I didn't need it!"

"What do you need it for?" I asked calmly.

Mom stalled. I knew that she was trying to think up a quick lie, and frankly, I didn't even wanna hear it. I shook my head at her, and then turned to head back out the door.

"Wait! T.J., why you gotta be like that, huh? I need it; I need it, I say! Why you gotta treat your mama like this?" My mom seemed to be almost shaking.

I sighed. She always did this, ranting and raving and making a scene whenever I would come by. Mostly I came back out of a feeling of guilt and necessity, as if I had to check on her, making sure that she was all right. The thing about it was that she was never all right; she was always high or stressed, her mind flying away, burned on crack. This was my memory of childhood. This choking, hot neighborhood that seemed to be crying out in pain and self-contempt. And nothing about it ever seemed to change, not even my mother.

"You should have food in the fridge, Mom, and the rent is paid up for the year; I made sure of that. I gave you five hundred dollars just last week. Why in the world should you be broke now?" I asked in amazement. I looked around at the unkempt house. The year-old living-room set was covered with sheets, stained with what could have been anything from ravioli to ketchup. Cleaning had never been a priority with my mother. I didn't have to guess why she was broke again. I knew exactly where her money always went, in her arm or in a pipe.

"I had some things I needed to take care of. Why do you have to question me all the time?"

"Because I know that you're using, that's why, and I don't want to keep on supporting you killing yourself," I said. "I don't know why you won't move away from this, from this neighborhood, from these people."

"Just give me what I need, please? Don't, don't worry about

me, T.J. I'm the mom; I know what I need. And this is my home; *these* are my people. I don't feel like I need to move in order to *up* myself and feel better than my own peoples!"

"So you think that's what I've done?" I sighed. It really wasn't worth waiting for her answer. I knew how my mom thought, or rather *didn't* think. I pulled out my money clip and gave her four fifties. She grabbed the money greedily, tucking it in her bra.

"Thanks, baby! Now Mama has to go, okay? You come around Sunday and I'll fix you a nice meat loaf dinner, okay?"

"I'll let you know; I'm not sure," I replied, in a hurry to go. "I have a business deal coming up, and I'm unsure of my schedule right now. Bye, Mom." I kissed her lightly on the cheek and left. Not that she noticed much; she was too busy shining a grin at her two hundred dollars.

Later that day, I sat in my study, sharing a cigar moment with Hawk. Hawk was my right-hand man. We had worked together for three years now. One thing that kept our relationship grounded was that we trusted each other, which is a rarity in this business.

"So what did you really think of this liquor chick?" he asked flippantly.

"Hennessy," I corrected.

"Yeah, you know what I mean."

I thought for a moment before I responded. That was something I needed to ask myself. "I don't know really. She was very different from what I expected."

"Beautiful?"

"Very!" I laughed, thinking about her hot temperament.

"You gonna fuck her?"

I choked, inhaling the cigar smoke. "Damn, Hawk! What kind of question is that?"

Hawk got up, pouring himself some Bacardi rum. Hawk was a short, extremely buff Italian man. He had always worked out religiously, trying, I suppose, to make up for what he lacked in height, by tightening and expanding his girth.

"It's a simple question, man. I always know if I'm gonna fuck a lady on first sight."

"Well, see, that's where you and I differ. Pussy doesn't impress me, and I don't feel a woman like that until I've come to know her mind. Any mindless chick can give you a nut, but I like a lady who caresses me mentally." I gave a smooth smirk, waiting for Hawk's reaction to my words.

"Get the fuck outta here!" Hawk laughed. "Who do you think you are, Denzel Washington or something? Caressing your mind, my ass. I just want a pretty piece that knows how to caress this mental mind between my legs," he finished vulgarly.

I shook my head, smiling down at him. "Well, you will get a chance to discern all that for yourself. I want you to meet her. You, Reynolds, and Mateo."

"So . . . since you want us to meet her, then you must already have decided to keep her, huh? We need to be more careful about shit like that, T.J." Hawk looked at me cautiously.

"No, no, I'm not saying I've decided anything yet," I said, shaking my head slowly. "But I would like you guys to help size her up for me. Also, I've already gotten Mateo checking out her background, to see if she's really who she says she is. That should take a day or so, and after, or *if*, all lines up good, we can maybe have dinner here or something, and you guys can shoot the shit and get to know her."

I walked over to the large scenic window overlooking the ocean. I was secretly hoping that Hennessy was clean, and not just so that I could stop my search for a female accomplice either. She interested me, and it had been a long time since a woman had caught my interest. I turned around after having cleared my face of all emotion, when my front door flung open; I gave Hawk a disgusted look, as he was the one who had left the door unlocked. In our line of work, security was a must. Fortunately, the interloper was Mateo, whom I was anxious to hear from.

"*La puta madre! Estoy caliente porque un hijo de puta me choco el fucking auto!*"

Both Hawk and I fell out laughing at Mateo's bilingual outburst.

"What the hell did you just say, boy?" Hawk laughed.

"It's not funny, man!" Mateo exclaimed with a strong accent. "You all be acting like shit be funny, man, this shit ain't funny, yo!" He looked at both of us with narrowed eyes.

"I'm not laughing," I said, holding my face tight, trying without success not to laugh *again.* "Just that you come in here screaming and shouting and talking in a language neither of us understands, and then you say that we are making light of things. I swear I'm not," I made a cross-your-heart sign with my hands. "Just calm down, my man, and tell us what's up."

"This drunk, old-ass hombre busted into my car and pulled off," Mateo panted out angrily.

"Did you get down his plates?" asked Hawk.

"Hell no, man! I was trying to catch de muthafucka myself, yo!"

I snickered at Mateo's sad attempt to calm himself. One thing about him, he had a superhot temper and an inability to control it, especially when he felt wronged. While Mateo stood huffing and puffing, ranting and raving about this guy who rammed his car, I half heard him, thinking about how I had originally hooked up with these guys who were now as close to me as brothers.

We were like rainbow stripes. Hawk was Sicilian; his actual name was Frank Mattucci, but he had long been disowned by his proud Italian family because of his run-ins with the law. Mateo, the young one of the bunch, was too fast with his temper, which often got him into trouble. Reynolds, who was a brotha like me, was one of my boys from Compton. He was still very much a ghetto ass, but the lack of fear of death that comes with boys from the hood was actually his strong point. We had all hooked up right after my release from prison, and of course Hawk's release. He had spent ten years in the federal pen in Florida for robbery. Mateo was new to the game, and Reynolds, well, his slick ass had never gotten caught.

"Okay, just calm down, papi," Hawk teased, grinning at Mateo.

"*I am calm!*" Mateo screamed, then took a deep breath and sighed. "Anyhow, T.J., I got that information on that broad."

"So?"

"So far so good; she seems to be clean; New York chica, college educated, journalism according to her records, but instead of taking up the pen after college, she's been working to pull off some small jobs on the East Coast. She's gorgeous, too. *Muy bonita!*" He winked at Hawk, who smiled, looking at me from the corner of his eye. "Looks like mocha pudding. I may have to have a spoonful of that, give her a chance to see how spicy Latino men can be."

Hawk laughed out loud. "Well, Mateo, my man, I think T.J. may have something to say about that, seeing that he met her first."

"You're a fool; you know that?" I said, shaking my head at Hawk. "Every beautiful woman I see does not turn my head, okay? Like I told you, pussy—"

"Doesn't impress you," he mocked, grinning. "Yeah, keep on saying that; one day you may believe it."

"Well, you best believe me when I say this is business, *only* business." Both Hawk and Mateo laughed at my insistence as I turned to refresh my rum. But secretly, I found myself not able to take the thankful smile off my face, glad that Hennessy had turned up clean, ignoring the little voice that was telling me to still walk with caution with her. All I could think about was getting some time alone so that I could call her and make plans to see her again.

# 3

*Beverly Hills, California . . . Hennessy*

I have never been able to stand waiting for something. It's the same as being stuck in an elevator to me. In a word, I'm hyper. The day, hours, and moments seemed to drag by as I waited for Tristan Jackson to call me. When had I started to think of him as Tristan, rather than T.J.? I had no idea, but maybe it was because the name seemed more personal somehow, even though I was clueless as to why I would want to start thinking of a crook in a personal way. I sighed while glancing at the softly ticking clock. The time was 12:15 P.M. It was of course still early in the day, but I had been up waiting to hear from him since nine o'clock that morning and couldn't help wondering what the delay in his getting in touch with me could mean.

The sound of my cell phone ringing jarred me out of my wonderment for a moment. I figured it had to Sebastian, wondering again if our plan was going to work. I picked up the phone with a sarcastic, yet airy, "Helloooooo."

"T.J. Jackson here," came the deep-voiced reply. I was flustered.

"Yes, um, hello, how are you?" I answered.

"I'm fine. Wondering if you are going to let me in so we can chat a bit?"

"Oh! You mean you're here outside my room?" I asked in surprise, jumping up suddenly and walking toward my hotel door.

"Yes, I am." He laughed. I opened the door without hanging up, quickly being rewarded with a devastatingly handsome grin from Tristan Jackson. "Um, I have to hang up now; a lovely lady-in-waiting just opened her door to me."

"Hi." I flushed slightly at his compliment. "Please come in." He eyed me with a penetrating stare, nodding his head in thanks as he strolled inside.

"Very nice," he commented on my room.

"Thank you," I said. "I've been hoping all day that I'd hear from you."

"Missed me already?" He raised one eyebrow in a cocked fashion, testifying to his humor.

"Ha, ha," I fake laughed. "Sorry, buddy, not a chance at that, but I was starting to wonder if the famed Tristan James Jackson was giving me the runaround. I came a long way to *hopefully* work with you, you know."

Tristan eyed me with amusement. "Well, there are some guys I want you to meet; they're waiting at my place right now," he announced, looking down at his watch.

I fought hard to keep myself from smiling. He was going to work with me. Yes! Swallowing my enthusiasm, I looked at him solemnly. "So are you *asking* me, are you telling me that you *need* me, darling?"

"Something like that. Leo called; I talked with him this morning."

My heart skipped a beat. Did Sebastian have any idea that our informant would be in contact with Jackson?

"And?" I finally said.

"And, he vouched for you, said that he sent you. I also checked you out and I've discovered that you aren't five-O, or a federal agent. At least I *hope* I'm not wrong." I tightened a bit

inside at his last words. Quickly gathering my inner compo-
sure, I fixed a serious look on my face.

"You have to trust me, Tristan. Otherwise we won't be able
to work together. I hope there is going to be a time when I have
won that trust."

He looked uncertain, yet hopeful. "We'll see, okay? I mean
everything takes time, Hennessy, and you are right, we do need
to be able to trust each other, so let's start to build on that."

"Agreed." I nodded, noting the sincerity in his words. It had
always amazed me how criminals could be so ruthless in their
crimes, yet at the same time hold such honor and ethics when it
came to other things, namely the trustworthiness of their *crook*
colleagues. Brushing off the slight tinge of remorse I felt that I
was going to be acting, lying, and basically betraying his trust
before this was all over, I reached out and took his hand, being
sure to look him in the eye as to seem as sincere as possible.
"You can trust me, Tristan." His face softened even more,
which was a good thing. "So, when are you going to clue me in
on things?" I asked.

"I'll do that at the house. I'm your taxi, miss; let's roll."

Tristan led me into a beautiful theater room in his home. On
the way over, he had described the three other men we would
be working with. I only had to glance a second at them to know
who each one was, and also to size them up. First he introduced
Reynolds, a tall, dark, black man who appeared to be somewhere in his early thirties, perhaps about Tristan's age. He had
big features, large nose, lips, eyes; too big to be considered tra-
ditionally handsome, yet he had a large build that showed
strength and character. I could easily see how some women
would be attracted to that appeal. Then he introduced me to
Mateo, who was a cute, fair-skinned Latino. He could almost
have passed for white if not for his dark Spaniard eyes and hair,
and the heavy accent. He was also a flirt, major, and can I say
again? Major flirt. Finally, there was Hawk. I could tell right
away he would be my challenge. He looked at me, his deep

brown eyes, beautiful eyes actually, sort of reminding me of the lead singer of Creed, but older, and shorter, definitely shorter, yet he had the demeanor of a man much taller. He had an *I don't trust ya* look in his eyes, and I discerned that I would have to win this one over, especially since Tristan had told me on the way to his place that Hawk was his closest friend and confidant.

"Now that you have all been introduced to Hennessy, it's time to get down to business." Tristan pulled down a white projector screen, then walked over to the projector and started it up. We suddenly had a front-seat view of . . . wow, Egypt.

"This is our target," Tristan announced. All eyes in the room looked at him  as we waited for a bigger explanation.

"Nigga, is that all you gon' say, this is our target?" Reynolds complained. "I thought you said this job was going to be in New York?"

Tristan grinned. "Hold up, people, I'm going to explain, all in good time, believe me. You see, we aren't talking about your regular penny-ante gig here." Tristan aimed a shiny black cane at the projector screen, clicking a button and pointing toward the ancient historical Egyptian pieces on-screen. "This is extensive," he said. "Inside these four walls are some of the most priceless ancient artifacts in the world. The original plan was to fly to Egypt and get inside these walls. But fate has decided to make it a bit easier for us, although in some ways, the job will still be just as risky." A picture of a golden slate entrapped within a glass casing appeared on the screen. "This, ladies and gentlemen, is the famous slate palette of King Narmer. It's thousands of years old, and if we can get our hands on it . . ." He paused, exhaling with a deep satisfying smile. "If we can get our hands on it, let's just say we can retire, each and every one of us, *quite* nicely. Right now this slate is located at the Egyptian Museum in Cairo, Egypt. It's about to take a trip, though, and so are we."

Mateo jumped up with a wide, excited smile on his face. "I like this already!"

"Tristan, how were you planning to get into a museum as tightly secured as Cairo?" I said.

"Nothing is impossible if you put your mind to it," he replied. "Besides, that plan, as I said before, has been altered."

"Hey, T.J." All eyes turned to Hawk, who was eyeing me suspiciously. "Shouldn't we wait before we give all the details of this gig?"

All the guys followed Hawk's glance to look at me.

"Look, I want this to work out just as well as you guys," I said defensively. "I didn't just come to you for this job. I was presented with the opportunity, so you have no reason to be suspicious of me." I looked over to Tristan. "Besides, I thought you said you had me checked out?"

"And I did," he responded. He looked me in my eyes, then said, "Look, guys, we have to move on this, we have to decide who we are going to trust, and we have to start practicing ASAP. Now I know that none of you really know Hennessy, and I can appreciate your wanting to be careful. But I asked Leo to find me someone and this is who he sent." Tristan looked around to each of his men. "We either go with Hennessy, or we keep looking, but I can tell you that we don't have much time. The slate will be transferred in a month."

"So tell us again what we need her for?" Reynolds asked.

"That's what I was about to do. You see, when this slate is moved, it would be suspected that any attempt to steal it would take place at that time. But that's not the plan. We will go for it *after* it is secured at the Met."

"The Metropolitan Museum of New York," Hawk stated.

"Exactly," Tristan said. "The movers will have security up the ass, and that is when they would expect a possible theft attempt, but we will give it a couple of days, and go inside the Met to get the palette. We won't be walking through the front door either, we will go underground to get inside, get the palette, and get out, and that's where Hennessy comes in, but I'll explain more about that later."

Tristan dug in his pocket, pulling out a gold cigarette holder.

Opening it slowly, he lazily pulled one out and lit it in one movement, then sat down comfortably in one of the theater chairs. "This is not going to be a hurried job. We take our time; we study and learn where every crack and corner of this museum is, and we plan our strategy carefully. I'm having a mock model of different rooms of the museum, rooms that we will have to have to access, built on my New Mexico ranch. We will be flying out there in a day or so." Looking toward me he said, "Hennessy, I think it would be best if you stay here on the beach with me for the next couple of days. I have a spare bedroom that you would find quite comfortable."

I protested. "Oh, um, no, I don't think so. I'm quite comfortable at my hotel, thank you."

"Look, it will only be for a couple of days; then we will be leaving for my ranch in New Mexico. Believe me, I'm not going to ravish you. Not unless you want me to," he said in a lower voice, drawing the laughter of the other three men. My face heated up in embarrassment.

"That's ridiculous!" I spat, looking away from him quickly.

His eyes sparkled in amusement. I was *not* amused. "Actually, Hennessy, my sista . . ." *Grrrr,* he was irritating me, I hated when black men called me their sista, when I was *not* their sister, and I definitely was not this fool's sister. "It's only going to be a couple of days, and then all of us will be leaving for New Mexico. In the meantime, there is no reason you should have to continue paying for a hotel room when there is plenty of room here. Besides, it will give us a chance to get to know each other better. Remember," he said, smiling, "you are the one who told me I needed to trust you."

I breathed in, wondering why this man got to me so easily, and with the littlest of things. Now here he was, making me eat my own words. "Yes, I see your point. But . . . I don't want to inconvenience you."

"Sweetheart, you're not inconveniencing me. In fact, I insist. I want you here because you are going to be a key player in this job. Mateo can drive you over and help you get your things." He nodded toward Mateo, who winked in agreement.

"This is not going to be a quick learn, people, but patience is going to pay off for us," Tristan said.

"Can't we use Mateo to slip through those tunnels?" Hawk suddenly asked. "Do you really need her?" He pointed toward me. I frowned slightly. He was really starting to get on my nerves.

"She's in, Hawk, okay?" Tristan responded. He looked around at his men. "Let's work together on this, people. We all have a lot to gain, but also a lot to lose, and we're going to need to trust each other. Now it was my call to count Hennessy in. Can you all trust my decision?"

The room was quiet for a moment before, finally, all the guys nodded in agreement. I looked at Tristan and smiled thankfully at him.

Mateo smiled broadly. "Well, it's all settled then! Whoa! I can't wait. It's been a while since I've been to Jackson's. Is that sexy *mamacita* still working for you, T.J.? Wha's her name? Aurora?"

"Yes, she's still with us, Mateo." Tristan chuckled. "I'm sure she'll be real happy to see you."

"What's Jackson's?" I inquired, unable to hide my uneasiness.

"Didn't you hear what he said?" Hawk responded impatiently. "It's his ranch, and it's where we will be training for this job. I mean how many times does he have to repeat things until you get it?"

"Well, excuse me!" I retorted.

"You never did say who our buyer was, T.J.," Reynolds reminded him, cutting in.

Tristan hesitated. "I'd rather keep that under wraps right now. But let's just say they are willing to pay us forty million dollars for this piece. That's eight mil apiece. So is it worth it, you think?"

I gasped. Forty million dollars! No wonder these men were going to such trouble to do this. I swallowed my surprise. After all, these guys thought I was part or their world and was a trained cat thief just like they were. I couldn't allow my face to give away my innocence in the fine art of robbery.

"Are you okay, Ms. Lewis?" Hawk asked, looking at me oddly.

"Oh, yes, I'm fine. It's just that . . . hell, that's a *lot* of money!"

Tristan chuckled. "Yes, it is, but believe me when I tell you, Hennessy, you will be working hard for that money. But we'll talk more about this . . ." He looked down at his gold Rolex watch. "Tomorrow. I wanted to go over more with you guys today, but I have to go to a quick appointment that I can't miss." He looked toward Mateo. "Why don t you run her over to her hotel now, man?"

"I can do that," Mateo agreed. He looked over at me, smiling pleasantly. "Ready?"

I really did not want to move in with Tristan, and I couldn't figure out why it got to me so badly. But with all eyes on me, awaiting my response to Mateo, I knew I didn't have much choice in the matter. "Yes, I'm ready," I said, grabbing my purse and hanging it on my shoulder.

"*Bueno! Después de usted entonces, hermosa,*" he sang out in Spanish. The other guys laughed, including Mateo, looking at me with his dark, perky eyes.

I surprised him though when I came back equally with perfect diction, "*Gracias, chulo. Y gracias por ofrecer tu ayuda a una desamparada como, yo.*" I winked at Mateo's surprised look, along with the shocked looks of the other fellas.

"What did she say?" Reynolds asked.

"Well, well, well. Seems like you have *many* talents, Hennessy." Tristan smiled. I had a hard time hiding my own smile, which was threatening to break loose all over my face.


*Elsewhere in Beverly Hills . . . Tristan*


I hate when I make plans to meet someone and they don't show up, and it seems like that's been happening to me more and more lately. What people don't realize is that a brotha fights hard to hold back his ghettofab personality. I had an appointment with one of my connections, an LAPD sellout money lover who would basically do whatever to fill his pockets, including working with the underworld. I have no respect for bad cops, but unfortunately, they are a necessity, and I always make sure to keep a half dozen or so on my payroll, especially when I am planning something new and big. It also paid to know what was up with the feds, who I knew knew me and were always eyeballing what I would be up to next.

I drove over to Keefers, a lil' joint in south LA that Lenox Rimes had told me to meet him at. Rimes was sleaze. I didn't trust him, never would, but like I said before, his type was needed. He had told me over the phone that he had some news to throw at me. What news? Who knows, but no news is not necessarily always good news. No news could mean I was being watched, so even when it was sleaze calling, I took note and listened. I waited forty-five minutes for the shiftless asshole and still no show. I looked down at my watch, sighing deeply. Looking around at the fancy cars and patrons of Keefers, I wondered if I had perhaps missed Rimes. He had never been late for a meeting with me before. Another fifteen minutes passed, and I finally decided to leave and contact him later to cuss his ass out for wasting my time. Just as I was about to pull out, I spotted his unmarked Lincoln Continental pulling into a parking spot across the street a few cars ahead of me. I was about to get out of my silver Lexus, when I noticed a tall, overweight brotha approaching Rimes's car. I paused, suspended, as he quickly pulled out a long pistol, pointed it inside Lenox's car, and fired five times. I gasped, looking around as upper-class Californians screamed, running for cover. I got out of my car, looking around myself as I walked toward the scene, trying to blend in with the screaming crowd. As fucked up as Lenox was, it was still hard to believe that the dead carcass with his head leaned against his car seat, eyes wide open, could be the same cocky cop I had had working for me for months. I felt a nervous twitch in my neck. Something didn't feel right, something didn't smell right, something told me that this murder could maybe have had something to do with me, but regardless, I knew that it was now time for me to make my way home and away from the murder scene before it became crowded with cops.

I swiftly made my way back to my Malibu Beach home, my mind in a puzzle over who could have planned this hit. And why *now?* Rimes had been adamant on the phone earlier that he had some big news for me that I would definitely be willing to pay extra for. I suppose with a man like Rimes, it could have been anyone. He had to have more enemies than Master P had cars. As I was working out in my mind who could have been responsible for this, my cell phone rang. "Hello?" I answered.

"T.J.," a gruff voice stated flatly, just *T.J.* The voice sounded vaguely familiar, yet still was hard to pin. "It's Earl, how are you doing, son?"

"Earl! My God, where are you?" I hadn't heard from Earl Walhman in months. Usually I would hear from my mentor during holidays, or birthdays.

"I'm out, T.J."

I shook my head, wondering if I had heard him right. "Out? What do you mean out?"

"I've been released early," he responded. I could hear the smile in his voice. Earl was like the father I never had, but my busy schedule and his being moved around a couple of times in the penitentiary system lately had made it hard for us to keep in touch. Still, his words that he was out couldn't have been more musical to my ears.

"Are you in Los Angeles?" I asked.

"You know it, and I want to see you."

"I'll come right now; give me an address!" I exclaimed quickly, excited about seeing him.

"Not tonight, son. I'm exhausted; haven't long gotten moved into my room, and I've spent the day unpacking. Can you meet me in the morning for breakfast?" Earl sounded tired, worn, as if he had something deep on his mind.

"Are you okay, Earl?" I asked with concern.

"Yes, I'm fine, and you know I'm eager to see you. Tomorrow?"

"Tell me where."

He paused for a second. "I'm at a halfway house in east LA called Maggie's House. Across the street from it is a café called Joe's. They have dynamite coffee and bagels. How about meeting me there in the morning around ten? We can have brunch."

"Sounds good. I miss you, man. . . ."

"I miss you, too, T.J., I love you, son. I'll see you at ten." I breathed heavily as Earl hung up the phone, thinking back to the last time I had seen him. His five-nine frame, slightly tanned, weathered skin, and tired, yet knowledgeable eyes. I missed him, missed his voice, missed his guidance. Guidance that I knew I still needed, even at thirty-two years of age. Earl would have spent a total of twenty years behind bars now, and although I was happy that he had had an early release, I knew those twenty years had been hard on him, and I knew something had to be up to explain his early release, even before his next parole hearing. Now it was a simple matter of waiting until brunch tomorrow to find out what that something was.

# 4

---

*Beverly Hills, California . . . Hennessey*

Mateo was a trip. After he realized that I was bilingual, he was nonstop *Español* all the way to my hotel. It was actually fun being able to converse with someone like him. He was fun, in the whoopee sort of way. It was always hard with some of the jobs I did, because with my spending months and months with these people, there was the tendency to get close to some of them, especially if outside of the fact that they were criminals, they had easy, likable personalities, like Mateo's. As for Tristan . . . well, that remained to be seen. The feeling I got from him and the feeling I got from Mateo were totally different, and living in his house . . . hmm, again, quite questionable.

The guest room was beautifully decorated, in dark green and plush, thick carpeting. After Mateo helped me bring in my bags and left, I sat on the edge of the bed for a few moments when it suddenly hit me: now was my chance to take a peek at Tristan's place, see if he had any hidden secrets that would help me figure him out. I stood up, feeling a rush of excitement. "I think I'll start with his bedroom," I said to myself, heading quickly for the door. I was in for a shocker though; his room door was locked! "Hmph, he's in for a surprise if he thinks something like a little ol' lock can keep me out of where I wanna be!" I pulled a bobby pin out of the bun of my hair, stuck it in the door lock, twist, push, turn, voilà! The door creaked as it opened, increasing my heart palpitations threefold. Damn! This guy had style, class, and good taste. His room reeked of him. The smell, the look, undeniably Tristan Jackson. I didn't know where to start or how much time I had to snoop. I looked over at the clock radio on his night table. I had already been here alone for thirty minutes, and had no idea when he would be coming back, so . . .

The first place I looked into was his closet. It was full of designer suits, shirts, and apparel. Above, on a top shelf were a couple of boxes with tops, and what looked like a picture album. For some reason, it was the first thing I reached for. Inside was what appeared to be his life history, pictures of him as a baby, hmmm . . . so cute! I smiled quietly to myself, looking around as if I were about to be caught. All his photos were of him, and a tall, thin, light-skinned black woman who must have been his mother. The pictures told a history of this interesting criminal, which is odd that I thought of him so, seeing the innocent hazel eyes of a child staring back at me in these photos. I could see the man he was now, and yet, I saw more, something deeper. I moved on to what appeared to be high school pictures, him looking all *thugged* out. I grinned, feeling sudden unexplainable warmth inside, when I heard the sound of the front door opening.

"Oh my gosh!" I exclaimed, slipping the photo album back onto the shelf quickly, but not before first grabbing one of his baby pictures and slipping it in my back jean pocket. I walked swiftly out of his room, locking the door quietly behind me. I was about to open the guest room door when I heard Tristan calling out my name.


*Tristan*


When I got back to my home, things were quiet. I felt jumpy, not only from the questions in my mind about Rimes's murder, but also I was on pins and needles wondering if Hennessy was around, and if Mateo had brought her things over. I wanted to remind her that she didn't need to totally unpack, being that we would be flying out to New Mexico in two days. The house seemed empty, until I heard a door creaking and realized it had to be Ms. Lewis.

"Hennessy?" I called out, walking toward the hall area. I peeped around the corner to see her coming out of the guest bedroom.

"Hey," she said.

She looked beautiful. *Whoa . . . did I just think that?* "So, all moved in comfortably?" I asked.

"Yes, thanks," she said. We both stood there, eyeing each other with smiles. For some reason, neither of us seemed to know quite what to say.

"So, Mateo took off?"

"Yes, he said he had some things to do. So I've been quite fine here alone. You know I really would have been okay where I was, but thanks for your hospitality anyhow," she said, looking at me kind of uncomfortably.

"You do understand why I wanted you here? I mean it's not personal." I laughed. I didn't know why I was laughing, but I always did when I felt these nervous, uncomfortable, yet elevated feelings. Feelings I hadn't had since Natalie. It had been ages since I'd let my mind even think of Nat, other than those dreaded nightmares. But it was crazy that I was thinking about a woman I had been deeply in love with and had lost, at the same time that I was with Hennessy Lewis, a beautiful woman, but one I really didn't know. I shook myself. "So, um, really, like I said, it's safer and you need not worry. I was joking before with the guys earlier, I really *am* a gentleman." Hennessy looked at me sideways as if in doubt. "Seriously, I am," I said, laughing.

"Okay, I believe you . . . not!" she spat jokingly.

"Listen, do I look like a man who would try to seduce a lovely lady like yourself?"

"Hmm . . . I guess not, but should the fact you say you

wouldn't be a compliment or an insult?" Her eyebrows rose, and her flirty words caused my heart to start a rapid beat; I could barely keep the involuntary huge grin from coating my face.

"What are you smiling about?" She laughed.

"Ahh, I don't know," I babbled out, feeling kind of foolish and wanting to find something to say. "Do you know you have really thick eyebrows?"

"Oh!" she huffed. "Go away!"

"You forget this is my house; where would I go away to?" I chuckled again.

"Well, you made me stay here. Why? Just to insult me?" Her lips drew together in a succulent pout. I laughed again, feeling rather captivated by this woman. I leaned a bit closer to her, whispering, "Hey . . ."

"What?" she asked, still pouting.

"I like thick eyebrows; never did find anything appealing about the plucked-chicken look a lot of women seem to dig. Your thick eyebrows are very nice, and my words were a compliment."

"Thank you," she whispered back. It took a moment for me to realize how close we were standing, and how very close my lips were to hers, almost touching, but not quite. I looked up from her lips and our eyes met, each of us poised as though waiting for the other to say something. After moments seemed to drift by, I cleared my throat, which had gotten suddenly very dry, and backed up a bit from her.

"Well, you should finish getting settled in, but I wanted to remind you that we will be flying to New Mexico in a couple of days so don't get too comfy." I paused for a moment before finishing up with, "Well, I have some things I need to do myself. . . ."

"Um, yes, you're right." She wrapped her hands around her arms, looking away from me. Just as I was about to walk away, she said suddenly, "Can you tell me more about our plans?"

"You mean clue you in separately from the guys? You mean just between you and me, on the *down low?*" I grinned, winking.

"Forget it; I'll wait."

My laughter filled the hallway as she hurriedly pranced into the guest room, closing the door behind herself.

The following midmorning I sat, sipping quietly on a cup of steaming hot coffee, waiting for Earl to show up at Joe's café. I looked down at my watch; he was already about fifteen minutes late. My mind flung back to someone else who had been late for a meeting with me just yesterday, and had ended up with a few caps in him. News about the execution-style murder of Lenox Rimes had bombarded the evening news with questions of who could have been responsible. Even though I hadn't liked Rimes that much, I still felt it was just plain fucked up how he had been taken out. I wondered more than a few times who could have had him killed. I especially felt it odd that someone had done him in only moments before our meeting, one in which he was supposed to be filling me in on what he had termed *news that was so juicy it would make my dick hard.* I had great suspicion about that whole scene, and had called Hawk and filled him in on what I had seen as soon as I finished my hallway conversation with Hennessy.

Hennessy. Now that was another puzzlement to my mind. I was attracted to her; there was no denying it. I wasn't even sure what it was about her; her beauty was undeniable, but I'd been around beautiful women before. It was part of the business, really. Money drew beautiful women, most of them being money-hungry gold diggers. But there was something else beyond beauty with Hennessy. She had strength about her features, and she was educated and cultured, yet not a prim and proper, whitewashed sista. Still she had a mystery about her, which normally would ring warning bells in me; but with her, I didn't want to hear warning bells, or use caution, I simply wanted to delve a bit deeper into the mystery that was her.

I was so into my thoughts of Hennessy and her beautiful, mysterious ass that I hardly heard Earl's voice, rallying me to attention. "What has your mind so occupied, young fellow? Let me guess, a woman?" I looked up to see his crooked grin, and jumped up to hug him tightly.

"Damn it! I missed you, Earl!"

Earl returned my hug with a tight grip of his own, loosening only after what felt like long minutes had passed. He looked at me warmly, unshed tears coating his eyes. "I missed you, too, T.J. How are you?"

"I'm good. Excellent now! So tell me what happened. How did you get out before your next parole hearing? Who did you pay off?" I joked, ribbing him good-naturedly. Earl sat down in the chair across from mine, as I gestured for the waitress to bring him a coffee.

He didn't look good. I couldn't put my finger on it, but I saw it in his eyes as he talked, telling me how he had gotten an early release and a semipardon from the governor. His eyes looked weak, tired; his faced looked drawn, far older than his fifty-five years.

"A pardon?" I exclaimed, "How'd that happen?"

"*Semi*-pardon," he said, correcting me.

"Okay then, *semi*, but since when has that made any difference in the great old state of California?"

Earl sighed, examining my face before speaking. "I've done twenty years, T.J. I've never once gotten close to making parole, but my lawyers were finally able to get me a pardon because of health reasons, health problems."

"O . . . kay . . . what kind of health problems, Earl? Come on, be straight with me, all right?" I felt this worried, sick feeling starting to come over me, and I knew that whatever Earl was trying so hard *not* to tell me could not be good.

"I have liver cancer, son. Doctors have said I have six months at the most. My lawyers were able to take that along with the consideration of my age and good behavior and have my time condensed to time served. It wasn't an easy feat, but I got lucky." I was speechless, watching the movement of Earl's lips, hearing his words but not able to summon up any of my own. "So I guess you couldn't even call what I got as a semi-pardon; it was more of a 'we pity your dying old ass so you can go free,' " he joked. I wasn't laughing.

"T.J., don't look at me that way. It's okay, it really is," he said firmly. He watched as my face reddened, with tears of disbelief threatening to spill over. Earl had always been like Superman to me. Nothing could get him down; nothing could hurt him. His strength got me through some of the toughest situations in my life while I was in prison, and he had been the main one who was there for me when I was trying to get over my grief at Nat's death.

"What, am I supposed to just not care?" I implored. "You're like a father to me; you know that."

"And you're like the son I've never had. And that's why getting to spend some time with you *outside* prison bars is like a gift from God to me." Earl gripped my hands, noting my shaken expression.

"Isn't there anything they can do? Chemo, surgery, medicines?" I asked. "Hell, there has to be something, Earl!"

"It's liver cancer, T.J, there is nothing that can be done about this type of cancer."

"I don't believe that shit, there has to be something!" I shouted.

I had to get a grip of myself. People sitting at the surrounding cafe tables eyed us curiously. I quickly wiped away tears, which had streamed down my face, feeling ashamed and yet at the same time not even caring who saw them. I had lost many homies growing up in Compton, death was part of life. But in reality, I knew that none of those homies had cared about me as Earl had, nor had schooled me on what life was really about, or how to be my own person and not feel that I had to follow the leader and do what I saw others doing around me, or act, talk, walk, or carry myself a certain way so I could be *down* or *cool* or walk the crip walk the way so many other dead muthafuckas had walked it. And even after I got out of prison, and he was still serving time, he still carried that father role for me.

Earl sighed. "I've accepted this. I love life, T.J. If there were anything that could be done, if I was not totally sure of what the doctors have told me, don't you think I would be fighting tooth and nail?"

"So now what?" I asked.

"Now . . . I live. The best way I can, for the short period of time I have, I live. And I'll tell you something else, T.J., I wronged you in a lot of ways."

"What are you talking about?" I asked, feeling a bit confused and overwhelmed.

"I know I'd always led you to believe that money was everything, but I was wrong. Twenty years is a long time to sit back thinking about what-ifs, and how-comes, and yes, I was just like you for a long, long time. I mean look at you, cocky, full of vigor and strength, not afraid of anything, not afraid of getting caught."

"I learned from the best, that's why," I said, complimenting him.

"Well, the best got caught, son. That's my point, and I wronged you when I made you think that I was somehow invincible. If I were, then I would never have spent over a third of my life locked behind iron bars. And I should never have taught you how to be a thief. I would never have shown you how to do the same type of work that got me a life sentence. Love should've made me encourage you to do something with that intelligent mind of yours, to go back to school, maybe get your degree, anything but live your life the way I've lived mine, and end up with regrets."

I had never heard Earl talk the way he was talking, or sound as though he was sorry for the things he had taught me. I knew it had to be his reflecting back, his being ill and feeling that he somehow had to seek redemption for his actions. I could understand his feelings, more than he even realized. I also had a lot I needed to redeem, or make up for. But not *yet*.

"I have no regrets, Earl. I've done what I had to do to survive, and I was doing it long before I had the pleasure of meeting you." The waitress came back to our table, refilling our cups before quickly walking away.

"So you have *no* regrets?" His eyebrows rose. I looked away from his knowing gaze.

"That's not what I'm talking about. There are some things I regret, which you know. But I'm not gonna be doing this forever, Earl, and I have no intention of ever being caught again. I won't ever be going back to prison, believe me."

"And that's the same thing I used to say, back in the days when I thought I was smarter than everyone around me. Don't allow yourself to get fooled by your own ego, T.J. It's the biggest trap. Everyone can get caught, everyone can die, and I don't wanna see either of those things happen to you."

I listened, but I was quiet. I failed to tell him about my upcoming plans, but then again, Earl had a way of knowing about things without my even saying a word, as if he could read my past, present, and future.

He finally stopped preaching, looking at me with his all-knowing gaze. "So, you're settled now, right? I know that what happened during the Renaissance robbery affected you deeply. That's it for you, right?" I didn't answer. My silence spoke for me. Earl sighed. "I have six months of life left, out of twenty and a half years of being locked away, six months. But if it is the last thing I do, the same way I taught you how to be the best thief, now I want to teach you how to *live*. How to live with dignity and with freeness of mind. Not having to worry about getting caught, or going to prison, or those serpents in your corner, or crooked cops, and all the bullshit that goes along with this life, T.J."

"Serpents in my corner?" I cut in.

"That's the biggest thing you have to worry about, son. You see, the devil, the original serpent, transforms himself into an angel of light, and so do false friends; so believe me, there are always serpents, backstabbers, people who you think you can trust but who in reality are in your corner, waiting for an opportunity to fuck you. I found that out myself, the hard way, and it's how I ended up losing over half my life in prison. I don't want to see that happen to you. I want to see good things, changes in your life, so you won't end up like me."

"Now you're getting churchy on me," I lamented.

"Not churchy, just real."

"Anyhow, I've already made plans to change, Earl," I cut in.

"Oh, you have?" he asked, unconvinced.

"I'm starting new, I promise, man . . . soon."

"Well . . ." Earl raised his cup up as if in a toast. "Here's to new beginnings, son, new beginnings."

# 5

---

Malibu Beach . . . Tristan

*She was so beautiful; even in death she had that same radiance that had attracted me to her from the start. She was dressed in a chocolate-brown nightgown, with soft fabric roses at the neckline, which rested just above her breasts. She looked as if she were asleep, being far too young and beautiful for this permanent state.*

*"And so we commend her soul to Jesus," the minister sang out, as the church of mourners looked on. I looked over to my left. A man's blue piercing eyes were glued on me, as they had been the whole service. It was odd, the way he was looking at me. No one knew who I was, or so I thought. And I wasn't sure who he was, but one thing was certain, he appeared to know me, and he blamed me for this. I blamed me for this. I was her murderer.*

*After the service, family and friends were allowed to view her loveliness one last time, forming a line to her casket for a final good-bye stroll. When I got up to her, my breath caught. I kissed two fingers, then reached out, pressing my fingers against her pale lips. She kissed them back. Slowly she opened her eyes. "Why, T.J.? Why . . . why . . . why . . ." she whispered to me. One tear traced down her cheek.*

*"I'm sorry, baby. Please come back to me!" I cried. Even as I spoke, her eyes closed again. I broke down, clinging to the rim of her cherry-wood casket.*

*"Come back to me, Natalie! Come back!"*

"My God, are you okay? Wake up, Tristan! Tristan!"

I heard Natalie, calling my name, but yet it was a different voice, softer, yet firmer of tone. Still I gravitated toward it, reaching my hands and arms out to hold on to her. "Oh God! God, babe! You came back! I'm so sorry!" I cried, burying my face in her neck. She smelled different, pleasant but different. I sought her lips as she rocked and cradled me in her arms, whispering that it would be okay. She gasped as my tongue slipped into her mouth, exploring its warm recesses, growing limp against me before jerking back suddenly and cutting on my night lamp.

"Tristan?" she whispered. As my eyes adjusted to the new light, I found myself looking into, not green, but big brown eyes, with thick, well-shaped eyebrows atop each one. Hennessy. It had been another Natalie nightmare, and Hennessy's face was a haven of embarrassment.

I swallowed, looking away quickly. "I'm sorry," I said blankly. Quietness filled the bedroom with me sitting there just praying, wishing she would get the hell out so I could cover my face with my pillow and disappear. I hated being seen, caught with my guard down, my shield yanked away, showing all the ugly shit that haunted my soul. When you are like that . . . people can get to you, tap into portions of you that aren't as strong as others.

"No, don't be sorry. Were you dreaming? You seemed to think I was someone else, someone named Natalie? Who was she?" Hennessy sat on the edge of the bed, expectantly.

"Listen, it was nothing, okay?" I said with a wide-eyed look. I looked at the clock that rested on the night table. "It's four A.M.; I'm sorry I woke you up but you need to get some sleep and so do I." I could feel her eyes searching for something in mine to see what my dream had been about. She stood up.

"So if you're sure? I mean I'm a great listener, if you ever want to talk about it. . . ." I felt myself stiffen at her words, and she must've felt it, too. She sighed deeply before saying, "Okay, good night then."


*Two days later . . . Hennessy*

Things were very tense. Since the night I had walked in on him having what must've been a hell of a nightmare, Tristan seemed to distance himself. And other than feeling his presence in the beach home, I rarely saw him. Instead of worrying about where he was, what I needed to do was contact Sebastian about New Mexico, and I needed to remind myself of who I was, not Hennessy Lewis, but Hennessy Justine Cooper, U.S. federal agent on duty to catch a thief!

I still cringed with embarrassment whenever I thought back to how I had reacted to Tristan's kiss. How my body had been *burning,* and my nipples taut against his chest. And that sudden, tingling wetness that welled between my thighs when his tongue had entered my mouth. And what was even worse was the knowledge he really wasn't kissing *me,* he was kissing Natalie, or at least in his mind he was. And me, I just *had* to respond and make a complete fool of myself.

I was in the kitchen spreading mayo over some wheat bread for a sandwich. Basically I had made myself at home at Tristan's place. It wasn't a huge house, although extremely well decorated and stylish. Although I tried not to think too much about the night before, my mind kept swinging back to it, and back to that kiss. The kiss . . . Gawd! Just as I took a bite into my ham and cheese sandwich and started daydreaming again, my cell phone buzzed silently against my hip. "Hello?" I knew it had to be Sebastian again; he was the only person who had my cell phone number.

"Can you talk?" he asked.

"No, he's home, in his room. You really shouldn't call me; let me call you, okay?" I whispered in a low tone.

"But you haven't been; what's been going on?"

Before I could answer him, I recognized the sound of Mateo's voice, and Tristan's. "Listen, I can't talk right now, let me call you back, okay? I'll call you before I go to bed tonight; I can tell you that tomorrow we are flying out to New Mexico. More on that later."

"Wait," he insisted. "Why are you going to New Mexico? Tell me what's going on, damn it!"

"Who are you talking to?"

I dropped my cell phone at the sound of Tristan's voice. "Oh my gosh, you scared me to death!"

"Sorry about that, now who were you talking to?" he pressed again.

My heart started beating fast as I worked hard to think up a quick explanation.

"I was calling New York to check on my father. He's been ill and I—"

"*Que pasa, mamacita?*" Mateo suddenly said, coming up behind Tristan.

I looked at him, gratefully. "*No mucho, y usted, querido?*" I grinned.

"*Estás muy hermosa hoy, bebé,*" Mateo whispered in a sexy, low tone.

"*Ohhhh . . . gracias, papichulo!*" I winked, flirting shamelessly.

Tristan looked at the two of us with an odd scowl on his face. "I really wish *both* of you would speak English and stop being so damn rude!"

He then turned directly to me. "Watch it with the phone calls. I don't want anyone knowing where we are going or anything about our plans. Not even your family. Got that?"

"I didn't," I exclaimed. "I swear!"

He walked out of the kitchen, then over to his wet bar and poured himself some ginger ale, plopping two big ice cubes in his glass before settling down on the couch. I looked at Mateo, who gave me a reassuring smile. Mateo then walked over to the bar to help himself to a drink.

"What time will we be leaving in the morning, boss?" he asked Tristan.

"Nine o'clock," Tristan answered, still looking a bit riled by our exchange. "I hope you've packed up your things, Hennessy."

"Yes, of course. I remember what time you told me to be ready." Our eyes met briefly, both of us looking away at the same time. Mateo looked at both of us as if he could tell something else was up besides the phone incident, but was polite enough not to question.

"So," I said suddenly, "why don't you guys tell me more about Jackson's?"

"It's my dream home. I've always loved the outdoors. Growing up I never had that clean-air feel around me, so when I was afforded the opportunity, I bought Jackson's, remodeled it, purchased some of the most beautiful mares in the West, and started breeding them." Tristan's face lit up as he talked about his ranch, pretty much showing where his heart was. As I listened to him and Mateo battle back and forth about the worth of the English purebreds he had bought six months before, I couldn't help but be amazed by him.

"So you're really into horses?" I asked, smiling in surprise.

"Definitely! Don't you know that *Bonanza* and *Big Valley* were my favorite shows growing up? Even if they were repeats."

"I remember *Bonanza,* with Little Joe. He was *so* cute." I giggled, "But he's dead, you know, Michael Landon?" I said sadly.

"Boo-hoo!" Mateo sniffed, teasingly.

"Oh, shuddup!" I laughed. It felt good to be laughing with

these guys, after the last two uncomfortable days with Tristan. Maybe it was that Mateo made things a bit more relaxed, I wasn't sure, but Tristan definitely seemed to ease up with the tension a lot.

It was odd, but I liked Mateo. He was so funny and a nice person. I felt bad every time I thought about what was going to happen to him once this big sting was over, and I had all the proof of their robbery in my hands. Basically, I would be betraying them all. Would I be able to stomach the look on these guys' faces once they realized who I was? I didn't know, and right now, I didn't want to think about it. This was the main reason I hated doing undercover work, and I had thought more times than once about a career change. Right now, though, I couldn't worry about that. I had to do the job that I had now, and I had to do it well. I knew that included finding out as much as I could, so that Sebastian could be schooled in properly, and also for my own protection. As far as I knew, these men could/would kill me in a second flat if they knew I was an agent.

I addressed Tristan again. "So you said the other day that you were having a model of the Met built on your ranch? Tell me more about that."

"Well, I've had it worked on for months now; it's makeshift, but it will allow us to get a visual of what we will be doing. We are going to learn the ins and outs of the museum throughout, and I have maps of every corner of the place."

"So basically, you're going to take us to robbery school?" I smirked. Tristan and Mateo both laughed.

"Basically, yes." Tristan smiled.

"How long do you think it's going to take, T.J.?" Tristan glanced at his watch at Mateo's question, checking the date most likely.

"Well, we don't have the luxury of time on our hands. The palette will be moved in a month, and I don't want it to get too comfortable in its new home. I don't want to take too long and risk someone finding out what we have planned, or worse yet, the feds getting wind of things or planting someone on us. You know how they *love* me," he said, laughing. I cringed inwardly at his words. I couldn't help but wonder if he maybe, kind of suspected something. But if he did, it didn't show on his face, or he was as good an actor as I was an actress.

Mateo hung around a bit longer, which was good by me; it helped me not having to be alone with Tristan. I thought about how, after tonight, we would be in New Mexico, surrounded not only by Mateo, but Reynolds and Hawk, too. Hawk seemed to frown whenever he saw me, the way he did yesterday. I don't know what his problem was, but he definitely was not feeling me at all. Nevertheless, I at least had Mateo in my corner. Reynolds I wasn't quite sure about yet. He was a quiet man, one who appeared always to be looking around himself. Tristan told me that he and Reynolds had grown up together in the hood in Compton. Now with Reynolds I could definitely see the ghetto in him. He used a lot of street slang and had this walk, this pimp-like walk that was funny as hell.

I excused myself from the men after we had a light dinner. Chicken salad, with anchovies. Now anchovies had never been something I could stomach well, but Tristan had excellent taste in just about everything, it seemed, and the anchovies set the chicken salad off tastefully. I excused myself as they did the wine and cigar thing, wanting to give Sebastian a call before he ended up with cardiac arrest and then I'd have his demise on my conscience. I snickered to myself at the thought. He was extremely into this case, almost unusually so, especially since I hadn't been in California or affiliated with Jackson and his crew long. But I kind of felt it might be because of what had happened to me a year ago.

I dried myself off, slipping on a powder-blue, soft cotton gown, which fell to my thighs. I had pulled my hair up in a ponytail, using a twister to hold it up, with it sweeping my shoulders just so. As I oiled my legs, I thought about my conversation with Sebastian. I had been right; he was worried because of how emotionally involved I had become in my last case. I had been sent undercover to Long Island, New York. Guy McNeal was an evil, crafty, meticulous man who had a child pornography ring that reached from the East Coast to the West Coast. What was so bad about him was that even though he made money off the sickos who got their kicks from sexually abusing children, he was not into it himself, he was into the money. I shivered as though I were still wet when I thought about some of the things I had seen in dealing with McNeal. I had gotten so caught up in my job that I failed to use the caution that I had been trained to use, first as a DC policewoman, and then as an FBI agent. When the evidence had been accumulated to the point that we had enough on some of the higher-ups and key players in the pornography ring, instead of leaving it alone, I wanted McNeal, and I was determined that he would not get away with what he had done. My determination landed me as his prisoner, trapped and almost dead from the beating he gave me once he realized how I had tricked him for so long, and realized that I had been the traitor in the ring. I was finally rescued just in time, with Guy McNeal receiving a round of bullets from SWAT, and me receiving a week's hospitalization, and a strong reprimand from Sebastian and other superiors for my failing to obey a direct order.

I sighed, thinking about the children who were still out there being victimized by animals like McNeal. I knew firsthand what some of them went through, kidnapped children used for the sick pleasure of adult men and women with no consciences. But this case with Tristan Jackson was a different type of thing. These men honestly didn't feel they were doing anything wrong. They just felt they were working, simply doing a *job*, and the more I got to know them, the harder it was to see them as criminals, and the easier it was to see and feel their compassionate natures. I knew that with all of this, it was going to become harder and harder to keep up the facade, and my attraction to Tristan wasn't making it any easier.

I pulled the covers to my shoulders after having shut off the night-light. As I closed my eyes, it wasn't the same disgust I had felt with Guy McNeal that roamed through my mind. It was this nervous apprehension, yet at the same time, a *sense of joy* that I would again be looking into T.J. Jackson's hazel eyes come morning.

# 6

———

*Los Angeles, California . . . Tristan*

Any time I try to make something happen on time, shit always happens to fuck up my schedule. We were supposed to be jetting out of California at 9:00 A.M. and yet here we sat, an hour and fifteen minutes later, still waiting on Reynolds, no one having a clue as to where he could be. The longer I paced the concrete, the madder and madder I got. The rest of the crew was waiting in Hawk's car, patient as hell, while I felt as if my damn head were going to blow like a volcano any moment now.

"Maybe something happened, you think?" I heard Hawk ask, as he walked up behind me. Mateo and Hennessy got out of the car and were strolling toward us, too. That was something else that got to me; those two were getting really chummy. We had work to do; I didn't have time to watch them make goo-goo eyes at each other and speak love words in Spanish all the damn time! I had thought all night about how I was going to tell them to keep that shit under wraps. When they got up close to me with Mateo's arm around Hennessy's shoulder as if she were cold, I lit into them.

"You know, I meant to tell you two, if you're gonna do this lil' love thing, flirt thing, fine, but keep that shit private, because I don't know about Hawk, but y'all are just about making me sick right now!"

"What in the world?" Hennessy had an incredulous look on her face. "Love thing? Flirting?"

"Yes *flirting,* whaa, are you having a hard time understanding me or something? Can you understand the words coming outta my mouth? Or must I say it in Spanish?"

Hennessy's cocoa-brown complexion turned almost ruby; her brown eyes were smarting with anger. "Man, you have a serious problem!"

"Naw, baby, *you* have a problem. I'm not gonna let my men be sidetracked by some pretty chick when we have work to do. Now if you're with us, fine; just cool it with Mateo!" Hennessy was tight-lipped, but I swear I could almost see steam tooting out of her ears, her eyes narrowing into little slits before she stormed off to sit back in the car. Mateo was laughing in the background, grinning at me like the Cheshire Cat. "Oh, it's funny?" I asked him.

"*Mi abuelita,* mi grandmother, would always read it to me, the old biblical proverb, *Jealousy is rottenness to the bones.* Better watch that, hombre." He winked.

"Yeah, whateva," I threw back, looking up to catch Hawk looking at me somberly. "She's gotten to you, hasn't she?" he asked.

"What?"

"You know what I mean. Just be careful, T.J., okay?"

"There's nothing to be careful about," I insisted. "I just don't want her fraternizing with you guys. It's not good business."

"I'm just saying that it hasn't been quite a year since Natalie. Give it time, man."

"Natalie has nothing to do with this." My eyes narrowed, as I felt anger building up at Hawk's words.

"I know that, I'm just saying—"

"Nothing," I cut in, "to do with this! Remember that!"

Just then, our hired pilot, Tim Redmond, walked up. "How

much longer, T.J.? I'm gonna have to charge you for this wait, bruh; time is money."

"I know, Tim, and you'll be paid. Don't worry, okay?" I glanced over at Hawk, apologizing to him with my eyes for my angry outburst seconds before. He blinked his acceptance to me.

"All right," Tim said, cutting in on our silent exchange. "But I have another run at four; don't make me late, bruh." Tim walked over to fiddle with his plane.

"Great!" I sighed as he left. "If Reynolds is not here within the next twenty minutes we leave without him." As soon as the words left my mouth, up the road came a stressed-out-looking Reynolds. He bounced out of his cab like a man possessed, rushing over to where Hawk and I stood. I counted to ten and then began my questioning. "What happened to you, man?"

"It's a long, long story, dawg. My brakes gave out on me on my way here. I don't know what da hell could be wrong with them. Like somebody tampered with 'em or sumpin'. But I got here as quickly as I could."

"Who would want to tamper with your brakes, Reynolds?" Hawk laughed.

"Somebody had to!" Reynolds shouted back.

"Well, whatever happened, you could have called or something!" I exclaimed. I looked over at the sound of Tim Redmond clearing his throat to catch my attention, and then pointing toward his watch. "Listen, I need to hear about this long, long story, so your ass is not off the hook, but right now we need to get going before we end up without a pilot."

We all made our way to the plane with our suitcases, packages, and gear. I had a lot of questions for Reynolds, but now was not the time. Once we were settled, I found myself in a seat next to Hennessy, who would not even look my way. I supposed I did owe her an apology, but the problem was I didn't even understand myself why I reacted as I did. Some of it came out of worrying where Reynolds was and my anxiety about that, but it was also something else. I didn't like the friendly way she and Mateo had with each other. I didn't like how she always seemed to have this warm smile for him, and yet for me whenever I looked her way, there seemed to be apprehension and a frown.

I looked over at her through my dark shades, thankful that she could not see me watching her. The curve of her lips, the dimples in her cheeks that were so deep and defined they were still visible even when she was not smiling. I couldn't help but be intrigued by her, more than intrigued. Yes, it had only been a year since Natalie's death, but still that's a long time to mourn for someone, and I missed a woman's touch.

Hennessy looked up, and then looked over toward me. When I opened my mouth and was about to speak and apologize for my bad behavior earlier, she frowned, scowled actually, and looked the other way.

It was going to be a long ride to Santa Fe.


*Hennessy*

I have to be Anne Shirley of Green Gables reincarnated, because just like her, sometimes no matter how hard I fight it, my temper always seems to get the better of me. It was not much different today with Tristan's sudden tantrum about Mateo and me. Anyone would think the man was jealous. I warmed at the idea, thinking about his comment about *pretty chicks*. Was he calling *me* a pretty chick? Really, it shouldn't matter much anyhow, but for some reason it did. He thought I was attractive, pretty? An unwilling Grinch-like smile was forming on my face, and try as I might, I couldn't shake the feeling. I looked over at him, soaking in his manliness. I swear if he was just your everyday businessman, cop, teacher, or, hell, even a trash collector, I would be all over him, but he just happened to be a thief, and I just happened to be, well . . . Special Agent Hennessy Cooper. He looked over at me before I looked away, and even though he had on sunglasses, I felt, rather than saw, his eyes meeting mine.

"Hennessy, I really owe you an apology for earlier. I know I insulted you and it was uncalled for," he said softly.

*Wow!* I thought to myself, sincerity! "I have not been flirting with Mateo, Tristan. I really don't understand why you think I have been."

He exhaled a bit, pausing as if he wanted to think a minute before he spoke. I always considered men who thought before they spoke of the superintelligent kind. Usually men like that, and women, didn't make too many mistakes of the tongue. This meant that I wasn't of the intelligent kind, because I never thought before I spoke. "It wasn't that I felt that you and he have anything going on, actually it's none of my business." Multiple expressions crossed over his features. "It was really important that we get out to Santa Fe and start looking over our plans. Sure we could just go with what's on paper but I want you all to get a feel for the real thing, as best we can. I . . . I haven't been myself the past few days, and Reynolds being late today sort of set if off for me."

"Ah . . . is it that dream you had?" I asked in a hushed tone. He looked at me with uncertainty, as if he wasn't sure he could open up to me. "Natalie, I take it she was someone you were involved with? Someone who meant a lot to you?"

Sebastian really hadn't told me much about T.J. Jackson personally, only about his reputation in the underground world. Seeing him in the vulnerable state he was in the other night told me other things about him, things that perhaps would help aid me in this case. That was the only reason I was concerned. I *knew* it was.

"Yes, we were in a relationship."

I sat up, reaching my hand out to touch his. "Were you married?"

"No. I mean yes! I mean . . . we were going to be; or rather *I* wanted us to be. It just didn't turn out that way. I never really got a chance to ask her, and then, then she was killed." The pain in his voice was so raw, I could feel a knot slowly rising in my own. *Natalie was killed?*

"How was she killed, Tristan?" I whispered.

"It was a year ago, we worked together," he croaked out, still in obvious pain from her memory. "She . . . she did the type of things on our jobs that required a delicate touch, sort of like you will be doing. She was . . . um . . . shot. It was . . ."

"Listen, T.J., you won't believe how this shit went down, man." I jumped at the interrupted noise of Reynolds's voice. I had been totally engrossed in what Tristan was saying. He, however, had a look of relief on his face, as if happy for the interruption. His face was flushed. "I think somebody tried to kill me today."

Jumping at the chance for a change of subject, Tristan said, "Why would someone want to kill you, Reynolds?"

"I don't know, but I will tell you this much. My brakes went out this morning. Just out of the blue, a vehicle that has never given me any trouble, brakes that weren't even squealing yesterday, suddenly today just give out completely? I ended up in a ditch when I turned the corner from my crib. And I'm lucky to have gotten here alive!"

"Ain't nobody tried to kill you, Reynolds, that hoe you was with last night probably drugged your ass and took your wallet, and you probably couldn't even wake up to get here on time. Now you're embarrassed and making up shit!" All the guys laughed at Hawk's analysis of things.

"See, y'all don't believe me, but I'm serious. I wasn't high last night," Reynolds insisted.

Tristan looked as if a thought had suddenly hit him. "You know, it's odd, but just last week someone damaged Mateo's car, too. Maybe it's a conspiracy." He laughed.

"When did someone damage Mateo's car?" I inquired. A look crossed Tristan's face, and I remembered how he didn't like me showing any interest toward his men. But the fact was I showed interest toward him, too, so really he didn't have a reason to be feeling as he was.

"That really had nothing to do with what happened to Reynolds," he said flatly.

"Okay," I said, flushing a little. To get my mind off of Tristan's quirky ways I enjoyed the sights through my window.

The West was warm and beautiful, and the closer we got to New Mexico, the more I could understand that radiant look that was on Tristan's face last night when he was explaining why he had chosen to buy a ranch in Santa Fe. I sat back and soaked in its quiet beauty as Tristan gave me a bit of history of New Mexico. New Mexico consisted of three major cultures, he explained, which I thought was very interesting.

"There are the Indians who are famous for their pueblos, the Spaniards whose exotic, impressive churches had ruled New Mexico lands for centuries, and the Anglos, you know, the white folks." He laughed. I giggled back, smiling at his warm tone. "Like they did in the rest of the states, the Anglos put their stamp on this land long ago. Today, it's what you see the most of, culturally speaking. So in the modern cities, you see the look, feel, and houses that could easily have been imported from Cleveland."

"Oh!" I exclaimed. "I have an aunt in Cleveland. So is Jackson's close to the city?"

"Actually no; my ranch borders a part of Santa Fe that's surrounded by adobe hotels and such. I bought my ranch from an old Spaniard who had clung to the ancient look and feel, which I personally love. We're only about fifteen minutes away now. Wait till you see the place; you're gonna love it as much as I do," he said, smiling with assurance.

"Well, I can't wait!" I smiled. Tristan smiled back at me, taking my hand into his and bringing it to his mouth for a soft kiss. And boy did I blush! Awww . . . what a sweetie! We sat in a comfortable silence for the next few minutes before making an uneventful front-door landing at Jackson's.

Even though you could see that the place had been remodeled, Tristan wasn't lying when he said it had an old Spanish look and design to it. The exterior had a dusty adobe look, with beautiful purple and white Mexican flowers encasing its walls. I was totally entranced with the whole scene, the serenity, the beauty and originality. I was especially taken in by how much this place revealed about Mr. Jackson. He had said this was his dream home, and aren't our dreams simply visions of what we desire deep inside ourselves? If this was his dream, as beautiful as it was, what could the person inside Tristan Jackson be like? And if I ever found out, would he hold me as captive and entranced as his dream home did?


*Santa Fe, New Mexico . . . Tristan*

As soon as we landed at Jackson's, I felt this instant peace. It's hard to describe, but where I am always does something to my persona. When I'm in LA at my beach home I feel comfortable and at home, far more comfortable than I do in, say, Beverly Hills, amongst the rich and famous, and I especially feel more comfortable there than in Compton where my mother lives, surrounded by the street violence that was so much a part of my life growing up. But not even my LA beach home can compare to the feeling of home I get whenever I am in Santa Fe. It isn't just the beauty of it, because to be straight-up honest about it, all of Santa Fe, and New Mexico in general, is *not* beautiful. But Jackson's is. I try to stay down at least three-fourths of the year, although I have to make frequent trips to LA and Compton, being that my mom refuses to leave the hood. I know her reasons are that she doesn't want me around her so much as to control or attempt to control her drug use and abuse. I can count on one hand the number of times she had been to Santa Fe, which she described as an old, boring corn state full of smelly old Mexicans and drunken Indians. Very few people can understand my attraction to the place, feeling it is so different from the sophisticated image I show everywhere else. Only Mateo, whom I had met in Madrid years ago, could feel and empathize even to the tiniest degree where I was coming from. Not even Natalie had completely understood, and it had been very hard to convince her to come down here with me the few times that she had. I guess now, though, it really doesn't matter. Natalie was gone, and she wasn't coming back. One day my sense of guilt will go, too, at least I hope it will.

\*    \*    \*

As we began grabbing our bags and luggage from the small plane, I felt even more at home at the sound of my young housekeeper Aurora's voice singing out as she ran from out of the house. "Señor Tristan, Señor Tristan, welcome home!"

# 7

---

*Santa Fe, New Mexico . . . Tristan*

Aurora was a young, beautiful Mexican angel I had had on my payroll for the last three years. She had been destitute really and desperately in need of a job. Not only was I happy for her sake that I had hired her to care for the main house at Jackson's, I was also happy for myself. There was not a better cook or housekeeper this side of the West Coast. After giving me lots of hugs and being introduced to Hennessy, she smiled a big, warm smile, turning her eyes and attention toward Mateo. Mateo seemed to have *all* the ladies these days, I thought with a frown, instantly shaking my head as the jealous thoughts flew through it.

I personally did not have a lot of bags. I had just as much of my clothing at Jackson's as I kept in LA. The person with the most baggage was, of course, Hennessy, who watched the guys like a hawk, specifically Hawk himself, who carried her makeup case. There was nothing worse than broken-up blush or eye shadow cases, she explained, and her makeup was Mary Kay, and *very* expensive. I had to laugh at that one. In my world of expensive things and with my knowing the taste of the extravagant ladies of Hollywood, Mary Kay was not what one would call expensive. But I noticed Hawk giving her a little frown but still carrying her makeup bag as tenderly as if he were carrying the queen's jewels.

"I'm not trying to be picky," I heard her explaining to Hawk, "it's just that you can never be too careful, you know."

I smiled as I remembered our first lunch a week before, with her *make sure the fish is well done* comment to the waitress at Shelly's. I was eager to see her reaction to my home, and could hardly keep my eyes off her as we all walked inside and down the long hallway. Her eyes lit up, which for some reason did crazy things to my heart.

"Oh, my gosh, this is so beautiful! I have always loved the old Mexican villas I used to see on television."

"I'm really surprised that you like it." I smiled, admiring with her the art adorning the sitting-room wall, which bordered the long hallway. "Actually this wouldn't really be described as a villa, but the mix of Spanish art and Indian carvings might give you that aura."

"I have a nice lunch prepared for you all," Aurora said, cutting in. "As soon as you all are unpacked, head on into the kitchen and enjoy!"

"*Gracias,* Aurora, it's going to be so nice not being the only female around now," Hennessy joked.

"Oh, you know you loved it," Mateo said to Hennessy. "Women always like *atención,* right, Aurora?" He winked.

"Oh, is that what I've been getting here with you guys?" Aurora giggled.

"I can give you a bit more if you want, *bebé,*" said Mateo. I looked at Hennessy, wondering about her reaction to Mateo's flirting with Aurora. I hoped she wasn't interested in him or else she would be in for a letdown. Mateo flirted with every female within a fifty-mile range.

"Let me show you to your room," I offered Hennessy. The other guys made their way to the back of the house where they knew the small guest-room section was. I walked her upstairs though, to one of the main bedrooms. Opening the door, I again was waiting for her reaction, but this time I wanted to see what she thought of what Aurora called *"asilo de una princesa,"* haven of a princess.

"Wow!"

"You like?"

"Did you have this fancied up like this just for me?" she asked expectantly.

I laughed, leaning back against the door as she roamed inside, caressing the ivory-colored quilt. The room actually was pretty enough for a princess. The walls were white and covered in white-rose wallpaper, which matched the quilt and draperies. I had told Aurora that we had a lady coming, and to ready the room. She had done so by including fresh white roses in a vase, which sat atop a circular glass table covered with a lace cloth, and sprinkled with fresh rose petals.

"Many of the rooms here were decorated when I came. This is one of them. Although I replaced some of the old decor with new, the coloring and style is the same. I thought that you would be very comfortable here, and not have your privacy invaded so much by being in a room right next to the guys, even though, believe me, you can trust all of them. There are no mad rapists in our bunch."

"Oh, I trust you there. I like the guys, and I really appreciate your thoughtfulness," she answered. I waited, not sure for what reason, before taking a deep breath and excusing myself.

"Well, I'll leave you to get settled, and we'll get the rest of your bags up here. We'll be having lunch in about twenty minutes, so I'll see you then," I said.

She nodded as I closed her door quietly behind me.


*Hennessy*

If I could get ghetto for a minute here, this room is *da bomb.* I love feminine, prissy things. Although I had not grown up poor, I wasn't born with a silver spoon in my mouth either. Both my parents had to work. My mother was a career woman, a social worker who toiled diligently to help lower-income kids reach outside the ghetto and see their true potential. My father had been a sergeant for the NYPD before his early retirement because of a back injury he incurred on the job. He had always been my hero. So although I had gotten my degree in journalism, and had thoughts of being a news reporter, my father's courage, his love for the law, and his determination to fulfill his role as a police officer, all of that led me to make a complete turnaround in my career plans, and led me to want to be the son my father never had. Although I have never been a tomboy, my father had always told me that my feistiness and determination to right the things that are wrong in the world would take me far. I started out small, thinking that being a local NYPD policewoman would be enough, but soon the Big Apple, even as big as it was, became too small for me, and I felt the need to branch out and test my wings. Eventually I applied to and was accepted at the Federal Bureau of Investigation.

I looked around the room again, and smiled. I wasn't materialistic. My sister, April, and I had been raised well and happy, not wanting for anything, yet at the same time not so wealthy that we didn't understand what dreams were, or how important it was to save for those special things. Considering all that, I felt like Alice in Wonderland. The room felt so cozy and smelled so good. I lay flat on the bed, bouncing up and down atop its soft mattress. Just as I jumped off gleefully to check out the paintings that were decorating the stone walls so beautifully, the door opened, with a smiling Aurora standing at its entranceway.

"*Hola*, señorita!" she said.

"*Hola.*" I smiled back. "I want to thank you for the roses, Aurora. They smell so good. This is a beautiful room."

"Yes, it is my favorite room to dust and clean." She paused for a moment before saying, "You know when Señor Tristan told me there would be a lady coming, I knew you had to be someone special."

I looked up at Aurora in surprise; she had gotten the wrong idea and I had to correct that ASAP. "No, Aurora, it's not like that; we are business partners working together. It's not at all personal."

"Hmm . . . Can I say something?" she asked.

"Please do."

"I know why you are here," Aurora said solemnly.

My heart hammered at her words. She knew why I was here? What could she have meant by that? I was starting to become too damn paranoid. "What do you mean?" I asked her.

"It is your *destino*. He needs you, and so you are here to soothe his heart, even though you may not know it." Aurora stood by the glass table, picking up a rose petal and bringing it up to her nostrils to smell its aroma. "The roses, they were his idea, not mine; you know this?"

"No, I didn't know that," I said, feeling happy that my paranoia was unfounded, but feeling an oddity nevertheless that it was Tristan who had asked Aurora to get the roses. What exactly did that mean? Sebastian had told me to flirt with Tristan, make him trust me, get on his good side. Was I somehow managing that already?

"Well, I better go set up the table. If you need anything, *mi hermana,* please let me know, okay?" Aurora smiled sweetly.

"Thank you, Aurora. I think I'm going to like it here. Santa Fe seems to be very beautiful."

"Oh, it is!" she exclaimed. "Can I call you Hennessy?" I nodded, happy to have someone close by that I felt so comfortable with. "Great! Remember what I told you, Hennessy: don't fight fate."

I had to laugh. Someone was going to be trying to play matchmaker; I could tell. "Oh, I hear you all right; I won't forget." She smiled as she turned to walk out the door, when a sudden thought hit me. "Uh . . . Aurora?"

"Yes?" She turned back around expectantly.

"Did you know Natalie?"

"He told you about her?"

"Well, a little, but our conversation got interrupted," I answered honestly.

"Yes, I knew her." Aurora studied my face, as though examining me. "You and she look nothing alike."

Hmm . . . I didn't know quite how to take that, but before I could question her further, she smiled again, and left.


*Tristan*


All of us were pretty much tired and fighting jet lag. I told Hennessy and the guys that we would relax, have lunch, and perhaps get started on our practice sessions early the next morning. I had showered earlier, so I was trying to relax myself. I walked over to the wide window, which faced my stables. That was another of my joys here in Santa Fe, my horses. I not only loved breeding them, I loved to ride. It relaxed me.

I took a swallow of my drink, feeling the strong liquor burning its way down my throat to my chest. Right now, I wasn't feeling very relaxed, I was feeling worried. I picked up my phone and dialed.

Even though I had tried numerous times, Earl had not been answering the phone at the beach house. I had given him the keys so that he could move in there while I was away. I knew I would see him in another week. I had promised myself that even though we would only be in New Mexico a month, I would fly back every two weeks to check on him. I knew that with his health problems, I could never be too careful. I had called three times since our having arrived in Santa Fe, only to be greeted with the sound of constant phone ringing, which became aggravating at best. I sighed as I placed the phone back on the ringer.

"This is crazy," I said aloud to myself. "I'm trippin' over nothing; he simply stepped out for a while." I laughed again at myself, my paranoia, then grabbed my jeans off my bed to begin dressing. I was suddenly feeling a great rumble in my stomach, which told me I needed to put something in it like *now*.

Lunch was delicious, but that was no surprise. I smiled at Aurora, thanking her for making our homecoming as comfortable as she had.

After lunch, I grabbed Hennessy's hand and showed her all around Jackson's, giving her more of its rich history. Although I had to deal with Mateo's teasing, claiming that I was vying for Hennessy's affection, Reynolds's complaints that we were wasting time and that we should be going over our plans ASAP, and Hawk's frowns and grunts in agreement with Reynolds, plus his insistence that he still didn't trust Hennessy, it still turned out to be a pretty good evening. When I turned in, however, I had a lot to think about. I couldn't help but wonder what type of men Hennessy was into, or if she had a boyfriend up in New York. There were a lot of things that I wanted to know that didn't have anything at all to do with the subject at hand, namely training and getting everyone ready for New York. But in the meantime, like the twisted saying goes, all work and no play could make T.J. a raving lunatic. That being the case, I resolved to spend more time with Hennessy, that is, if she was free and willing. I had never been shy, or unsure of my own charms.

I went to my door, and looked out, glancing toward the princess room. Hennessy had not yet closed her door, and I was taken by surprise when she walked past, beautiful as always, with her hair caressing her shoulders. My eyes followed in the direction of her cleavage. The cocoa-colored swell of her breasts was barely covered by the long silk night robe she wore. My eyes slowly moved up from her breasts, to her eyes. They had an almost smoky glow to them.

"Good night," she whispered.

"Good night," I stammered out. Hennessy closed her door before I finished my words. It was at that moment that I realized how fast my heart was beating.

We were blessed with a warm, beautiful morning for our first practice round. I opened the cellar door, and instead of an old mildew smell there was the scent of fresh paint.

"Here we are," I announced. The cellar door gave a welcoming creaking sound.

"It's underground?" Reynolds asked, perplexed. He was referring to the model rooms I had had built in the cellar.

"Yep, and wait till you all see it; it's perfect."

I had gotten the cobwebs and oldness swept away months earlier, and with day-by-day diligence, now had a perfect replica of the rooms we would be working in at the Metropolitan Museum. Hennessy was the last one to make it down the narrow stairway. I reached out to help her, grabbing her around her waist, and pulling her close for a moment before setting her down with a sigh. I didn't know if she noticed it. I *hoped* she didn't notice it, but that one breath of a moment left me with a raging hard-on.

"Goddamn, man!" Hawk screamed. "You've totally changed this place. How long did it take to get all this done?"

"It's a work of art, huh?" I grinned. I was feeling pretty proud. A few months prior, I had made numerous trips to New York and the Met, so I knew what to shoot for. I had hired men I knew I could trust, whom I had worked with for almost six months to reconstruct things, and they hadn't let me down.

"Damn straight it's a work of art." Hawk laughed. I observed Hennessy's impressed look, not that anyone could be anything but impressed. Whatever I did, I did one hundred percent, including pulling off a forty-million-dollar robbery. Although the rooms were narrower, I had copied more the architecture of the place than the surface design.

"As of now, they are planning to place King Narmer's palette in this room." I walked toward one of the rooms I had reconstructed. "We would have a hell of a time getting it from this entrance, as you can see." I walked everyone over to a full wall map I had put up, and began pointing to various guards that had been drawn in on the map.

"See, they have it so secured, not only because of the Narmer palette, but also because on the other side, in the room across, are the ceramic artifices from old-emperor China that were given to Roosevelt after World War Two. They think that by putting the Egyptian pieces nearby, no one would dare try to get them." All eyes were on me as I went on to explain our strategy and plans.

"Hey, maybe we can get a few of those Chinese vases while we're there," Reynolds suggested.

I shook my head. "We don't need to press our luck. Besides, the alarm system in that room is much harder to get around than the room the palette will be in. I'm sure that eventually they plan to install the same system, but I have a feeling that they won't have it set up by day two of just moving the palette in. But that really doesn't matter at this point."

"Because we are coming from *under* the Met we won't even have to worry about alarms," Mateo said, as the realization of what I was saying hit him.

"You smart bitch, Mateo, you figured it out. Duh!" Hawk joked.

"Suck my dick, papi!" Mateo laughed back.

Hawk snickered, good-naturedly. "Yeah, that's right; I forgot your ass was *sexually challenged.*" I heard Hennessy clearing her throat uncomfortably at their teasing vulgarity.

"All right, guys, no dick sucking today; y'all forget we have a lady in the house," I spat out, winking when Hennessy looked at me, shaking her head. I held my hand up, stopping everyone in their tracks as they started to walk into the room that was modeled after King Narmer's slate palette room.

I stopped walking, looking toward my group seriously again. "This"—I waved my hand toward the door of the room—"is the farthest we will go into the Narmer room. And we will be going in . . ." I snapped my fingers, nodding my head for everyone to follow me. "Here . . ."—I pointed toward a small iron-covered hole that was reachable from another room in the cellar. By now it looked more like a huge redone basement than an underground cellar—"is our entryway. The other side of this is a gutter, which will be located twenty feet north of the Narmer room.

"Now our handler for this job, who by the way will of course be Ms. Hennessy, will be going in through this hole. You will have twenty feet to worm your way, in the dark, to this tunnel. So you know what that means, right?"

Hennessy was looking flabbergasted at my whole description of things, so I had to repeat myself. "Hennessy?"

"Uh . . . yeah?" she answered.

"You know what this means, right? We won't be feeding you a lot of strawberry shortcake this month," I quipped. I knew what was coming next.

"What the hell is that supposed to mean?" she shouted. "I've told you before, I am not *fat*. I am a size seven, a *petite* seven at that!" I, along with Mateo, Hawk, and Reynolds, laughed heartily at her outburst. "Okay, so it's funny, huh?" she huffed. "Can one of you *funny* guys tell me how my *tiny* body is supposed to fit through that little hole, get the palette, and get it out without so much as a dent, seeing that I have to crawl twenty feet in the gutter?"

"Mateo and I will be with you. We can go twelve feet into the tunnel; then we turn left and the hole will get even smaller. That's where you come in. You can make it the rest of the way by yourself, Hennessy, believe me. Mateo and I will be waiting for you on the other side. Hawk and Reynolds will be waiting for all of us with the car. You get the palette, and all of us are forty million dollars richer."

"The one thing I have to say, guys, is that you know how valuable this piece is, and you know that if we are caught, I'm not going back to prison. They will have to take me fighting, or dead. I can't make any decisions for any of you, but the question is, how much is it worth to you, all of you?"

No one spoke. I supposed everyone had a lot to think about. The money, the risk, the excitement, all of which went hand in hand with the career we had all chosen. One I secretly hoped to retire from very soon.

# 8

---

*Malibu Beach*

Earl had no idea who could have been following him. He had had this odd premonition all day, and rarely was he wrong about things like that. After having gone for his doctor's appointment, he had driven to T.J.'s place to take some of his things over. T.J. had told him he could stay at the beach house, which Earl himself had to admit was going to be much more comfortable than the halfway house. But at this moment, comfortable could hardly describe how he was feeling. From the time he had left Maggie's house with his luggage till now he knew someone was behind him, watching his every step.

He pulled up in the driveway, looking around before shutting off the engine. He was alone, maybe, but Earl knew his imagination was not running wild, and just to be sure, he felt his waist for the .38 special he had been keeping close to him in case some idiot in LA decided to test an old man. Sensing that he was alone, he got out of the car, deciding to unlock the door to the house before dragging his bags in. Since his sickness, his strength had slipped away little by little.

Once Earl was comfortably inside the house, he let out a breath of relief, feeling tired from the overexertion, but relaxed at the same time. After having fixed himself a sandwich and coffee, he turned on the evening news. Listening to the latest goings-on in south central LA, drive-bys and the like, he thought to himself, there was always some type of urban catastrophe going on. Life hadn't much changed from twenty years prior, when he had been locked up in the pen. He thought about T.J.; there was work he had to do with him; the last time he had talked to him, he could tell that some of what he was trying to say was getting through. Although he hadn't hoped to get him to cancel his upcoming plans for the museum in Cairo, he had gotten T.J. to promise this would be his last job. It wasn't that he wanted to be pushy or preachy, but he didn't want T.J. to be sitting in the position that he was in. He wanted him to understand that there was more to life, and other choices besides the ones that they had made. Earl wanted to rectify his life's mistakes, and having no children of his own, having not stopped long enough to build his own family, he had adopted T.J. as his. He wanted the best for him, and he knew that his own life was not one to emulate. With the TV on and with all these thoughts mulling around in his head, he didn't hear the window that was being opened, nor the soft footsteps as they crept ever closer to him.

A tall man, dressed all in black, walked up to the back of the couch that Earl was sitting on, and as quietly and elegantly as a panther pulled out a large-caliber pistol. Earl turned around suddenly at the sound, only to be confronted with the weapon at his forehead. "Who are you?" he exclaimed.

"Have you made your peace with God, old man?" the tall, Nubian-dressed man asked in a whisper, before slowly pulling the trigger.


*Santa Fe, New Mexico . . . Tristan*


It just didn't make any sense. I knew for a fact that Earl wouldn't be away from the house *this* much, not with him feeling as bad as he had been telling me he felt sometimes. A few days passed, and even though I kept busy, and kept the guys and Hennessy busy with the training, my mind still could not get rid of the scary suspicion that something was very, very wrong. I wanted to get someone to check on him, but at the same time I knew how private Earl was and didn't want to invade that privacy by having him checked on as if he were a teenage boy who just might have a wild party while the parents were away.

I decided that I needed a break from the relentless discussions and training for the New York job. Besides, Mateo and Hawk had been getting into these little joking battles over everything lately and my anxiety about Earl didn't make me very tolerant of them. I left them to their bickering, and went in and changed to my riding gear. Just as I was coming out of my room, Hennessy came past.

"Are you okay?" she asked.

"Yeah, I'm fine, just needed a break from the noise."

She laughed softly. "Yes, I can understand that; those guys can be a handful. So where are you heading?"

I thought a minute before answering her. "Do you ride?"

"Ride?"

"Horses," I answered. "Have you ever ridden before?"

Hennessy perked up. "When I was a little girl, my father took me and my sister to visit family in North Carolina. They had the most beautiful mares there. I tried to ride, but of course I was a straight amateur. That was the first and last time I rode."

"Well, here's your chance." I smiled, throwing my bag with my riding gear over my shoulder. "Come along with me; I'm sure there is something we can find at the stables that you can fit."

"Oh my gosh." She giggled. "I guess I can . . . try, but if I get thrown, I'm holding you accountable, Tristan Jackson."

"Trust me, does this look like a face of a man who would fool you?" I winked at her, with her laughing back at me as she led the way down the narrow hallway.

I picked a young, calm mare for Hennessy; didn't want to frighten her with a powerful, fast one and have her vow never to ride again. I had Alonzo, one of my stable men, suit up

Parry, a beautiful, white, docile babe I had purchased three months prior on a trip I had taken to England. Hennessy smiled as Alonzo introduced her to the mare.

"You guys talk as if she were human." She grinned.

"But she is," I insisted. "Horses are the closest thing to humans you will ever find; the only thing they do differently is they don't kill each other."

"Huh?" She looked perplexed.

"Well, they eat, sleep, and play just like children. The ones fresh out of adolescence even *make whoopee*," I whispered close in her ear, as if telling a secret.

She looked at me, her cheeks flushing slightly. "Well, thank you, that's just what I needed to know, the sexual habits of horses. Now my education is complete thanks to you."

I winked. "Anything for a lady. Okay, let's go!" I had saddled up my own horse. A black stallion, which was one of my first purchases when I bought the ranch.

"So what's his name?" Hennessy asked.

"Bond, James Bond." I fixed my voice in an English accent, smiling as she shook her head.

"You really are a trip, you know that?" She laughed.

"No, I really did name him James Bond, no joke." I smirked. "Let's go, milady."

I couldn't recall an afternoon that had ever flown by as fast or as peacefully as this one had. Although she was an obvious rookie, it didn't take Hennessy long to get the hang of things, and she and Parry seemed to be a match made in heaven. She looked beautiful, her glowing caramel skin upon the whiteness of the mare. And as Hennessy joked, Parry must've liked her too, seeing that she didn't throw her. She laughed as she told me about her first time riding as a child, and how the horse had made her hit rock bottom again and again. She had this sense of wonderment that was intoxicating. Every time she saw something new, she would get all giddy with the excitement of a child. She reacted exactly as I had when I first saw Jackson's, before I had decided to purchase it. We rode for about an hour, then stopped at a heated stream to catch our breaths.

"So could you get used to this, you think?" I asked her as I helped her off of Parry.

"For sure I could." She laughed. I gripped her around the waist. She wrapped her hands around my neck and hopped down to stand in front of me. I held her there. I could sense her puzzlement, her eyes growing wide in curiosity.

"So . . . do you have a man?"

"Um . . . where?" she gave a lil' laugh. I ran my hands up and down her hips, still not letting her go.

"You know what I mean. Are you seeing someone in New York?" I didn't know what I was gonna do if she snubbed my advance, but my heart was beating fast at the thought, or it could have been just beating fast at the knowledge that she hadn't pulled away yet. I pulled her closer, drawing her hips up snuggly against mine.

"No, I'm not," she whispered back. Neither of us said anything for a minute. Hell, I didn't know what to say. *Is that her heart beating? Or is it mine? Maybe I should try to kiss her. Maybe not. Maybe . . .* I waited too long to decide. She pulled back, looking at my nose, not my eyes.

"Excuse me," she breathed. I backed up, slowly dropping my hands from her hips, and letting her past. I closed my eyes wanting to kick myself for passing up that chance. She had walked up closer to the stream, wrapping her arms around herself as if chilly.

"Are you cold?" I asked her. "It's usually cooler here by the water for some reason." I took off the thin jacket I was wearing and walked up behind her to wrap it around her arms. Damn . . . I couldn't help it, she was either going to have to slap my face or . . . She felt so good. I heard her sigh, moaning a little. I pulled her back against me, and started kissing and sucking at the crook of her neck, slowly moving one of my hands up to press against her rib cage, almost daring to cup her breast. Hennessy turned her eyes up to me as if about to say something, and I seized the opportunity, covering her lips with mine. Her mouth opened automatically, grabbing at my tongue as I explored her. She tasted so good; I could feel a heat flash coursing through me from head to toe. I reached my hands down her belly, to her hips, to press her back against my hardness. I trailed my lips from hers, down her cheek to her jawline, leaving a wet line of kisses. She sighed my name. "Tristan, yes. . . ." Then she gasped, "No! Oh, my goodness, what is wrong with me? I can't be doing this!"

"Turn around," I whispered. "I just wanted to kiss you. Please?" She turned around, putting her hand on my chest. "You said you didn't have anyone."

"And I don't. But—"

I pulled her close again, finding her lips and tracing them with my tongue. She moaned. I pulled back a little, locking her eyes with mine. "But what? I'm not seeing anyone either, and I'm interested in you. I have been from the moment I first saw you." I saw hesitation in her eyes. "See, I've put myself on the line here so you can't embarrass me." I smiled.

"I'm not going to embarrass you," she said shyly, "but I didn't come here looking to get into anything with anyone. And . . . maybe I'm not your type."

"Am I your type?" Did I really want to know the answer to that? "Okay, I'll let you off the hook." I laughed, finally letting her loose, but not before bringing her hand to my mouth for a kiss.

"You know, you really are a sweetie," she said, sighing.

"Not as sweet as you." I winked. We were both quiet, neither of us knowing where else to take this scene. I decided to change the subject.

"Listen, I was gonna fly back to LA for a short break. I need to check on someone. Do you want to come with me, or would you feel more comfortable here with the other guys?"

"Oh, I would rather go with you. Who is it that you need to check on?"

We both got settled on our horses. I gave James Bond a pat on the ass for the welcoming strut he always gave me. I was delighted that Hennessy had said so quickly that she would join me. Not that I was worried about leaving her here with the other guys, but it was always good to have a traveling companion, and I loved being around her, period. I had decided not to push her though. Something was there, in her eyes. I wasn't sure what it was, I was almost certain that she was as attracted to me as I was to her, yet something was holding her back. Whatever it was, I didn't want to push my luck and have her draw away from me completely. I would just bide my time, and wait her out.

I needed desperately to get to LA. I had thought about it for hours, and I could come to no other conclusion. Now I only needed to get in touch with Tim Redmond.

"Tristan?" Hennessy broke me from my train of thought. "Who was it that you needed to get in touch with?"

"Well, remember I had mentioned before about this guy who I had gotten pretty close to while I was, um . . ." It felt weird as hell to be sitting here talking to her about having been in the pen, for some reason. I watched her sitting on Parry, her face looking serene, and understanding.

"Are you uncomfortable talking to me about this?" she asked.

"No, but it's getting late. I need to get us a ride to LA at this late hour, *hopefully,* and, um, I guess it doesn't feel too cool sitting here talking to the woman I just tried to seduce about having been in the big house." I laughed weakly.

"Well, it would be pretty hypocritical of me to down you for that, seeing the reason that I came to meet you." I looked at her oddly, not sure what she meant. "The Met," she said pointedly.

"Oh, yeah, I almost forgot." I laughed. "Earl helped me get through some rough times when I was in prison." We began a slow gallop toward the ranch as we talked. I continued, "I was young, scared, and nervous as hell. I was this scrawny badass kid suddenly hooked up with the real deal. My mom always used to tell me that one day I was gonna meet up with someone bigger and badder than I was, and she was right. But Earl, he was there for me, gave me protection and taught me a lot of things. You could say he's like a father to me now. I never for-get those who have my back, you know?"

"I'm pretty much the same way," she said.

We rode the rest of the way back to Jackson's in a comfort-able silence, both of us lost in our own individual thoughts. Alonzo greeted us at the stables. "Did you have a good ride, señor?" he asked.

"*Sí*, we did, Alonzo." I looked over at Hennessy, noting her blush. She brushed imaginary lint off of her backside, looking around as if lost. Alonzo grabbed the reins of our mares and exited with them to the stables. I grabbed Hennessy's hand. "So I'll get in touch about getting Tim Redmond, the pilot that brought us out here. I'm sure there won't be a problem getting back to LA with late notice like this. He's usually pretty flexible as long as the money is flashing."

"Okay," she said, "I'll go pack a bag."

"Hennessy . . . I really did enjoy our ride, and everything else, too."

She hesitated, but then said honestly, "So did I, Tristan."

# 9

---

Hawk and Reynolds had been livid about our leaving. Reynolds carried on about how we had only just gotten to New Mexico, and how with so much money involved we needed all the practice time for the robbery that we could get. Their ranting didn't seem to bother Tristan though. I was very impressed by the diplomatic way he spoke with his men, yet he was still able to leave them knowing that *he* was in charge, not they.

After I had gotten back to my room after our horseback ride and witnessed the small-scale argument between Tristan and the guys, I felt breathless almost to the point of hyperventilation. I have to say my mind was just about gone. I could hardly believe the intimate exchange by the stream had really happened, that I had let him kiss me that way, that I had kissed him back. That I had sucked on his tongue, and could feel him all hard against my butt. In fact, I wanted to give it a little wiggle if the truth be told. Tristan had asked if I had a man. The truth was I had been in two prior relationships. The first was with my high school sweetie, Tevon Martin. There was never really an official break up with Tevon. We simply grew apart, especially since we ended up going to different colleges. I took a break from men and focused on my career for a while after that. Second, was my last relationship that ended only six months ago. I had nothing but stars in my eyes for this smooth talking, chocolate-skinned Casanova named Vincent. He was a fellow FBI agent who had played me like a flute, and it was all good till I found out he was a multi-talented musician, of the heart that is. He had been seeing other women as well. After finding that out, it didn't take long for the beautiful music he was making with me to stop playing.

When I was at the stream with Tristan I heard all kinds of tender melodies. Maybe it was time for me to take up dancing, and leave the music thing alone.

Tristan had been right, it had been very easy to convince Tim Redmond to make an unexpected trip to Jackson's in order to fly us back out to LA. Once we were on the plane on the way back to LA, my mind was still in an uproar over the intimate situation.

"Ugh," I said aloud.

"What's wrong?" Tristan asked. We had been quiet for the past fifteen minutes of the ride.

"Oh, nothing, had a slight cramp in my leg; that usually happens with me when I'm flying."

"Well, it won't be much longer," Tristan said. He looked anxious, and quiet, causing me to lie back myself, not wanting to disturb whatever had him preoccupied. I kinda knew it was the thing about not having heard from Earl. It was odd to see a black man who was raised in the ghetto, hood, or however you wished to phrase it, who was so very attached to an old Jewish man. But it was pretty easy to see that his attachment was no pretense.

After about another thirty minutes of flying in total silence, Tristan jerked me out of a sleep-like state with, "Okay, we're here." Tim Redmond gave us a smooth landing, which was a relief to me. I never did much like flying. Usually when I went to visit my family in New York from DC, I'd rent a car and drive, which I also hated. I hated traveling *period*.

Since we had driven to the landing base with Hawk a couple

of days before, Tristan had ordered a cab to be waiting for us. It was right on time. We scurried out of the plane with our luggage.

"Thanks, Tim," Tristan said. "I'll be in contact with you in a day or so."

"No problem, T.J., just holla." Tim looked over at me and nodded a good-bye.

It was an odd feeling riding to Tristan's beach house. I could sense and feel his anxiety the closer we got. I don't know exactly what he thought was going on, but I could tell he didn't think it was good. Also, my own premonition as an agent told me something was up. As we pulled up in the sandy drive, I noted a black Olds in the driveway. Tristan noticed it at the same time.

"That's the car I rented for Earl!" he exclaimed. He jumped out of the cab, leaving our bags, before the cabby, who was obviously Jamaican, informed him, "You have to get those bags, mon!"

"Oh, sorry," Tristan said, grabbing both his and mine. I grabbed my small makeup case and followed him to the door. He walked in long, hurried strides. My heart was beating rapidly. Unlocking the door in a hurry, Tristan burst inside, both of us immediately seeing an open window, blinds flapping at the warm air that breezed through.

"Oh, God . . ." Tristan said.

"What's wrong?" I asked, following him toward the couch. It took two seconds for me to see what was wrong. A body and splatters of congealed blood and brains told the complete story. I swallowed back nausea, grabbing my mouth to keep in the contents of my morning breakfast. Tristan let out a squeal that sounded like a wounded animal as he reached out to hug the remains of what must've been Earl.

"Oh, my God! Oh, my God! Who did this?"

"We should call the police," I said, breathing deeply. I rushed over to the phone, dialing 911. Tristan's cries had grown to a full weeping now, as he rocked Earl close to him.

"Earl, Earl, who did this to you? Who did this?"

"I'd like to report a murder. Yes, a murder. One moment please." I put the operator on hold, asking Tristan for the address of his beach house. He was so torn up he could barely get it out, but eventually did. After hanging up, I walked over to Tristan, who was still hugging Earl's body close to him, and crying.

"I'm so sorry, Tristan. . . ." I could somehow feel his pain roaming through my body, wreaking havoc with my emotions. Never had I been affected like this working undercover. I had to keep reminding myself that this was Tristan's world, T.J. Jackson's world, that he was not some poor innocent man who had found someone he loved murdered. That he, too, had probably murdered many, and this was probably a hit because of his own deeds, or the deeds of Earl. But I somehow couldn't see it like that. Tristan's pain was real; his obvious love for this man was, too. And I liked Tristan, cared about him more than I should. It hurt me to see him hurting. Tristan looked up at me with tears floating in his eyes, as if dazed, then back down at Earl. I caressed the nape of his neck, trying to comfort him a little until the police got there. It only took about eight minutes before we heard the sound of the sirens roaring up the Malibu beachfront.

I stood back once the LAPD was on the scene. Actually, I was afraid that I would recognize one or two of them, or that they would recognize me, and I could not have Tristan suspicious under any circumstances. Both he and I answered the questions posed to us the best we could. That we had only just flown in, that we had found the body with no clue as to who could have been responsible, although I felt an itch that Tristan might have kinda, sorta known the culprits. After about an hour of interrogation, the LAPD finally took their leave. The coroner had removed Earl's body earlier. I felt exhausted, not only from the questioning of the police, but just from the trauma of the whole event.

"I'm so sorry, Tristan. I know how much he meant to you," I whispered. Tristan had disappeared in his bedroom. His back was away from me as he watched the beach water, washing against the bank of red sands, through his window. He was silent. I walked into his room, searching for words to ease the quiet. As I walked up behind him, I saw the twinkle of a large-caliber pistol shining in the sunlight, Tristan rubbing it as if prepping. I gasped. "What are you gonna do?" He ignored me, then walked over to the bureau, pulled open a drawer, and took out bullets to fill the gun.

"What are you going to do, Tristan?" I said in a panicked voice.

"I'm gonna find out who did this shit and blow da hell outta 'em!"

"Tristan, it's not worth it; you won't bring Earl back by going after someone else. You'll only end up hurt yourself, or end up in prison again!" I exclaimed, feeling a nervous ache coursing all through me. He ignored me still.

"Tristan, pleeeease . . ."

He looked at me finally, and then fell weakly to his knees. His eyes went glossy. And seeing him like this ripped at my heart.

"God, I can only imagine what you're feeling right now. But what good is it to go storming out like this? Do you even have a clue as to who could be responsible?"

"Maybe . . . I don't know," he whispered. "But, Hennessy, can't you see I have to do something? I can't just sit here. I really can't believe he's gone. . . ."

As I was stroking his hair tenderly, Tristan's tearful stance seemed to change back to the vengeful spirit he had shown minutes before. He placed his gun in his gun belt, then pulled a second, smaller .22 out of the drawer, and hooked it in an ankle belt. "I need to go out for a while."

"I'm coming with you."

"Suit yourself."

I followed him into the living room, grabbing the cashmere sweater I had worn on the plane. *I'm coming with you,* I had told him. To what, and to where, I had no idea. I only hoped I wasn't getting in too deep again.

## Los Angeles, California . . . Tristan

It wasn't fair. Life was never fair. I had always known this. It had never escaped me that bad things usually happened to good people, and the assholes were usually the ones who were never held accountable for anything. Earl hadn't long to live as it was, and only wanted to spend the remaining months he did have in comfort, and with the one person he loved and was close to, me. And yet Rolez decided to come now, to pay back an old debt. I really wasn't sure that Rolez was responsible, but I still needed to talk to him, talk to someone, *do* something to curb this ache inside; do something to show Earl that his death would not go down as just another ex-con who couldn't make it in the outside world.

I swallowed hard, determined not to let the tears drop again. I could feel Hennessy looking at me, watching me pensively. I was feeling regrets now that I had allowed her to come with me, but regardless of that, I wasn't going to let her company stop me from taking care of business. I didn't want my anger and rage to cool off. I wanted to look Rolez in the eye, see for myself if there was a touch of smugness in his eyes. I wasn't looking to hurt anyone, and I wasn't a murderer, although I had been involved in plenty of drive-bys in my youth, and bullets from my gun had maybe taken a couple of brothers out in the past, but I had managed to put that behind me, to rebuild myself. Now I was a *businessman*, it was all about money, not respect or territory as it had been when I rolled with the crips. Rolez had been someone I had known from back in the day, back when I had first gotten out of the pen. We had done some work together, drug related. Rolez and I had both gone in different directions after working together for a while. Eventually, he had been caught and arrested for drug smuggling, and for some odd reason was convinced that I had turned him in, and had sworn vengeance. I had almost forgotten about the situation. How and when he got out of the pen I had no idea. But I knew how Rolez worked; I had dealt with him long enough to know him well. Whenever he had paid back a debt, as he would always put it, he would leave something behind, and one specific thing had been left, purposely, to make sure I knew who had been in my house, and who was responsible for Earl's murder. Rolez had been sure to leave a red signature scarf, with his infamous *R* embroidered on it. The police had found the scarf, but I had told them it belonged to me. The last thing I needed was LAPD trying to fight my battles. Never had I had anyone fight for me. Weakness was not part of my character; never had been, and never would be. Justice for Earl would never be served through the pigs. I was the only one who could bring him true justice, and that was exactly what I was going to do, whether it was really Rolez, or some other sick fuck who had smoked Earl.

"Tristan, you're making me nervous. What are you gonna do?" I heard Hennessy exclaim, breaking into my mental venting.

I sighed. "Sit tight, okay? It's gonna be all right." We rode in silence. I was having a hard time getting used to the gears in the rental vehicle that I had gotten Earl, but after a couple of jerks and random grinding of them, we were rolling. Hennessy was silent all the way as I drove to Rolez's place, but I could almost read what she was feeling. Again I vowed within myself that I couldn't let that deter me. Again I saw the dead expression on Earl's face, my Earl. I coughed back tears.

We pulled into the circular stone driveway. It was dark, and quiet. I quickly made my way out of the car, walking over to open Hennessy's door. I didn't have a plan, and I just wanted to talk, or at least that was all I wanted to do *for now.* We walked around to the back patio. I was hoping to confront him by surprise, but as we crept around the side panel, a heavyset black woman met us.

"Yes?"

"I need to see Manuel Rolez," I said.

"I'm sorry, Mr. Rolez is not here at the moment," she said impatiently, obviously startled by our intrusion. I could feel Hennessy letting out a deep breath in relief. "Who should I tell him called?"

"Hmm . . . I'll just come back; I'm an old friend; I wanted to surprise him," I said. "Sorry to have bothered you."

"No problem," the housekeeper said. "Just come back another time."

On leaving, Hennessy touched my arm, whispering, "That should be an omen for you."

"No," I said, starting the ignition. "Not necessarily an omen, but it gives me more time to think about what I want to do."

"Do you have many enemies?"

I laughed sarcastically. "Don't we all?"

"Then couldn't it have been someone else?" Hennessy reasoned. "Think hard. Who else do you know that would want to hurt Earl? And even if Manuel Rolez had something to do with it, why would he want to hurt him, especially if it was you he was after?"

"I have no idea. I keep my shit on da low, and my business is not all in the street where I'm dealing with mofos that would do something like this. *It had to be Rolez,*" I said, more to myself than to Hennessy.

She sighed in frustration. "Don't assume, Tristan. Let's just go back to your place and rest up and give you a chance to calm down some, okay?"

I was quiet, too deep in my own thoughts to pay much attention to hers.

"Okay?" she pressed again.

I nodded my response to her. That seemed to calm her down some, but I knew that for now, nothing would calm me down but answers.

Later I had come in from a run. I needed it badly; anything to get my mind off the awful evening I had had. Hennessy had been good enough to clean and rearrange things in the living room. She really was a jewel, and even though she had seen a side of me that I wish she hadn't early in the day, the thought quickly came to my mind as I surveyed her handiwork that I could use a woman like her in my life. I needed someone, something in my life, period. I really didn't know what my next plan of action would be. Did I take Hennessy and go back to Santa Fe, thus renewing our plans for New York? Or did I stay here and work like hell trying to figure out who killed Earl and get payback for him?

"I hope you don't mind that I rearranged the furniture a bit."

I turned at the sound of Hennessy's voice. "No, as a matter of fact, I was just thinking how nice it looks. Been a while since I had a feminine touch in my life." I bit my tongue as soon as those words came out, I didn't need her asking me about Natalie again. For a moment, her eyes looked aware, as if that was exactly what she was going to do, but instead she started asking me about our plans.

"I know that you have to stay and bury Earl. Are you going to send for the other guys for the funeral?"

"No," I said, shaking my head. "Actually they didn't know him very well. Hawk did, but only through me. No, I'll see to the cremation; no funeral."

"Does he have any family to speak of?" Hennessy asked. She sat down on the couch, planting one leg under the other as she waited for my response.

"I was his family," I stated firmly. She looked at me with warmth and understanding in her eyes.

"Tristan, afterward can we leave? Please don't go after this Rolez person. . . ."

I leaned forward, taking her small hands in mine. She had tiny fingers, tiny well-shaped fingers, made for touching and driving a man wild. I brought them to my cheek, needing to feel her touching me. "Tristan . . ."

"I just need to know who's responsible for this, okay? Whether it was Rolez or whoever it was, I need to, for my own sake, find a conclusion to it. Maybe I can get someone on it, someone to look into things while we're gone. But I have to arrange something. I can't just leave and go on with our plans when someone I loved deeply has just been murdered in my own home; I just can't." I wanted so much for her to understand me for reasons not even known to myself.

"Yes, but earlier you were talking about killing someone."

I gave a bitter laugh. "I wasn't going to kill anyone. I just wanted to talk to him, that's all. You're panicking for nothing, babe. What do you expect me to do, let the police handle it? Come on now, Hennessy, you're not new to our business; you know they don't care about people like us."

"Well, no . . . I mean I wasn't saying that." She seemed a touch nervous. "I'm just saying that maybe it would be better if you waited till after we finish the job, and then you, Reynolds, Hawk, and Mateo can figure it out together, instead of you trying to go this alone or hiring some hit man to go after some unknown assailant. It's too dangerous, and you scared me earlier, you really did."

"I'm sorry. I promise I won't do anything just yet. But you do know that we can't leave until after the LAPD gives us the clear." She nodded. "So we're cool then; no more going off the deep end on my part, and you'll wait patiently with me until I can put Earl to rest?"

"Yes," Hennessy answered, "that sounds fair."

We smiled at each other, both of us more than a bit worn from the events of the day. As we made our way to the kitchen to get some dinner started, many thoughts flew through my pained head, the biggest one being my wondering who, who was responsible, and questions of why they would do this, and how I could get payback.

# 10

*Malibu Beach*

"What the hell is going on, Hennessy? You're supposed to be keeping in touch. I haven't been able to contact you at all." Sebastian was obviously riled. It had entered my mind that I needed to call him when I rose the morning after arriving in LA, after all the stress and hoopla had died down.

"I'm sorry, okay? Yesterday was wild, and I just wanted to get some much needed sleep." I smoothed a touch of bronze lipstick on my lips while using my shoulder to balance my cell phone. "Besides, it's only eight-thirty A.M.; it hasn't even been twenty-four hours since we last spoke."

"So, do you have any idea who killed Earl Walhman, or does Jackson?"

Did the man have an extra sense or what? "Wow, you know about that already?"

"Of course I do." Sebastian laughed. "There's not much that I don't know about within moments of its occurrence, especially if it involves Jackson."

I sighed, thinking back to the grisly scene the day before. "Well, it was awful, just awful. Tristan was so upset when we saw the body. He was very close to Earl Walhman. He cried like a baby." I frowned, thinking about the look on Tristan's face. "Like I said, it was awful."

"Hmmm . . ."

"What are you humming about, Sebastian?" I asked.

"Well, you sound mighty *concerned* about Jackson's emotional well-being."

"What?" I said indignantly, "Aren't I supposed to be concerned? Come on, man, make up your mind here!" I knew where my defensiveness was coming from; I also knew that I was much more concerned about the personal welfare of Tristan Jackson than I should have been. But hell, Sebastian was irritating with his know-it-all he-man tactics at times.

"Calm down." He laughed. "I was just joking, okay? I know you're a sensitive soul." I could hear him smiling over the phone line.

"I'm not a sensitive soul. I'm human, and it's only human to feel compassion at someone else's pain." I paused, trying to gather my wits about myself; I could feel myself overreacting to things. "Anyhow, I need to go, all right? I'll be in touch." I hung up before Sebastian could say good-bye, just knowing he was gonna call me on it next time I talked to him.

I had gotten up early, showered, and dressed, and was now feeling in great need of some breakfast. I hadn't seen Tristan all morning, so I was expecting to see him somewhere near the kitchen, but instead, as I walked out into the foyer with my orange juice, I heard the front door open. I turned to see it was Tristan.

"You've been out?" I asked him.

"Good morning," he said. He looked tired, and tense. He had a newspaper in one hand, and had obviously been out running from the look of him with his workout gear.

"And good morning to you, too." I smiled. "Have you been running?"

"Yeah, something like that."

I couldn't put my finger on it, but Tristan seemed very evasive. "Did something happen, T.J.?"

"Yep," he said without hesitation. "Guess what was in my mailbox. Nicely packed in a box and gift wrapped."

"What, a present?"

He pulled out, wrapped inside a tissue, a large pistol from his back pocket. I gasped, bringing my hands to my mouth.

"Tris . . . Tristan, that was in your mailbox? You didn't put your fingerprints on it at all, did you?" I asked, the five-O in me raising its little head.

"No, I have more sense than that. But guess what." He leaned toward me, showing me the underside of the pistol. There was a letter on it, an obvious signature initial, *R*.

"Rolez?" I asked.

"Yeah, it's his sig all right."

It just didn't seem right; it appeared that someone was going out of their way to make sure that Tristan knew or would assume that it was Manuel Rolez who had committed the murder, making it seem, at least to me, highly unlikely that he, Rolez, really had been responsible. Almost like a setup. I voiced my feelings to Tristan.

"Maybe I'm wrong, but . . . but doesn't this all ring a little untrue to you? Why would Rolez put his gun in your mailbox? Why would he point the finger to himself like that?"

Tristan's eyebrows rose. "I see we are thinking alike here. I mean, yes, at first I was thinking that it was Rolez. But after this," he lifted the gun up, "it seems like someone is trying to run a number on me, like maybe whoever it was who killed Earl wasn't really after Earl at all, but instead maybe it was some sort of game to get me here, start me playing hide-and-seek with Rolez." Tristan's voice got higher and higher as he contemplated. "Shit, I don't know; all I know is that Earl is gone, I don't know who did it. Mateo, Hawk, and Reynolds are in New Mexico waiting for us to get back so we can get ready for the heist. I just need to get my mind clear of all this, and focus on something else for a while." He stopped and looked at me, then whispered. "You . . . you're so damn beautiful. . . ."

My mouth opened and closed in surprise. I was *not* expecting that, and from the look on Tristan's face, he wasn't expecting to say it either. My heart did a little flip-flop, and again I silently wished that Tristan had another profession. As I puzzled over my wishes, Tristan leaned over and kissed me lightly on the lips, his eyes soft and tender.

"Yesterday I was thinking that I was sorry I got you to come back to LA with me, but now, I'm so glad you're here."

"Are you?" I whispered back, feeling touched.

"Very glad," Tristan said. "Nobody can be a rock all the time, you know, and although I try not to, sometimes I just need someone." We both stood, looking at each other with open honesty. It hit me suddenly how attractive he was, and not just outwardly. His sensitivity and strength of character were beautiful. I remembered when I had walked in on him having a nightmare about Natalie, how young and needy he appeared. A desire to envelop him in my arms and protect him with my heart came over me, frightening me with its intensity. Unthinking, I stood up on my tippy-toes, and parted his lips again with my own. He didn't kiss me back; he stood completely still, moaning as I softly sucked his lips. I pulled away as I felt my body getting hot and my heart expanding. His face looked enraptured. He cleared his throat, sounding hoarse as he said, "I need to shower and change; I'm all sweaty. Be right back."

After Tristan left, I put my hand on my stomach, catching my breath. I didn't know what was coming over me, but I was quickly losing my equilibrium. *I'm Hennessy Cooper, federal agent,* I said to myself. *I have a job to do, I'm losing myself here and I need to get a grip!* But the biggest realization that hit me was that Tristan Jackson was not evil; he was not the devil's seed as I had once thought, and although I had a job to do, a job I loved, instead of trying to entrap him, God forgive me, I was going to find a way to *save* Tristan Jackson, for me. . . .

## Tristan

The water at first was warm and relaxing, but I didn't need warm and relaxing. Hennessy's lips had been warm enough to last me till Armageddon. I needed something to shake me, wake me from this desire that was building inside me for her, a desire that way surpassed lust. I reached for soap, lathering up and trying to take my mind off of her. Just as I had got into a scrubbing rhythm, I heard a pop sound. Gunshots!

"What the hell?" I rushed out of the shower, not even bothering to grab a robe. Dripping wet, I ran into the living room. I called out for Hennessy. "Are you okay? Hennessy?"

"I'm here!" she whispered out loud.

She had her back pressed up against the wall between the kitchen and the foyer. Holding her hands closely to her.

"What in the world happened?" I asked. Did you hear gunshots? Are you hurt?" I rushed over to her, noting her looking at me with wide-opened eyes. I looked down, following the path of her eyes. Her eyes were resting on the rise between my legs, a rise that was steadily growing, as I noted the heated look in her eyes. I put my hands to my hips, as if posing for her. "Are you okay?"

"Um . . . yes, I was heating up the oven to fix some cheese toast, and the door to it just flew open all of a sudden. It scared me but I'm fine."

"I've been meaning to get someone out to look at that; it has this problem with gas buildup, especially when I don't use it often. It hasn't done that in a long time though. I hope it didn't scare you too much." I knew I was rambling. But I wanted her and I had to have her. I could see her nervousness; I could see she wanted me, too. She looked down at my manhood again, and licked her bottom lip tentatively.

"Tristan?" she said, as she looked into my eyes. I walked slowly over to her, picked her up, and walked us into my bedroom.


*Somewhere in LA*

"What's taking him so long to go after Manuel? I thought by now Manuel would be one dead muthafucka. Is T.J. turning punk on us all of a sudden?"

"I honestly do not know, I think maybe it's that bitch he has with him. I never thought he'd take her with him."

A tall, lithe figure of a man stood, his body casting a shadow over the high-rise balcony. He picked meat from his teeth as he spoke on the phone, flicking the soured bits and pieces over the edge. Bringing his attention back to his long-distance caller, he said, "So why did he bring her? You said there wouldn't be a problem; she seems to be a problem."

"I don't know, man, she seems to be getting real close to him, like he's feelin' her or sumpin'. I don't even know where he found her at, but listen, don't worry, okay? I have everything under control," the phone caller said.

"Has he been in touch with any of you at Jackson's? When was the last time he called?" the tall man asked, flicking another piece of meat from his teeth.

"No, I haven't heard from him, and I don't think any of the others have either, or they would have told me for sure." He sighed. "So what do we do now? You think he's gonna go after Rolez?"

"I don't know, but he fuckin' better, or I'm coming after your ass."

"Man, come on now. I've done everything I promised to do."

"No, I've done everything I promised to do, including poppin' the old man to get T.J here, and now wassup? You told me that T.J. still had grief with Manuel, and based on that, I had my boys hook it up so that T.J. would think him responsible, yet ain't shit happened yet. Wassup with that?"

"I told you, he took the girl with him. I didn't expect him to get all into her like this, or for her fancy ass to weasel her way in with him."

The tall man threw his toothpick over the balcony's edge. "Well, my friend, you may feel it's not your fault, but it will be all on you if things don't work out after all my efforts. We need a body, and I want that body to be Rolez; I'm depending on that, and I'm depending on you to make sure we get that palette. Don't fuckin' let me down. . . . I have people who are depending on me. As for that fancy bitch you mentioned, I'll take care of her. . . ."

*Tristan*

I unbuttoned Hennessy's blouse. She was breathing so rapidly I had to look at her to make sure she was okay. "You want this?" I asked her. I moved my hand to cup her chin. She was quiet, yet her eyes spoke in volumes. "Please tell me you want me, too," I begged. She nodded yes, turning her face so that her lips were in the palm of my hand. Kissing it, she turned her eyes back toward me. She was shaking. I unbuttoned her blouse the rest of the way, it fell from her shoulders to the floor like a silk curtain. I was surprised that she had a small butterfly tattoo at the swell of her right breast; I placed my mouth on it, licking around its delicate lines as I lifted her skirt, cupping her bikinied front to my nakedness. We moaned at the same time at the heated electricity that grabbed us both as we touched. I had never been with a woman who had set me on fire as quickly, not even when I had been with Natalie. I licked between her breasts, and then ran a wet trail of kisses to her right nipple, sucking and licking it hungrily.

"Oh!" Hennessy cried out as she let her skirt drop to her ankles with a breathy sigh.

"Tristan . . ." she whispered. She was finally revealed before my eyes, with breasts so beautiful, a waist so tiny and well formed. Suddenly I remembered again her insistence that she was not fat. As my throat tightened and constricted at the sight of her, I could only shake my head at how right she was. Watching her, I forgot how naked I was myself, that is, until I felt her hand touching me, stroking my hardness back and forth. I gasped, moaning at the pleasure, and at her boldness.

"Oh, that feels so good," I moaned. My head fell back in a sigh as she continued to stroke me, and suck at my neck. She pulled me forward, both of us falling back on the bed with me atop her. I devoured her, kissing her neck, her breasts, her stomach, moving down to kiss and run my lips along her hips.

"I want you inside me. Now, Tristan, please; I can't wait any longer," she pleaded. I looked down at her swollen sex lips, her clitoris stood out proudly, almost seeming to beg me for attention. She was clean shaven, every inch of her revealed to me; I bent my lips to her and began to lick her bud, sucking it into my mouth. I sucked and flicked my tongue; her clit seemed to throb as I tasted her. "Oh my God, oh yes!" she cried out as she arched up at my mouth.

"Mmmm . . . don't stop, please . . ." she moaned. I moaned, too, against her, fed on her sweet wetness that was so intoxicating, it seemed to grow sweeter and sweeter as I tasted her. I opened her up wider with one hand, inserting two fingers inside her with my other, stroking upward and caressing her inner hotspot as I suckled. She pushed my head closer, thrusting her hips up in a dancer fashion. "Oh . . ." she moaned. As she grew closer to her climax, her thighs started trembling. I could feel her inner muscles gripping my fingers in spasms. "Oh!" she moaned again. I opened my mouth over her mound, my tongue still flicking at her button, and growled. Suddenly Hennessy's body stiffened, she screamed out, jerked twice against me, and came and came, her inner muscles squeezing my fingers in a repetitive motion. I kissed and licked her softly till her climax finished, then moved up slowly over her as she breathed in hiccupping sobs, kissing her deeply and exploring her mouth, sharing her taste between us. Suddenly, she flipped me over to my back, sweat rolling down between her breasts, as she guided me inside her, sliding down onto me full-length in one downward movement.

"Oh, baby . . ." I gasped. As my head fell back against the pillows, I saw lights flashing behind my eyelids. Hennessy began a slow, grueling, up-and-down motion with her hips. I thrust up as she swiveled downward. I looked up into her lovely face. Her eyes were pressed shut, her face reddened and filled with ecstasy. She played with her berry-colored nipples as she rode me, and as I thrust back upward to meet her dance, I cried out, knowing at that moment, I had found forever in Hennessy's arms.

We both were quiet after our lovemaking, neither of us knowing what to say, or how to express what we had felt. At least I didn't have any words. I was almost afraid if I talked I would somehow say the wrong thing, ruin the magic of it. Hell, I was feeling poetic, like I wanted to start humming some Babyface tunes to her or something. After a while even though it was midday, it seemed as if she had fallen asleep, still with words between us left unsaid.

I got up, moving her slightly to the side. Just as I was about to stand up to grab my robe, she reached her hand out to touch my arm.

"Where are you going?" she asked.

"Just to the bathroom, and maybe to get a bite to eat. Are you hungry?" I looked down her body, licking my lips remembering how good she had tasted. She noticed my look and blushed. I laughed. "Well, are you?"

"Well, I guess I could use a bite. I need to shower first though."

"All right, I'll go fix us some omelets; you can use my bathroom if you want," I offered.

"No, that's okay; I need to change." Her brown eyes bore into my hazel ones. I knew we needed to talk. She rustled around, trying to find her clothes.

Handing her a pajama top, I said, "Here you go; put this on till you get your robe." She walked out of the room toward her bedroom. At first I was going to head to my own bathroom, and then start on the omelets, but after standing in the middle of my room for a moment, and feeling the chill that instantly came over it after her leaving, I looked toward where she had left, and followed her to her room. She was already stepping into the shower. She looked behind her, noticing me standing and watching her. She stepped inside, turned around, reached her arms out, and beckoned me to her. I walked to the shower, stepped in, and closed the glass shower door behind me. . . .

# 11

*Los Angeles, California . . . Hennessy*

There are so many times in one's life when one knows what one should do, and also what one should not do, and yet the two conflict with each other, neither being the correct answer. I remember when I was a little girl, and my mother would get after me about something I had done, and she would spank me, then sit me down and explain to me what I had done wrong. I remember how upset I would be at her at times, because my sister, April, would do the same things that I had done, and yet would receive a lesser punishment. And I could never understand that; to me it was a show of favoritism. Mama would soothe me after I got my butt spanked. She would tell me how if one knows how to do what is right, and yet does not do it, it is a sin for that person. Well, this was one of those times when one (me) knew what was right, yet did the opposite. I knew that I had had no business being with Tristan as I had been; I had gone at him like some fevered cat in heat. But I couldn't feel sorry; it was too beautiful to feel sorry. For even with the other two relationships I had had in my twenty-eight years, no one had ever made me feel as beautiful, as desired and worshiped and loved as a woman, as Tristan Jackson had.

Ramifications be damned, and I knew there would be many. I could only imagine Sebastian throwing me off this case, and bringing me up on dishonorable conduct charges. I had never betrayed my oath as an agent before; I had never even been tempted to do so.

We spent the whole day discovering each other, and making love. And it was truly making love. Tristan was so open with me with his feelings, not hiding or fronting on them as some men tend to.

Now in the middle of the night, I was having a hard time keeping my mind off of him. He had stepped out to get me some microwave popcorn since I was having a big craving. I was getting antsy though, not that he had been gone a long time, but the room was too quiet. Tristan had a stereo system that was wired to a speaker in each room of the house, so I got up to head to the living room and see what kind of tunes he was into. Wrapping his navy blue terry cloth robe around me, I tipped into the living room.

We had different tastes in music. He had a lot of rap, DMX and 2Pac, Eve and Master P. Although I liked some rap, I was mainly into neo-soul, a die-hard Maxwell and Erykah Badu fan. I pouted. "Dang, what's up with the gangsta rap, geez!" I would have thought that a man as classy as Tristan would have a different music flavor. "But," I said out loud to myself, "you can take da man out da ghetto, but cha can't take da ghetto out da man." I laughed, thinking about his sexy smile and boyish charm. His eyes looked like a swirling caramel sundae when he was aroused. And that last time we had sex, he had moaned out my name again and again, telling me how good I was making him feel. He was so well endowed, he had me full to the brim. "Mmmm . . ." I moaned, "I need to stop."

Sighing at my flashbacks of our night, I finally came across something I wanted to hear. I slipped the Macy Gray CD in and as the sultry-voiced singer began to croon, I crooned right along with her. "Try to say good-bye and I choke, try to walk away and I stumble, although I try to hide it, it's clear . . ." I suddenly heard a tapping noise, disturbing my musical flow. I looked toward the door; it was kind of dark since I had only the lamp by the stereo system on, but I could still see shadows of light. "Tristan, is that you?" I called out. Silence. After a moment, I figured I had to be hearing things, being in an unfamiliar place alone at night.

Finally, being content with my music selection, I walked into the kitchen, opting for a Seagram's cooler over the ice-cold Coronas that were in the fridge. Sipping the cool, sweet, alcoholic beverage, I tried to figure out how I could convince Tristan to cancel the Met robbery, without having him get suspicious of me. He didn't need the money from the heist. His position was totally different than what I had thought when I first took this case. With his ranch in New Mexico and his horse-breeding farm, he would never be poor. He could easily give up the criminal life. The question was, did he want to? And what would it take to convince a man who had lived his life on the other side of the law since his teenage years that he didn't necessarily have to live that way? And what about me? Was I in love with Tristan Jackson? I caught my breath at my thoughts. In love? That's a big word of four single letters, with a lot of meaning behind them.

"Wow, okay, I've had enough of this," I said, referring to the cooler. I put the remnants in the sink. Then I heard something knocking again. "Tristan?" I called out again. I suddenly had a sort of eerie feeling, as if something wasn't quite right. Turning around to head back into the bedroom, I almost screamed out as a big hand covered my mouth, some person grabbing me from behind. I jerked, fighting to free myself. A swift slap across the face knocked me quickly to the floor. The slap was so hard that my ears started ringing. I wobbled to my feet, knowing I had to get to the front door, or some door, to make an exit. As I turned to flee, my hair was grabbed from the back. I felt my neck being yanked before the guy brought his knee up into my stomach, knocking the wind out of me. Just as I was trying to get my balance, I felt a hard punch to my eye, knocking me sideways into the stove. "Oh, God," I said out loud to myself, "this cannot be happening to me again." Those were my last words, before I saw through one eye a big foot coming down into my face, chest, and ribs, stomping me again and again, until I saw darkness.

*Tristan*

Talk about slow. Being that it was after 10:00 P.M., I didn't expect the Safeway to be so crowded. On top of that, the two cashiers they had were just plain slow. I felt hyped to get back to Hennessy. Just thinking about her warmed me, and gave me a rush. But be that as it may, I didn't want to leave her. Baby wanted popcorn, so popcorn it was. I smiled as I stood in line, thinking about how after her last orgasm she had breathed, "Now I'm hungry again." Even though finding Earl like that had been and still was a nightmare, the beauty and love of Hennessy was like a soothing salve. She was just what I needed. Maybe what I had always needed, it was hard to tell. We had been so wrapped up in lovemaking, we hadn't gotten much into talking about what it all meant, or if we were going to try for a relationship.

After finishing my purchase, I got into the rented Olds, thinking that I needed to get the car back, being that I had only rented it for Earl; my own Lexus was still in storage. I felt uncomfortable in the Olds, too, as if I were surrounded by ugly memories, and yet before I had come back to LA, I had never seen the car. I knew that the memories were mainly my thinking about the horror that Earl must have gone through.

The loud beep of a horn cleared me of those thoughts, for which I was glad. I didn't want to get all down and depressed. I couldn't get anything done when I let my mind get that way, and I knew that Earl wouldn't want that either. There were so many more pleasant things to think about, like Hennessy.

I pulled up to my place, secretly hoping that she would still be in bed. Not that I was some sex maniac or anything. Hmm ... was I? When it came to Hennessy, I could be.

I unlocked the door, noting that she had put on some music. "Hey, I see you're resetting the mood," I said, calling out to her. "Hey, lady, stop being so lazy and come help me pop this popcorn you slaved me out to get!" I laughed, heading toward the kitchen, fully expecting to soon see her smiling up at me. Instead of seeing her smiling, though, what I did see shocked the breath out of this brother. I rushed over to the feminine body curled up by the stove.

"Hennessy!" I cried out. I was about to pull her into my arms. A feeling that was as sharp as the pain I felt when I saw Earl's body went through me. Her face was bruised; her right eye swollen shut and blackened. Someone had beaten the hell out of her! She stirred suddenly, moaning out in pain. She was alive!

"Oh, thank God!" I breathed, caressing her hair back. "What happened, baby? Who did this?" She moaned again. I laid her carefully back to the floor, realizing that her being conscious or not, I needed an ambulance here, and fast!

I waited and waited in the emergency room with not a soul telling me how Hennessy was. Finally, after an hour, a heavyset nurse came up to me. "Do you have the number of her next of kin?"

"Can I see her now?" I asked, ignoring her question and rising quickly.

"Are you the next of kin?" the prune-faced nurse asked me, looking at me up and down.

"I'm the person who brought her here, damn it! Now when can I see Hennessy?"

She shook her head. "I'm sorry, sir, only next of kin is allowed to see patients here."

I almost growled. "Bitch, if you don't let me fuckin' see Hennessy!" The nurse gasped in shock, as did half the people sitting in the waiting room. I was immediately sorry, especially when I saw a security guard rushing up to us. *Fantastic, just what I need is to get kicked out of here.*

"What's going on here?" I heard a man's voice ask as he was coming up behind me. I glanced at him; he had to be either a doctor or a technician since he was dressed in a white jacket. Good, I thought, maybe he could help me. I opened my mouth to speak. . . .

"This man should be escorted from the premises," the prune-faced nurse said angrily. Just then, the security guard grabbed my arm. I jerked back.

"Get the hell off of me," I said, giving the guard a warning look.

"Wait," the guy in the white jacket said. "You brought Ms. Lewis in, right? Her ID says Hennessy Lewis."

I felt a quick relief brush over me. "Yes, can you please tell me how she is? I've been waiting an hour and no one has told me anything."

"I'm Dr. Edgerton. Follow me please, and we can talk."

I followed Dr. Edgerton, giving Prune Face and the over-stuffed security guard a cocky look. Settling into what was obviously the emergency room doctor's office, he pointed to a chair, getting comfortable in his own.

"Have the police talked with you yet?" he asked.

"Yes, and I told them exactly what I know. I came in from the store. I had only been gone about thirty minutes maybe, and I found her in the kitchen."

Dr. Edgerton ran his fingers through his receding locks. "She was beaten pretty badly. Outside of the cuts and bruises she has a sprained neck and bruised ribs. I'm surprised they weren't cracked, but the bruising is almost as bad. There is a dark bruise on her lower right back, and X rays showed severe bruising to one of her kidneys. Obviously she was kicked there. Actually, that's the most serious of her injuries, and we'd like to run more tests on her."

"Damn. . . ." I closed my eyes, swallowing convulsively. I could only imagine how horrible it had to be for her. My sweet, beautiful Hennessy. Who would want to hurt her? She wasn't even from LA. Something was going on here. First Earl, then Hennessy . . . something that cried out for an answer.

"Did you hear what I asked you?"

I looked up to see the doctor looking at me curiously. "Huh? Um, I didn't get what you said."

"I asked if you are involved with her," he asked boldly.

I shook my head. "What would that have to do with anything?"

"Well, for one thing, we checked to see if she had also been raped, and while we didn't find any evidence of forced injury, she had recently been sexually active. And there were traces of semen found."

I flushed at his words. I really hadn't even thought about them checking for rape signs. Or that the doc would have pulled me in here to ask me about it.

"Um . . . yeah, we are involved," I said quietly.

"And she will verify that?"

"Of course she will!" I said heatedly. Like what was this muthafucka trying to say?

"Good, so we have that straightened out. Next question is, do you know her next of kin?"

"No, I don't, but listen, does the fact I'm not blood kin mean I can't see her? That's what all the trouble was about earlier when you walked in. I know for a fact that Hennessy would want to see me," I insisted.

He smiled, standing. "Don't worry; come with me. It will be okay."

Hennessy was resting quietly in a side room off the emergency room entrance. Her brown curls lay matted against her face. Walking up to the edge of her bed, I took her hand in mine.

"We've given her pain medication so she's pretty out of it. They should have her upstairs in a little while, as soon as some test results come back." I nodded at Dr. Edgerton's words.

"Can I be alone with her?" I asked.

Looking at his watch, the doctor nodded. "I have a few more patients to check on, but you can be with her for a short while. If she awakens and needs more pain medication, just ring for the nurse, okay?"

"Okay, and thank you," I said, still watching her face intently. Her right eye was black and swollen, with a greasy ointment or salve on it. The side of her lip was busted and red. Her right jaw swollen and bluish. I felt an intense anger surge through me at seeing her, an anger that must've shown on my face.

Dr. Edgerton touched my shoulder saying, "She's going to be all right, trust me." I nodded again.

I pulled up a stool and sat, waiting, hoping she would awaken so that I could talk to her, get a clue maybe of who had done this, and also just so I could see for myself that she was okay. About thirty minutes later, she stirred. I rushed up, touching my hand to her bruised cheek.

"Hey, baby, I'm here," I whispered.

"Tristan . . ." She cringed as she tried to move, putting her hand up to hold her stomach.

"Shh, don't move, I'm here; I'm not going anywhere." I felt my eyes moisten, watching her pain. She opened her one good eye. Even with her bruises and contusions, her beauty was still so radiant. "How you feeling?" I asked her.

"Like I just got my butt kicked," she rasped.

I frowned. "Did you see who did this?"

She nodded, pointing toward the water pitcher for a drink. I poured her water and waited for her to speak. "No, I had the lights off but for the lamp in the living room. And he caught me from behind. I was so scared, all I could think about is what happened to Earl, and that I was going to be next . . ." Her voice broke, she coughed, gasping out in pain and grabbing her stomach again.

"Don't, baby. I'm not gonna let you out of my sight from now on, not until I find out what's going on, and who's responsible for hurting you and killing Earl. I'm not letting some crazy person hurt and kill everyone I love and get away with it."

Hennessy looked at me intently. "What?" I asked her.

"You do?"

"Do I what?" I questioned, unsure of what she meant.

"Nothing. . . ." She looked down.

"No, tell me please," I pleaded.

She sighed slightly, then looked up and said, "You said that you were not going to let some crazy person hurt and kill everyone that you love and get away with it. Do you love me, Tristan?"

My heart hammered. Just as I was about to answer her, a nurse came in.

"Okay, Ms. Lewis, we're going to take you upstairs now."

# 12

*Washington, DC*

Sebastian was impatient. Things were not going at all according to plan. One thing that bothered him was that he had sent Hennessy on this job even after seeing her obvious attraction for Jackson. He had hoped her professionalism would prevent it from being a problem, but Sebastian knew that professionalism had nothing to do with matters of the heart; he knew that better than anyone. His mind pictured the auburn innocence of Natalie, an innocence tainted and destroyed by one man . . . Tristan James Jackson. It would have been so easy just to smoke the bastard, but knowing Jackson, if he had a preference between death and the pen, Sebastian knew which one he'd choose, and he didn't want to give him anything that would have been his choice.

Standing up to pour himself another bourbon, Sebastian thought of a year ago, when he had first gotten the news about Natalie. She had been so carefree and happy, so beautiful. Having been his late wife Kate's godchild, he had seen her grow up from a shining newborn to the voluptuous auburn-haired beauty she was when they first started their affair. Sebastian thought back to her touch, her warmth. He sighed. T.J. Jackson had taken it all away from him. His mind refused to admit that moving to LA had been Natalie's choice. His mind refused to acknowledge that his wife Kate's finding out about them had been the last straw that had broken her already weak heart, and that the guilt from that, and Kate's fatal heart attack, was what had really run Natalie away. As far as Sebastian was concerned, Jackson was the real villain, not his infidelity. Jackson made Natalie fall in love with him. Jackson was the monster who killed her. Jackson had to pay. When Sebastian had found out how she died and that she had been involved with a burglary ring, he had been livid. Upset at first with himself for allowing such a thing to happen, and then with Natalie for getting involved with it, for her leaving him as she had. But it had really been Jackson who had gotten involved with her, stolen her heart, then left her to face the firing squad that assassinated her. Left her, like the coward he was, to swallow the bullet that was meant for him.

"The bastard!" Sebastian exclaimed to himself, taking another swallow of his bourbon. The only words that ever came to his mind when he thought of T.J. Jackson were bastard, dirty, rotten, low-down scum.

There had never been enough proof to convict Jackson on first-degree robbery charges, and no one could pin a thing on him, but Sebastian knew better. He knew that Jackson had been involved, and had made it his duty ever since to know every step he made in order to seal him for good. What he hadn't expected was all the trouble that was brewing because of his getting the wrong people involved. He had found out who Jackson's enemies were in LA. One being Manuel Rolez, whom Jackson once worked with, but who now was his sworn enemy because of a drug deal gone bad. Another was their trusty cohort, Alfred Majors. Majors had been partners with Jackson and Rolez, and had worked with them on several jobs that he of course refused to give enlightenment on. Probably for fear of incriminating himself, but Sebastian knew what a lowlife he was. At this point, though, Sebastian needed the lowlife to get what him what he wanted, T.J. Jackson's head on a platter.

Rolez was a real joker. At first he had pretended to agree to help Sebastian get Jackson, but soon his motives became evident when he asked for more than fifty percent of the take from Jackson's upcoming robbery booty. Sebastian had to turn that down, but he had made the mistake of filling him in on too many of the plans, and the asshole informed Sebastian that he would have to pay for his silence. Big-ass mistake on his part. Being a smart man, Sebastian had Al Majors as his ace in the hole. Although Majors wasn't to be trusted either, he did hate both Jackson and Rolez enough that Sebastian could use him to get rid of the bigmouthed Manuel Rolez for trying to squeeze him and set Jackson up for murder at the same time. A murder rap would be far easier to stick than the robbery; a murder rap would get Jackson the death penalty, or even better, land him for life in the one place he didn't want to be, the penitentiary. Problem was, Jackson hadn't played according to the plan, at least not yet he hadn't. He hadn't yet reciprocated for the Earl Walhman murder, which was a *big* problem. Also, Hennessy had come with him back to LA, another problem. Sebastian was starting to realize that maybe it was time to pull Hennessy off the case; she was too smart a cookie for him to keep things from her for long.

At this thought, the phone rang. "Rogers here," Sebastian said.

"I had to scare that chick, man."

"You had to what? What are you talking about? What chick?" Sebastian asked. He recognized Al Majors's voice right away.

"The one that was with T.J. She was trouble. Had to quiet that bitch up, teach her a lesson."

*"What the fuck did you do to Hennessy?"*

Al Majors laughed. "See that? I knew she was one of your people. So why didn't you tell me you had planted her, Rogers? We could easily have killed that broad and then think of the trouble you'd be in."

"You did know; I had told you we would have someone there watching things! Besides, Jackson has her involved in the

New York job. Her testimony will be vital once we nail him," Sebastian said angrily.

"Calm down, tough guy. Listen, you aren't calling all the shots here, ya dig? The reason T.J. hasn't gone after Manuel yet is that that chick is making him soft. I know him much better than you do. Besides, I have my sources who know the deal, too."

Sebastian was seething. First that mishap with that LAPD cop, Lenox Rimes. After finding out that Rimes had dipped into confidential files and found out that Hennessy was an agent, and was about to blow her cover to T.J., it was pretty obvious that something had to be done about him. That was a big-ass mess, but fortunately Rimes had been dirty enough that it had been easy to get a hit put on him, and have it suspected as a Mafia hit. Rimes had his hands dirtied in just about every drug deal on the West Coast. Sebastian knew that the hit was necessary, but his new partner, Al Majors, who had led the hit, was a hothead, and seemed hell-bent on getting rid of any- and everyone who got in their way. Although Sebastian had to agree that the Rimes situation had been a necessity, he was starting to feel like things were getting a bit out of hand. It was only supposed to be about Jackson. Now with Hennessy having been targeted, it was time to put a warning lid on Majors.

"Don't you ever touch her again, do you hear me?" Sebastian warned. "Where is she?"

"Los Angeles General last I checked." Al Majors laughed. "Don't worry, it was only a scare. My man got a little overzealous though, but she has nothing majorly wrong with her. She'll be a'ight. Does she know that we're setting T.J. up?"

"No. As far as Hennessy is concerned this is a legitimate sting. So you made a big mistake touching her."

Al laughed again. "Sowrry, boss."

Sebastian sighed. He needed to get in touch with Hennessy to make sure she was okay.

"So . . . do you want me to get rid of Rolez since T.J. is taking so long to bite?"

"You're a hothead, do you know that? Where's your patience? This shit is gonna take time."

"Time is all I've had ever since those two double-crossed me. Now it's *their* time, so don't tell me to be patient," Al snarled.

"What did they do to you to make you hate them both so much?" Sebastian laughed.

"I told you they cut me out, made me feel like I was the garbage they had to get rid of. . . ." Al's anger was tangible, even over the phone.

"So, you got fired." Sebastian smiled to himself.

"You acting like this is all so funny to you," Al spat. "I was cheated, I told you this before. And then later, even after how they did me, I figured, okay, we can't work together but we still cool. But neither one of them would help me when I was down. They *owe* me! And this thing with you, this is *my* payback."

Sebastian thought for a minute, allowing Al to vent before he finally said, "Okay, I feel where you're coming from, and you'll get your payback, but let's give it a few more days. It's only been two days since he's been back in LA. Maybe he's still distraught over finding the body. I mean he hasn't even buried the man yet. Give it two, three more days, and if he doesn't act, we will."

Vent time being over, Sebastian heard a loud burp in his ear. Al Majors had always given him the impression of being an ill-mannered muthafucka. "Ahhh . . . sorry, my man, have a touch of colic here," Majors gurgled out, laughing.

"Yeah, right," Sebastian said disgustedly. "Just call me in a couple of days. And keep your filthy hands off of Hennessy. . . ."

Majors laughed again. "Uh-huh, whateva. Ciao!"


## Los Angeles, California . . . Hennessy

My whole body hurt. I was lonely, bored, I missed Tristan, and I was just basically in need of some good ol' TLC. After two days at Los Angeles General I was feeling much better, and yet Dr. Edgerton still wasn't comfortable sending me home yet. He was concerned, he said, about kidney damage, because he had found some blood in my urine. One important thing I hadn't done, though I knew that I needed to, was call Sebastian. Lord, just thinking about his reaction gave me goose bumps. I couldn't let him take me off the case, and knowing him, that's exactly what he would want to do.

Thoughts of what could or would happen if another agent was assigned to Tristan floated through my mind. Another female perhaps? Would he find her attractive? She would him, I knew that for a fact. I frowned at the thought, pushing away the rolling cart with my afternoon lunch on it still untouched.

Now the question was, how would I keep my condition secret from Sebastian until I was released from the hospital?

Just as those thoughts filled my pained head, the phone rang. "Hello?"

"Hennessy, are you all right?"

Sebastian's voice made me sit straight up. "Hey! How did you know I was in here?" I asked.

"I told you before; I make it my business to know everything. What were you trying to do? Keep this shit from me?"

I swear Sebastian loved to play the bitching mother's act. I snorted, then regretted it when pain rumbled through my bruised rib cage area. Taking a deep breath I said, "No, I was not trying to keep anything from you. As a matter of fact, I was just thinking about how I needed to call you and let you know about this."

"So what happened?" he asked.

"I thought you already knew everything," I joked.

"Hennessy . . ." he said warningly.

I laughed. "Okay, okay . . . I was at T.J.'s beach house, and some asshole attacked me."

Sebastian was quiet for a moment. I could hear his mind working without him even saying a word. "Hennessy, this is getting too dangerous for you."

"It's a dangerous job; I knew that from the start, Sebastian," I said pensively.

"You know what, Hennessy, I'm gonna be straight with you. I want you back in DC when you leave LA General, no questions asked."

I knew it! "I can't come back to DC, Sebastian, what about the case?"

"Fuck the case. I'll put someone else on it."

"No!" I shouted, feeling my face getting hot. "There is no way you are going to be able to get someone else to get as close to these guys as I have. And this soon before New York? No way! And there's no way I'm going to let all my hard work and efforts go down the drain either."

"Are you saying you are going to disobey a direct order again?" Sebastian quizzed. "I'm the one running things here, and I say get your ass back here. Make up some excuse. Your injuries are excuse enough, but either way, it's over."

"No, it's not over, and I'm not coming back until I've completed what I came here to do." A curious thought came to my mind suddenly. "Sebastian, I still cannot understand why you knew so much, long before I contacted you. You never have on any other cases I've been on. What's so different and important about this one?"

Long seconds passed without Sebastian saying a word. Then finally he said in a low, calculating voice, "What is this, Hennessy, am I under interrogation now?"

Just as I was about to respond, the door to my room creaked open. It was Tristan, smiling warmly at me with a small bouquet of red roses in his hands. "Listen, I have to go. I'll talk to you later," I told Sebastian.

"Wait! I meant what I said, Hennessy, I want you back here as soon as we can arrange it. I mean it—"

I cut him off. "I have to go. Bye!" I said, slamming down the receiver.

"Hey, you." I smiled at Tristan. He walked over, kissing me softly on the lips.

"Hey, yourself." He pointed at the roses and winked.

"For me?" I asked, acting coy and surprised.

"All for you, baby girl." He smiled. "Let me put them in water for you." I felt warm and loved as I watched Tristan arrange my roses in a hospital vase, then pour water from my pitcher into the vase. There were only about six of them, but they were beautifully shaped, and the aroma filled the whole room, and my heart.

"You are sooo sweet," I crooned. My eyes were getting misty. Never had I had a man give me so much attention and show so much caring toward me. I couldn't help but think how cruel the gods could be, that the one time I would get this loving feeling, it would be wrapped up in so much chaos.

Tristan put the roses on my end table, then sat down on my bed beside me.

"Who was that on the phone? Sounded like they were upsetting you," he noted.

I had to think quick. "Um . . . it was my ex-boyfriend, calling to see if I was all right; he always gets on my nerves." I laughed nervously.

"How did he know where you were?"

I reached out and touched one of my rose petals. "Well, I had called my mom, of course, and I told her that I had had an accident but that I was okay. I'm guessing she contacted him and told him where I was. She always did like him, and always thought we would be together again one day."

Tristan gave me a sideways grin. "Well, that's because she's never met *moi*," he said cockily.

"Oh, is that so?" I smirked.

"Yep, and you know it. Okay, so, wassup with the boyfriend? It's all over with him, right? And, Hennessy, you are being careful with what you say to your family and friends, right? Remember I told you we have to keep this quiet. . . ."

"Tristan, my family thinks I'm in LA for business. Trust me, please?"

"I do trust you," he whispered, touching my cheek softly. I swallowed guiltily, and bit my bottom lip. "Again, what about the boyfriend?"

"Oh, that's been long over and done," I said. I swear I was making stuff up so quickly I was starting to forget what we were even talking about. I absolutely hated misleading Tristan like this, especially with him looking at me so trustingly. I looked up at him; he had a jealous look on his face.

"What's wrong? Don't tell me you're jealous?" I laughed.

He slipped his arms around my waist, holding me tenderly so as not to hurt my bruised ribs. "You and I, we, um . . . So what are we doing here, huh?"

I swallowed. "That's what I was trying to ask you the other day, when they were bringing me up here."

The warmth in Tristan's eyes seemed to glow into mine unblinkingly. I felt this tingling feeling inside. I lay back against my pillows, suddenly feeling very weak.

"Tristan," I whispered, "do you believe in love at first sight?"

"I really don't know," he said honestly, "but I will say this. You're making me feel things I've never felt before. I don't know if it's love; I don't know what it is, because I have been in love, but I have never felt this strongly about someone, this quickly. And I do want to explore the possibilities with you, and I don't want you exploring them with anyone else."

I frowned inside, and smiled inside, too. He hadn't said *I love you,* but at least he was honest. But whether he had said it or not, I knew that for me, the moment I had seen his picture my interest had been piqued, and the moment I had seen his actual face, he had stolen my heart.

# 13

---

*Los Angeles, California . . . Tristan*

Thankfully Hennessy was released from the hospital after four days of observation and tests. While she was there, I had time to iron out the details for Earl's cremation and also to plan a private memorial ceremony for him. Earl didn't know too many people, or rather he didn't trust very many. Earl had once told me the more friends you have the more enemies you have, and the more problems. He was right of course, because I was almost certain that one of my so-called friends was the person who had ended my mentor's life.

Only Hennessy and I and a distant cousin of Earl's attended the service at the funeral parlor, which wasn't so odd being that Earl's list of family and friends was very limited. I had told my mama about the time and place, but like I figured, she was probably too high to remember, or to even put forth an effort to be there.

I sat staunchly beside Hennessy, listening to the assigned minister talking about life in the hereafter, and the everlasting hope. I sure as hell didn't know if Earl warranted a heavenly calling, but he certainly had been the angel on my shoulder when I needed one, time and time again. I could only hope that if there was a God, and if there was a heavenly realm, that God would remember the good that Earl had done, and not just the diamonds and pearls he had stolen.

As if sensing my apprehension, Hennessy grabbed hold of my hand during the prayer, and held on tightly. Outside of my sad feelings about Earl and worrying about the memorial service and getting back to our training schedule for the Met robbery, she had been my anchor, my strength. I was afraid to say I love you when she had asked me days before. I mean I hadn't even known her a month, and here I was having all these wild and all-consuming feelings, emotions that were even more overwhelming than what I had felt for Natalie. She had asked me if I believed in love at first sight. I wasn't sure if I did, but I was sure that she had tapped at the inner me from the day she walked into my home.

"You okay?" I heard her whisper in my ear.

I looked over at her. I could see she was tired. It had only been a few days since her hospital release, and although she had been resting and recuperating well, I knew that she really needed more time to get herself together physically. Yet she had insisted on coming with me. My baby was like I said, my anchor, and I knew that after we finished this upcoming job, I wanted to have her in my life, in a permanent way, in some form or another.

"Yeah, I'm fine," I answered, forcing a smile upon my face. She smiled back, squeezing my hand again.

There really wasn't much more to say after the ceremony. I shook hands with Earl's cousin, who of course wanted to know if Earl had left a will, and wanted to let me know that he was Earl's only living relative. I should have known the big-nosed, fat-necked asshole wasn't here to say any good-byes. He was only here hoping he had been left something, and wanted to make an appearance. I controlled a burning desire to snap his neck at one of the lines and creases that folded over its layers and layers of excessive blob, and curtly informed him that no, Earl had not left a will, and had been, if he didn't know, incarcerated for the past twenty-odd years. The look of disappointment on his cousin's face told me even more so where his heart was, as if I hadn't already known. He looked almost resentful that he had wasted his time coming to the service, and took off without so much as a good-bye.

"Dang," Hennessy said, disgustedly, "people are so readable."

"Ain't it the truth?" We watched as Earl's cousin walked out of the funeral parlor. I wasn't even going to try for a church or synagogue. I could see Earl rolling over about that even now if I had.

I sighed, and ran my hands over my freshly cut hair. "So are you ready?" I asked Hennessy. She looked at me oddly. I suppose she was wondering about my hurry to get away from the place. But I was tired of thinking about it. Tired of the whole morbid deal; and I knew that Earl wasn't about this type of thing. Hennessy nodded at me, but just as we were about to leave, the door to the funeral home opened. In walked my mama.

"Mama, I wasn't sure you were gonna make it," I said in surprise.

"Didn't I tell you I was?" she replied. "I didn't know him that well but I always try to pay my respects to the dead. And you said he was good to you."

My mom looked over at Hennessy, eyeing her up and down. "And who is this? Something new?"

I felt a flash of irritation. How could my mama comment on my *something new* when she had never even tried to get to know my *something old* back when I was seeing Natalie? Her biggest concern back then had been that Natalie had been white, not whether or not her son was with someone who treated him well.

As if reading my thoughts, she said, "Well, at least you're staying within the race this time, T.J." She spoke to Hennessy. "I swear these black mens today be running after dem white gals, don't they? It's a shame! They be forgetting that dem white girls are the ones who be screaming rape back in the day, especially down South where my daddy's peoples are from. See, I almost peed my pants when I found out T.J. was seeing a white gal. I'm not prejudice, but I don't forget shit. I don't forget where I'm from. I don't—"

I had to shut her up. I could see Hennessy's eyes getting bigger and bigger. I'm pretty sure she had never met anyone like my mama before. Sober she was almost scarier than when she was high.

"Mama, this is Hennessy," I said, stopping her verbal rampage. Hennessy put her hand out, giving my mom a warm smile.

"It's so nice to meet you, Mrs. Jackson," she said.

My mom laughed. "Naw, honey, not Mrs., Miss. Girl, you know don't no niggas marry no sistas today. They just hit and run and leave us with the baggage, or either they leave and go find a white gal!" She hooted again. "Lawd, I swear, whoa! So, T.J., am I too late or what?"

On the ride home, I was quiet. We had dropped my mom off, after listening to more of her sober confessions, and it had just about worn me out. I don't know, I think that I had always been proud of my transformation, my ability to appear classy, cultured, and aware of good living. Although Hennessy knew that I was originally from Compton, I knew that she had no idea how ghetto my mom was, or what my upbringing had been like. I had been embarrassed by my mom, and the fact that I had been was embarrassing also. My mama had said more than a few times how she never forgot where she came from, and I also remember her telling me a few weeks ago the same words about where *I* came from, as if I had forgotten. It didn't feel too good knowing that your mother thought you a snob. *Was* I? Earl had taught me that knowing proper English did not make you uncool, or snobby, and that it would also knock down doors that were usually sealed. His cultural education had helped me a lot, but it had also caused a breach with some of my people from around the way, all but Reynolds, that is. He was the only one from the old neighborhood that I was still cool with. The rest, my mama never failed to remind me, I had outgrown.

"Shhh . . . you're talking too much."

I glanced over at the sound of Hennessy's soft, teasing voice. "Sorry, babe, my mind was wandering."

"It's okay. I guess you've had an emotionally charged day." We were both quiet for a few minutes. Then she said, "Your mom is something else!"

"Don't I know it." I sighed.

"Oh, come on, I found her refreshing." She laughed, punching me in the arm. She noted my exasperated expression. "You two don't get along, I take it?"

I tried to keep my eyes on the road. LA traffic, especially at night, was rough. "I don't know if it's so much that we don't get along, more so that she's never been sober or not high long enough for her to try and get to know me. But hey, I'm not bitter."

"Hmm . . . but she came tonight, right? I mean that had to mean something to you?"

I laughed sarcastically. "Yeah, she did, she also needed money."

Hennessy frowned. "You're so pessimistic. Maybe, just maybe, she did come out of love and concern for you, you know?"

"It's hard to be anything but pessimistic and distrusting when you've had the truth drilled into you all your life, Hennessy. The truth about what people are really like. I care about my mom, but I'm under no illusions about her feelings for me." We pulled up into the driveway at my house. Home was looking very good to me tonight, and the thought of bed was even more appealing. I looked over at Hennessy, seeing her still frowning. I took her hand.

"There are very few people that I trust, my mama is not among those people."

She nodded. "I understand."

"But guess what," I told her, smiling. "You are."


*Hennessy*


It was about 4:00 A.M. I could hear the sound of Tristan's sleep voice, singing out to me from his pillow. I sighed as I watched him. I loved watching him sleep. I loved everything about him. *Almost.* But now that I knew him better I understood more how he had gotten into a life of crime. He had never really had a foundation of love, or trust; he had never believed there could be anything trusting when it came to relationships. His mother had been the root of all of that. There were always reasons why people did the things they did, and I suppose being raised in the jailed atmosphere of the hood, without a true mother's love, had caused Tristan to gravitate toward gangs and the false sense of loyalty that they gave. The false sense of actually *belonging* to something or someone.

My eyes watered when I thought about his words, that he trusted me. I actually was the last person that he should trust. Forget the fact that it was Tristan who was about to do a criminal act of robbery. I was deceiving him in matters of the heart, and that was far worse than anything that he could do.

Tristan didn't have to tell me that he loved me. I felt it, saw it in his eyes. It was the reason for his jealousy toward Mateo. I felt it when he touched me; I saw it when he looked into my eyes. I *knew.* I didn't even want to think about how he was going to react once he found out who I really was. I could only imagine that he hated with the same passion that he loved. Most passionate people were like that.

Tristan's armed tightened around me. "Are you awake?" he whispered.

"Yes."

"Are you okay? You're having a hard time sleeping."

I turned around in his arms, wanting to see and smell his manliness. His lips found mine, and he kissed me ever so gently. As his kiss deepened, I felt enveloped in him, not wanting to think about the thoughts that had been permeating my mind all night. I didn't want to think about him hating me, only the love. His tongue explored the recesses of my mouth. He moaned as if he was feeling the same feelings I was. And I kissed him back, wanting him to know, to *know.* He slowed down with his kisses, his breathing harsh and his heart beating rapidly against my breast.

"Tristan . . . Tristan, no matter what, promise me you'll remember the sweet moments," I pleaded. He kissed my neck, nibbling softly.

"No matter what? Baby, I don't have to remember moments. We'll make more and more. I'm not going anywhere. I'm yours as long as you want me here."

He kissed my eyes, tasting my salty tears. "Now tell me those aren't sad tears."

"No," I lied. "Never sad, not with you, never."

An hour later, Tristan had drifted back to sleep, with me still in his arms. I got up and headed for the kitchen, cautiously though, remembering what had happened to me the last time I had ventured into Tristan's kitchen alone. I needed something familiar, and looking at the kitchen clock I realized that my family in New York were on eastern standard time, and that Mom would be awake, and probably looking at *The Morning Show*.

I put on some coffee. I walked back past Tristan's bedroom, grabbed my cell phone, headed for the bathroom, and then dialed my home number.

"Good morning," my mother greeted cheerfully.

"Hey, Mom," I said.

"Hennessy? Oh my goodness, you live and breathe and exist! You've actually called your dear mammy." She was being funny and sarcastic, I knew, but it was so good to hear her voice. I tried not to contact my family much when I was undercover. It was never safe to finger those who were close to you, lest they got caught up in the mix somehow if things went wrong. Besides, Jocelyn Cooper was far too emotional for me to keep her on pins and needles worrying about me. Usually I would just tell them that the bureau had sent me on a business trip and that it would be a few months before I could call regularly. My father usually could tell what was up though. At fifty-four, he was still young, and still a cop, at least in spirit. Although retired, he kept up with the goings-on with the NYPD, and was so proud that his baby girl had followed in his footsteps in law enforcement. Usually I would offhandedly let him know I was on an undercover job, but even with him I wouldn't reveal too much. He and my mom were too close for him to keep big secrets from her, and I didn't want to obligate him to keeping them.

"Yes, I'm alive." I laughed.

"Sooooo . . . are you okay? What's wrong?"

I sighed. "I just wanted to hear your voice." I could feel myself ready to cry, and swallowed repeatedly trying to hold the tears back, but my mother wasn't a bit fooled.

"Hennessy, this is me you're talking to, all right? I can tell when something's wrong; now spit."

"Nothing, Mom . . . it's just . . ." I paused, thinking, and catching my breath before I spoke. "It's just that sometimes my work can get to me." I paused again. "Mom, sometimes what you know is right conflicts with your heart."

"You mean you're having a man problem," Mom stated.

"Yeah," I admitted, wondering how she knew right away I was talking about a man.

"Sweetheart, don't you be letting no man make a fool out of you, hurting you."

I wiped at the tears that were steadily falling from my eyes. If only my truths, the truths I was hiding from Tristan, truths that I knew were going to destroy the newness of us, could be wiped away as easily, things would be okay.

"It's not a man that is hurting me; it could be the other way around though." I sighed again. "I just don't want to lose love before I really have it. It's hard to explain, Mom."

My mom's silence was golden, because even though she probably didn't completely understand my spotty dialogue, I knew she understood somehow. A woman always understands another woman in matters of the heart.

"Hennessy, remember what I always used to tell you. The heart is more traitorous than anything else, and it is desperate. Don't ever go against what you know to be right."

More tears rolled down my cheeks, falling to my lips. "Well, I don't know what my heart is doing right now, but I know I've never been so scared of losing something I care about."

"Tell me what's wrong, baby," my mom pleaded.

"I can't. I gotta go, Mom." I hung up, feeling a sudden chill. I closed my eyes and wished my mind to go blank.

It didn't work.

# 14

*Malibu Beach . . . Tristan*

"Hawk! What's up, you big-headed bastard!"

"You mean wassup with you? Man, you've been gone all this time, and we only have, what, two weeks before we fly out to New York? Time is ticking away, man!"

"Oh, come on, Hawk, I left a message letting you know what had happened to Hennessy. Was I just supposed to fly back without her? Anyhow, we need her to get better before we can even go on this," I explained. I could tell that Hawk was irritated, and probably the other guys were, too. With so much money involved, we did need to get rolling on our plans. Actually I couldn't wait to get out of LA. I was seriously thinking about selling my beach home and making Jackson's my permanent address, especially since Hennessy liked it there as much as I did. Since Earl's murder and Hennessy's attack, the beauty of the beach and of this house just wasn't the same. This place had too many ghosts for me now.

"So," Hawk was saying, "D day is still in two weeks?"

"Yeah, of course, nothing has changed, although it's gonna be hard for Hennessy with her just having gotten out of the hospital."

"Who in the hell would want to beat the shit outta her like that?" Hawk queried. "I don't know, man. I don't like this. First Earl, then her?"

"Yeah, I feel the same way. . . ."

"So do you think she's gonna be well enough to carry it out?" he asked.

"I hope so. If not, we may just have to postpone things."

"Postpone? Oh, I don't think so. You said yourself that we do this now or we may not get another chance, and that's a lot of money to postpone." Hawk paused for a second, then said, "You know, T.J., you don't sound as convinced as you did before that you want to do this. What's happening with you?"

I was starting to get a little irritated with Hawk. Actually he was right about our time delays, but I wanted to do the job. It had been all planned out, and forty million dollars couldn't be ignored. But then on the other hand, the actual thrill of the chase that I used to have was gone for some reason. I don't know if it was because my mind was on something, or someone else, namely Hennessy, or if it was because of the words Earl had said to me that day at the café.

"Man, where the hell are ya? I'm talking to you," Hawk demanded.

I pulled my attention back to him, using my shoulder to keep the phone to my ear as I tied my Timberland boots tightly. "Sorry, I was just thinking about what you said, and yeah, you may be right. It's not that I've changed my mind, it's just that so much has happened. It's like Hennessy had said once, like a bad omen, you know?"

"That's superstitious nonsense." We were both quiet for a moment. I knew that Hawk needed this money. Time and again he would whine about his gambling debts. All of the guys had their reasons for needing or wanting this money.

"Look, whatever you decide, I'm cool, T.J.," Hawk finally said.

"Don't worry, I won't let you guys down. Don't I always have your back?"

"And I always have your back; always have, always will," Hawk said sincerely.

I smiled at his words. "That's because you're cool like that. Always have been, always will be."

Hawk laughed heartily. I could almost see the big grin on his face. "I'm a regular Capone. When them other ones be gone, who do you call?"

"You're one corny bitch is what you are." I laughed. "See you in a few hours, man."

"As you say, Captain. Peeeeace!"

I snickered after hanging up from Hawk. I missed those guys. Even though it had only been a little over a week since Hennessy and I flew out here, it felt more like a month. So much had happened in that week and a half. I closed my eyes and thought of her, my loins hardened. Since Hennessy's release from LA General, we hadn't been able to do any repeats of that night. I knew her body wasn't up to it, and I was happy and content just being close to her at night. But she had felt so good. I had used those images in my mind while relieving sexual tension a couple of times, and just the remembrance of touching her, tasting her, and her riding atop me had made my body explode again and again.

"Was that Hawk?" I heard her voice ask me from my bedroom door.

"Hey," I greeted her with a smile, then walked up to give her a bear hug. "Yeah, that was Hawk. I was just letting him know that we were flying back to Santa Fe this afternoon."

"Oh, okay," she said.

I sighed, shaking my head. "I don't know about you, but I've had just about enough of LA to last me a lifetime. And I also would feel much safer where you are concerned for us just to get out of here."

"Hmm . . . okay," she said again quietly.

I flopped down on the bed, moving to sit up at the head of it. I held my arms out to Hennessy, pleased when she rushed right into them. "Is something on your mind, babe?"

"Nothing much, but, um . . . I heard you talking to Hawk just now, about New York?" She looked at me from the side.

"Yeah, what about it?"

She laughed lightly. "I guess this week has just seemed so long, I almost forgot about it. I mean, I'm not saying it's a bad idea now. But I'm not as sure as I was before that I can do it. I'm sore and off balance and then there is Earl's murder and still trying to figure out what's up with that."

"So, you saying you're scared to do it now?"

"What?" she spat. She moved out of my arms as if upset.

"What's wrong?" I laughed, looking at her and smiling. "You're saying you're feeling a lil' nervous? *Chicken, chicken, chicken. . . .*" I laughed again.

Hennessy moved off of me, looking indignant. "Forget you then. I wasn't saying I was scared or chicken. I'm saying that things are off balance, and . . ." She jumped up after looking at the slightly amused look on my face, I suppose. She had been so weak and needy the past few days, I had almost forgotten about her sexy feistiness.

I pulled her back down on the bed. "Hey, I'm just messing with you." I winked. "Listen, I was just saying the same thing to Hawk on the phone just now, that things seem off, not quite right. But he reminded me, and he's correct too, that we don't have long before the big day. We are talking millions, Hennessy." I started counting in a mock way on my fingers. "See, so many dollars I keep losing count." I laughed.

"But what if something goes wrong?" she pressed.

I smiled reassuringly. "Nothing is going to go wrong, baby. Trust me on this."

## Hennessy

I think Tristan must have a thing for that word *trust*, or maybe it was me and my guilty ass. I was going a bit crazy. I almost felt like I wanted to confess things to him, but then again,

I really had no clue how he would react. I mean what if he completely lost it and put a bullet between my eyes? He was, after all, no Boy Scout.

I felt rushed as I packed while Tristan was out for his daily run. I snapped the last buckle on my suitcase just as my cell phone buzzed at my hip. My nerves jumped at the feel of it. I did not feel like battling with Sebastian.

"Yes, Sebastian?"

"You have not been answering your phone; you have not been returning my calls; and you're pissing me the fuck off, Hennessy. . . ."

"That sounds like a personal problem to me," I said flippantly.

"Damn it, Hennessy! You don't know what game you're playing here. You're playing hardball now with the big boys, and it's time to pull you off the field!"

"And maybe I don't wanna come off the field," I said in a strong, quiet voice. "Sebastian, you sent me here to do a job, and I plan to do just that. You have absolutely no valid reason to pull me off this case and you know it."

"Fine then," he said, "come back here and file a formal complaint, but as of right now, this case is closed and you are off it. As a matter of fact, I want you to take some time off, go to Yonkers, and spend a month or so with your family."

I almost laughed. Sebastian said those words in such a hopeful way, he really sounded like he thought that would make me jump for joy. Obviously he didn't know me, but mainly I knew it was that he didn't know how I followed my heart. Right or wrong, I followed my heart.

"Great," I swung back at him. "Since you want me to take some time off, I will. I'm going to spend my vacation in New Mexico."

"Shit!" he said under his breath. "Hennessy, if you fly out with Jackson to Santa Fe, you are fired."

"On what grounds?"

"Insubordination. . . ."

My head was spinning. I didn't know what had come over Sebastian, or why he was reacting as strongly to things as he was, but with a clear and articulate voice I said, "I'm going to finish this job. If you want me back in DC or Yonkers, you're gonna have to come and *get* me, understand?"

"Oh, don't test me, Hennessy, because you know I'll do just that. . . ."

"Oh, really?" I laughed. "You know what, Sebastian? Fuck . . . you."


*Washington, DC*


Sebastian stared at the phone in his hand. It was humming out a tone that told him Hennessy had hung up in his face. Anger surfacing through him, he growled as he threw the phone base against the wall, breaking the glass of one of the art pictures that hung there.

"Fuck me? Damn you, Hennessy!"

The door to his office opened. With a shocked expression on her face, his secretary, Lillian, was looking back at him. "Uh, Agent Rogers, there's someone for you on line two." She glanced at the phone. "Should I tell them to call back?"

"No . . . no, I'll get it; thanks, Lillian," Sebastian replied. Lillian closed the door quietly. Walking over to retrieve his wounded phone, Sebastian was glad to hear it was still in working order. He replaced the receiver, then pushed line two.

"Rogers here."

"They're heading back to Santa Fe right now," Al Majors announced.

"Yes, I know that," Sebastian said. "I tried to tell Hennessy not to fly out with Jackson, and she refused."

"What? Why would you try to tell her not to go? We need her to help T.J. get the slate. I found out that he has her as the courier. If she's out, he'll cancel the whole thing."

Sebastian sighed. "Listen, it was you and your people who

beat her up. Did you really think I would let her stay around after that?"

"All right, all right," Al hissed. "I'll admit it went a bit overboard. She was only supposed to be scared a bit, and it got out of hand. But I want that money, Rogers."

"And I want the money, too, but I have a lot to lose, and I don't plan to be sloppy with this."

Al laughed. "Oh, you want the money, but you are more concerned about T.J. I'm smart enough to know how to get both without getting irrational."

"I'm not getting irrational, but if something happens to my agent I'll have a lot of explaining to do," Sebastian said.

Al Majors was quiet for a moment, then said, "The hell with her! I want that slate, I want that money, and I want my payback from T.J. and Manuel, and if you fuck me on this—"

"Don't you threaten me, Majors. . . ."

"Oh." Al laughed. "I'm not threatening; I never make idle threats, I make promises. You keep your end of the bargain and I'll keep mine, *comprende?* We need to keep your girl on board so we can get that slate in two weeks; I'll take out Rolez after T.J. gets back to LA to exchange the goods for the cash, because it's obvious that his weak ass is not gonna do it, and my connection will get the slate and bring it to me. I get what I want; you get what you want; then both of us will be happy and rich."

Sebastian frowned. "Let's hope it all works out that way."

"It better," Majors warned.

Sebastian heard humming again. He needed some Tylenol, badly.

*Flying back to New Mexico . . . Hennessy*

Soft jazz hummed in my ear as we flew back to New Mexico. I felt so relaxed, especially as I sat quietly beside Tristan. He had relaxed me even more before we had met the plane, giving me a nice back massage to help loosen up my tight muscles, he had said. I smiled as I thought about the tender way he'd handled me.

"Glad to be going back?" Tristan smiled.

"Mmm . . . yes." I turned around to lay my head against his shoulder. "I love your home. And I miss Mateo, too," I teased, winking at Tristan's sudden frown.

"Don't miss that crazy Rican too much," he said, his eyes narrowed.

"Oh, you are jealous, I see!"

"You're damn right I am; you forget, I know Mateo. Let him find his own señorita and leave you alone before I have to get ghetto on his ass."

I reached up, caressing Tristan's freshly shaved cheek. He was so handsome. I thought about what my mom and my sister, April, would say if they got a look at this gorgeous man. A bright grin coated my face at the thought.

"What are you thinking about?" Tristan asked.

"Oh, nothing." I laughed. "Okay, yes, something. I was thinking about what my sister and mom would say if they got a look at you. You're quite dashing, you know."

He blushed. Then said something I didn't catch.

"Hennessy?"

"What did you say?" I blinked, still smiling.

"I asked if your family knows what you do."

I had to think hard to try to remember just what I did do. But slowly it registered to me what he meant, meaning I had to quickly take off the real and put on my acting skills. I lost my good mood all of a sudden, but of course I couldn't show it, so I smiled and said, "Yeah, I tell Mom about all my exciting crook adventures."

"Now you're trying to be funny." Tristan frowned. I laughed again.

"I just want to get to know more about you," he explained. "You're really very mysterious."

"I'm not mysterious, I'm just Hennessy, and really there's

not much to know about me." I pouted. "Besides, I'm tired of talking, and I want you to be quiet so I can lie on your shoulder and wake up and already be in Santa Fe, so shh . . . you're talking too much."

Tristan laughed, giving me a little squeeze. "Okay, anything for you. . . ."

# 15

Santa Fe, New Mexico . . . Hennessy

I didn't need to open my eyes to see when we landed in Santa
Fe; I was like that long-nosed bird on the Fruit Loops box, the
one that always sang to follow your nose. The fresh smell of
New Mexican flowers overwhelmed my senses as soon as we
landed. I felt myself smiling with the familiarity of it, although
I hadn't been at Jackson's long before flying back to LA with
Tristan.

After we got up to the door of the beautiful adobe haven,
Mateo met us with his cheesy smile. "Hola! Hola, T.J., and
Hennessy, mmm . . . estas muy bonita, as always, chula."

I giggled. "And you, too, chulito, just as handsome as you
wanna be." I noted right away Tristan's frown, but then again I
expected it, with his jealous, sexy self.

Pushing himself past Mateo and me, Tristan went for his
mail drawer, where there were loads and loads of old mail for
his inspection.

"Where are Hawk and Reynolds?" he asked Mateo.

"I don't know where that Reynolds is, but Hawk is out running; you know how he is. He thinks he's Superman or some-

thing, eh?" Mateo laughed. "So, um, I'm sorry about Earl, T.J. I know how much he meant to you, amigo."

"Yeah, thanks, man. My biggest upset is that he had to go like that. Hell, he was better off in prison; at least there, he was alive," Tristan said sadly.

Mateo nodded in agreement, before turning his attention toward me. "And you, *bebé*. What sicko want to hit a woman? We should hunt them down and kill dem fuckas, T.J."

"Agreed," Tristan said, glancing at my fading bruises along with Mateo, anger on both of their faces.

"Listen," I said, "nobody has to go out and kill anyone, okay? It was probably a robbery attack or something."

"Then why didn't they take anything?" Tristan questioned, his eyebrows raised.

I picked up my small bag, anxious for a shower. My body was literally aching with tiredness. "I don't know. I'm only saying that they didn't come back, so maybe it was a mistake. Anyhow, I'm tired, I'm sleepy, and I want a shower, so I'm out for a while, guys." Smiling sweetly at Tristan I said, "See you at dinner," and exited for the princess room.

It was just as I had left it, beautiful. It felt even more special knowing that Tristan had added some extra loveliness just for me. The same ivory roses smiled at me. I breathed in the clean pleasant scent that floated ceremonially around the room. Fresh white rose petals again blanketed the side table, falling delicately to the floor beside it. I felt at home, oddly enough, more so than at my own high-rise apartment in DC.

I set my small makeup case on the floor beside my bed and flopped down to catch my breath for a moment. Just as I was taking off my sandals, the door opened. Aurora stood there smiling.

"Señorita! It's so good to have you back!"

I smiled, more than happy to see her. "It's good to be back, Aurora. I hadn't been here long, but I missed it like crazy."

Aurora walked up, giving me a big, warm hug. She was many inches shorter than I, and had to look up at me. Right away, she paused, looking at the blue bruises on my face.

"*Mi Dios!* What happened to your face!" she exclaimed.

I reached up and touched my face. Honestly I sometimes forgot that I didn't quite look myself since my attack. "Well," I explained, "while we were in LA, someone came into the house while I was alone and attacked me."

"What? How horrible! Are you all right? Did they catch that bad person that did this to you?"

"No, afraid not." I bit my lip slightly, slipping my foot under me on the bed. Aurora sat down beside me. "Actually some really bad things happened in LA. When we got there, we found one of Tristan's good friends dead, in Tristan's home." Aurora gasped in shock. "Yes, I know." I nodded. "Then Tristan had gone out a couple of days later, and that's when I was attacked. I was sure he had phoned here and told everyone."

Shaking her head, Aurora said, "I really don't know things that go on here much. I usually don't want to know, but I'm going to fuss Mateo. He knew I would want to know something like this, like you being hurt."

I took her hands, smiling at her concern. "Well, I'm okay, but thank you, Aurora, for caring."

"But of course I do. I know how much Señor cares for you. . . ."

"You do?" I felt myself blushing furiously. "We are kind of, sort of seeing each other, if you want to call it that."

"Mmm, I knew it. *Destino, querida; destino* is what has brought you two together."

I looked at Aurora, amazed that she would say such a thing. Could it really have been destiny? Were things somehow arranged in the stars that Tristan and I would meet, and fall for each other? Could it perhaps also have been *destino*, destiny, calling me to save him from himself? I wasn't sure, but it sure sounded good, and if it was destiny, perhaps, just perhaps, he and I had a good chance of making it. My heart beat a bit faster at the thought. I had been trying not to think too much about the chance I was taking with him, and about my job. That is, if I still *had* a job.

My face must have mirrored my disturbed thoughts. Aurora looked at me curiously. "Are you okay, Señorita Lewis?"

"Hennessy," I reminded her, "call me Hennessy, okay? And yes, I'm fine. I'll *be* fine. Like you said before, it's *destino.* . . ."

## Somewhere in LA

Al Majors sat in his black Expedition, chewing slowly on a mustard-covered hot dog as he waited for the light to change. He thought about how crazy his plans were going. One thing Al hated was for things not to go his way, and little by little, he felt his control slipping. Control had always been something that Al treasured. When he had hooked up with T.J and Rolez, they hadn't wanted or appreciated his ideas, and had in fact cut him loose when he moved ahead with some things on his own during one of the jewel robberies they had planned. T.J. had conjured up the plans and ideas, but it was a partner thing as far as Al was concerned, or at least it was supposed to have been. T.J. hadn't wanted to see it that way. He ended up not only telling Al he wasn't the kind of partner he was looking for, but calling off the job altogether. And Rolez, the punk bitch, had gone along with him. Al had been depending on the money from that last job. Once the brakes were put on it, he'd had a loan shark chasing him down. He ended up putting a cap in that pain-in-da-ass fool, but none of that helped the fact that he was still at that time flat broke. Living on the edge of poordom, something that Al had never thought he would have to do again, he had gone to Manuel Rolez for help. Even though Manuel hadn't had his back when T.J. had decided to trash their plans, he'd figured that Manuel would at least give him a loan to help tie him over for a while. Wrong again; the son of a bitch had laughed in his face, and kindly told him to kiss his Latin ass. His day would come, Al thought to himself. Manuel's day would come when he would get his ass kissed with a bullet.

Then there was Sebastian Rogers. That stupid fuck was letting his emotions take control over his good sense. So worried was he about T.J. and getting him that he was letting the chance of a lifetime, millions of dollars, go to risk. Al's concern was always about the dollars, and he couldn't have been happier when Rogers had contacted him about T.J., and about this job he had going down, and the type of money that would be involved. Being that he was very good about feeling people out, Al could tell quickly that Rogers's mind wasn't wrapped too tight. Yeah, he was able to front like he was all intelligent and shit, but the most intelligent people were also the stupidest.

The light changed. Al stuffed the last of his hot dog in his mouth as he turned down the one-way street, which led to his condo. He wasn't living too badly, but as far as he was concerned, his old cohorts were living much better than he was, and that shit he could not have. His former buddy Manuel was about to be in for the shock of his life; and T.J., the green-eyed nigger who thought *his* shit didn't stink, proper muthafucka . . . Al got a rush just thinking about the pleasure it was gonna be, just watching T.J. squirm when the cops come tapping at his door and finding the evidence linking him to murder, evidence that was going to be planted, that is.

All of that was the easy part, but making sure that before it went down T.J. would do him the honor of carrying off a master robbery plan was something else.

Walking into his condo, he headed for the phone, anxious to find out how things were going with T.J. and his crew of sporty thieves.

*Santa Fe, New Mexico*

"Oh, yes! Fuck me, baby! Yes!"

Reynolds grabbed Sylvia's plump hips, pulling out to thrust back deep inside her. She pushed back, grinding on his dick as if riding a buffalo. Feeling the familiar tingles starting to encase his erection, he worked faster, moving his mouth to the base of her neck and biting down on her skin. She howled in pleasure.

"I'm gonna come! Shit! Shit!" she squealed.

Reynolds bit down even harder when his own climax hit, almost forgetting that he was fucking flesh and blood that actually bled.

"Goddamnit, Reynolds! That's my neck you biting, fool!"

Reynolds fell back on the bed, fighting hard to catch his breath. He reached down, grabbed the used condom off of his still erect penis, and threw it across the floor. "Oh, get a grip; you know you like that shit."

"Get a grip, my ass," Sylvia spat out, jumping up to slip on her robe. "And your time is up, buster, you only paid for thirty minutes."

Reynolds smiled, watching the swaying movements of Sylvia's behind. "How about a blow job? I'm still hard, boo."

"If you want me to suck that fat dick of yours, it'll be another fifty; ain't no freebies around here," Sylvia said, as she lit her cigarette. She blew out a circle of smoke, moving her mouth in an open-and-close fashion. Watching her, Reynolds could almost feel her doing the same lip movements, but on him.

"Besides," she continued, "for me to swallow that big bone I should charge you a hundred."

Reynolds laughed. "Naw, you wouldn't do that; I'm your favorite customer. Besides, I'm probably the *only* one you ain't gotta fake it with, right?" He winked.

"You just full of yourself, ain'cha?" Sylvia smiled, slowly walking over toward Reynolds. She got down on her knees, inching her mouth toward his penis. She slipped him in her mouth and started a slow suck, leaving Reynolds sighing in contentment. Just then, the buzzing of his pager jerked them both out of their sexual daze. Reynolds reached over to the table, picking it up to see who was paging him.

"Igg it, baby," Sylvia demanded, nibbling at his mushroom head. "I have something for ya."

But Reynolds's attention was gone. After seeing the number on his pager, he knew this was a must call.

"Wait, wait. I have to make a call." He pushed Sylvia away.

"Hey! I don't have time for you to waste; this is gonna cost you whether you come again or not, you hear me?"

"Fine!" Reynolds shouted, throwing her another fifty. "Now bounce." Grumbling, Sylvia grabbed up the fifty and made an exit for the bedroom door.

"If you want me to finish you off, it's gonna cost you another fifty!"

Reynolds dialed the Los Angeles number that blinked from his pager, a nervous itch running down the base of his neck.

"Reynolds?"

"Yeah, it's me. Wassup?"

"Listen, man, I want you to fill me in on what's going on now. I know that T.J. and that agent are back there."

Reynolds sat up abruptly. "Wait a minute, what agent, Al?"

"The bitch; she's five-O, man."

"Oh, shit! How long have you known about this?" Reynolds asked anxiously.

Al Majors laughed. "Calm down, son, it's okay. I've known for a while that there were plans in the works to infiltrate an agent on T.J., but I only found out who it was a few weeks ago, after I talked to you and then found out from my sources who she really was."

Reynolds, though, was already thinking about how to get rid of Hennessy. He should have known something was up with her . . . most smooth, sassy hoes like her had some type of agenda.

"You don't understand though, Al; she knows everything, and I mean everything, about the job. She'll probably have FBI waiting for us as soon as we land in LA from New York."

"Nope, wrong again. We need her to get the slate, and once she's in LA, there will be no cops waiting. Like I said, I got this under control, okay?" Al said with a quiet confidence. "When the time comes, we will be silencing Hennessy Lewis, if that's even her real name."

"But how do we do that, when the feds obviously got a good wind of what's going on with us here?" Reynolds pressed.

Al snickered. "I have friends in high places. Believe me, the feds know more than you think they do. Reynolds, everything that appears shiny ain't clean, a'ight? Trust me; all will go smoothly as long as you make sure that you all get that slate."

Reynolds nodded in agreement. "Okay, sounds good."

"Can you imagine?" Al laughed again. "T.J.'s know-it-all ass is flying around with five-O in his pocket and he don't even know it. Looks like the King of Thieves is getting jeweled." He laughed again. "Get it? Fooled-jeweled? Get it?" The loud hoots over the line made Reynolds pull the phone away.

After cringing, then putting the phone back to his ear, Reynolds laughed at Al Majors's joke, as required, and bade him good-bye.

Reynolds hoped that things would be winding down soon. His decision to go traitor against his longtime friend and partner had not been an easy one. But as far as he was concerned, where he had always had T.J.'s back, T.J. hadn't always had his, choosing instead to trust and rely more on Hawk, or even his so-called adopted Jewish daddy, Earl. Time and time again he had voiced to T.J. the reminders of how he was the only one who had been with him, stuck with him through thick and thin, besides the fact that he was his brotha in the racial sense. But brotha or no, T.J. had somehow forgotten who he was.

That being the case, when Al Majors had approached him two months prior about what T.J. was up to, and getting the splits at higher odds than T.J. was offering, he accepted. Not readily, 'cuz straight up he couldn't trust Al as far as he could throw him. But then maybe he couldn't trust T.J. either. He couldn't trust any brotha who'd allow his surroundings to make him forget that he was just another nigga from round the way, always had been, always would be, and that all the proper lingo, expensive clothes, and Lexuses wouldn't change that fact. Now, Reynolds thought, it was about him, Reynolds, and getting his.

There was a loud knock at the door. "Are you finished yet? I need my room!" Sylvia shouted.

"Yeah, come on in."

On entering Sylvia caught sight of Reynolds, still buck naked, lying against the silk covers, holding his black, Mandingo dick straight up in the air. She smiled. Though not a handsome man, he was so fuckin' virile. He waved at her with his hardness, eggin' her with it to come closer as though it were a finger.

"Fifty more dollars," she announced, walking over to him, then rubbing her fingers up and down his shiny knob.

Reynolds laughed and grabbed her arm, yanking her down to him. "Shut up and suck."

# 16

Over a week had passed since our return to Santa Fe, and even with all that had been going on in LA, I kind of missed the quiet privacy that Tristan and I had had at the beach home, although I knew that finding Earl's body there had ruined any love affair he may have had with that place. We had had our sweet moments, not just our delicious night of lovemaking, but just being together with no interruptions.

Since coming back to Santa Fe, we had been so busy going over plans for the robbery that we hadn't had much time to just share space. After breakfast, though, he had whispered in my ear about going for a ride with him later in the afternoon. Now can I say that I was literally aching in anticipation? I had started getting this worried feeling that I was making a complete fool of myself thinking that our feelings for each other were mutual. And seeing all that I was giving up to be with him, namely my career, the last thing I needed to think was that he had gotten with me that time for unsavory reasons, or that he was doing a Limp Bizkit thing, you know, in it for the nooky? I laughed at myself while tying my Nikes. I swear the things we women think up, but then again men are such untrustworthy beings at times, turning us into the insecure creatures that we sometimes are. But they are oh so needed, too!

Tristan had told me to meet him at the stables at noon, and it was already five till. I needed to hurry, or rather I wanted to, or rather I was becoming obsessed. *Not good, Hennessy . . .*

Just as I was about to make my way out of my bedroom door, I felt the familiar buzz of my celly.

"Damn it!" I said to myself, "I'm gonna leave this damn phone here, maybe even hide the mickie flickie!"

"What do you want, Sebastian?" I hollered in the receiver. This was the third time Sebastian had called me; the first two times I did what I should have done now, ignored the call.

"You want to stop being so stubborn now and hear a bit of reason?" he asked.

"Whose reasoning, Sebastian? Yours?"

He sighed. "Okay, look, I've thought about all you said and fine, you can stay on the case. I hope you know that I just care about you, Hennessy, and I don't want you to do anything that could get you hurt."

I felt myself softening. Sebastian really was a sweetie, and I knew that he was only doing his job, and trying to protect me. It wasn't his fault that I had allowed myself to fall for a criminal. But then again, I knew that Tristan was so much more.

"Sebastian," I groaned, "I'm sorry about everything, all right? You know that I'm not the type of person who quits anything, so with this job, I want to finish what I've started. I'm a big girl, sweetie; you don't have to baby me."

"Hmm . . . are you sure about that?"

"Yes, absolutely positive," I assured him. Dang, I thought to myself, I was getting worse and worse with the lying. But there was no way, feeling as I now did about Tristan, that I would allow him to wind up in prison again. There was hope for him, and hopefully I could find the words to help him see that he really didn't need to do the things we had planned.

"You've fallen in love with the guy, haven't you?"

I paused, not having expected the question from Sebastian. "Sebastian—"

"You have, haven't you?"

I took a deep breath. "No, I haven't. I don't know why you would think such a thing."

We were both quiet, each waiting for the other to break the thick tension. "Okay," Sebastian finally said, "tell me this, how can you work with no bias, having those feelings?"

"I'm fine. Don't worry, okay? Now I have to go; I'll talk to you later." I hung up. Sebastian was right. I wasn't unbiased at all. I was determined.


Even though I had feared being late getting to the stables, I got there before Tristan did, or so I thought. Alonzo met me at the stable door entrance.

"*Hola*, Señorita Lewis." He smiled. "Señor Tristan asked me to lace up Parry for you; she is ready whenever you are finished changing."

"Where is Señor Tristan?" I inquired.

Alonzo smiled mysteriously. "He told me to tell you to meet him at the waters, that you would know where. I laced Parry for you, okay? And you get changed."

He was a demanding little man, that Alonzo. I smiled at him as he walked away, and I headed for the stable changing rooms to put on some riding gear.

Tristan wanted me to come to the waters. He must have meant the stream where we had shared that first kiss. I felt my face getting hot. If that man wasn't the sweetest thing next to cherry cheesecake, I didn't know what was.

Parry was as docile as she had been before, acting almost as if she remembered me. I patted her ivory mane and galloped toward the stream in search of Tristan. When I got close to it, I could see him sitting on a blanket, picnic basket beside him, and a humongous "I'm so proud of my romantic self" grin on his face.

"Just look at you." I smiled. "You think you're something, don'cha?"

"Well . . ." He held his arms out wide, looking like one of the *Price Is Right* models, showing off a prize. "I did go through all this trouble for you. Don't I warrant a kiss?" he said slyly.

"Hmm . . . I'll think about it." I giggled, dismounting Parry. I walked over to his blanket and picnic spread. Getting down beside him I peeked into the basket. He had fried chicken, potato salad, and ice-cold pickles. "Yummy, this looks good. I think maybe it does deserve a kiss." Looking over at Tristan, I noticed that he didn't hesitate to pucker up as soon as those magic words were out of my mouth. I laughed. He opened one eye, looking at me and frowning.

"What?" I giggled.

"You really gon' leave me hanging like this? I need some Hennessy, lady; wanna get drunk off you. . . ."

I flushed, smiling coyly as I moved forward to press my lips against his. They were so soft and pliable. We kissed for a quick minute; then just as I was about to curl up in his arms to deepen it, he pulled back.

"Oh!" I protested. "Why'd you do that?"

"Because . . . I'm hungry. I wanna eat, and I wanna talk," he said, kissing me on my neck, then moving away to grab a bagful of paper plates and forks, and two wineglasses.

"You're all prepared, aren't you?" I smiled.

"Yep, always for you. And oh, must not forget the wine," he said, pulling out a bottle of vintage. "Pichon-Lalande 1989," he read, "nothing but the best for you, baby."

"Oh, wow." I grinned, thinking to myself that I had no idea what Pichon-Lalande was, but trying to be sophisticated, I played along. "Nineteen eighty-nine was a very good year," I commented.

"Not for me." Tristan laughed. "I was locked up in prison in eighty-nine." I bit a pickle, cringing at its bitterness. "That bad, huh?" he said.

"Um . . ." I shook my head. "No, just a strong pickle. So how long were you locked up?"

"Well, I was at California State Pen for nine years, but of course I had spent years in and out of boys' homes before then."

"Ah, okay." I nodded. "So you were a bad boy."

"Yep, but I'm really good at heart," he said, laughing.

"Okay, I believe you." I laughed back.

We both sat quietly. He picked up my hand and started playing with my fingers.

"Tell me something," he asked slowly.

"Yeah?"

"How long have you been doing this type of work, and why?"

I started choking on the pickle this time. Tristan banged me on the back, trying to help me catch my breath. I swear I didn't know what to say to him half the time. In one way I was happy that he wanted to know more about me, that he was actually interested in me. But then on the other hand, I couldn't really show him *me*; I had to show him a made-up Hennessy Lewis, knowing full well that he wouldn't like the real me at all, the real woman that I wanted so much for him to love.

I went back in my mind and remembered my cover information. Recovering quickly I spilled out, "A couple of years ago, I met with Leo Jenson. We had met through a mutual acquaintance. He said he had heard I was looking for money to start an independent publishing company, which I never did start, by the way. And it went from there."

"So whatever happened to your dreams?" he asked, eyeing me intently.

"I don't know." I laughed weakly. "I mean dreams are just that, aren't they?"

"True. Usually make-believe, popcorn dreams never become more, unless you want them to."

We both shared a silent moment of agreement, deciding to chill with the melodramatic talk and dig into the delicious lunch Aurora had prepared. We chowed down, not only on the food, but also on the expensive wine. I was thinking as I swallowed down the tasty liquid what my mother would say about a bottle of wine that cost a week's worth of groceries for a family of four. Giggling inside at the thought of her reaction, I felt something cold running down my back.

"Oh! What are you doing, Tristan?" I shouted. He had obviously poured his Pichon-Lalande down the back of my shirt. He laughed. I glowered at him. "I can't believe you did that. Ugh! I'm gonna be all sticky now." I pulled my shirt off, feeling the wine dripping down my back.

"Oh, I feel so bad," he said teasingly. "I guess now you're just gonna have to get into the spring and take a bath."

I looked at him, not even being able to stay angry with him as I watched his cute, goofy expression. "Oh, I just bet you do feel soooo bad."

He leaned close to me, fiddling with the button of my riding pants. "Hey," he whispered in my ear, "why don't you be my *cup?*"

"Your cup?"

"Stand up," he said, his eyes burning into mine. After I stood he slowly unzipped my pants, then pulled them down my hips. A wind blew, a warm spring breeze that I could hardly feel, my body was just that hot. Tristan did away with my riding pants, then he started with my panties. My heartbeat tripled as I stood there naked and bare before his eyes.

"Lie down, baby; I'm so thirsty."

I moaned, knowing what he was about to do and almost dying at the thought of it. But he shocked me again, pouring some of the cool vintage wine on my neck, sucking it off, then down between my breasts, lick . . . suck. He dribbled some on my stomach, licking and sucking and kissing softly there, paying special attention to the still visible bruises that covered my rib cage. He kissed them tenderly.

Finally he pulled my legs up and over his shoulders, lifting me up to him. His wineglass empty, he picked the bottle up and poured a generous portion between my legs. My head flew back. I looked into the clear blue skies above with my mouth gaped in ecstasy as he drank his wine from my cup.

What felt like hours later, we lounged in the hot spring. There were so many rocks in the spring that Tristan was able to sit atop one with me straddling him face forward. I felt so good to be with him like this, it almost brought tears to my eyes. We had made love again and again, and even now he was semierect inside me, and singing soft, romantic R&B tunes in my ear. It hit me suddenly how much I needed this man. I needed this soft sweet thing he was giving me. I thought of how I was going to lose it if he did the planned heist. I could not allow that.

"Tristan?"

"Yeah, babe?" He kissed my shoulder, holding me closer to him.

"How important is it that we do this? Getting the Narmer slate, that is?"

"What do you mean how important?" He smiled. "It's big *moola, bebé*. You know, that green stuff?"

I bit my lip, searching for the right words to say to him.

"But you're already wealthy, aren't you? And you have your ranch. Would it be so very terrible if you didn't do it?"

He moved me backward to look into my eyes. "Hey . . . you're really serious, aren't you? You don't want to do it now?"

"Tristan, remember I told you before that I could feel when something was a bad omen?" I asked him anxiously.

"I remember."

"Well, I feel it with this job; I feel it here." I pointed to my heart. "I love you; I don't want anything bad to happen that may interfere with that, or with me doing the best I can to get you to love me back." I was afraid to look at his face, afraid of what his reaction would be to my love confession.

"Dang . . . do you really think I don't love you, too?" He brought my chin up, forcing me to look into his eyes.

"Well . . . you didn't say yes before when I asked you."

"I told you that I had never felt about anyone the way I feel about you," he said. He smiled tenderly, moving slightly inside me. I wiggled down a little on him, causing him to wince as if in pain, the good kind of pain though.

I laughed. "Uh-huh, too much for ya, ain't it?" He moaned

this time, burying his face in my neck. I moved slowly up and down, the water washing over us as we danced the lovers' dance.

"Tristan . . ."

"Yes," he choked out, his heart beating fast.

"I like the words 'I love you.' I need to hear them. They make me feel secure."

*"Te amo, bebé. . . ."*

Reynolds watched the two lovers from a distance. So wrapped up were they in their "moment," Reynolds thought, they didn't even sense that they had company. He should have guessed that something like this was going on, that the hoe would use her wiles to trick T.J. She had a sexy body though. Reynolds smiled, watching her moving, prancing and dancing atop T.J. "Would love to tap that ass myself," he whispered to himself.

But sexy body or not, she was trouble. He had been close enough to hear her trying to talk T.J. out of the Met job. He knew that he would have to do something to quiet her, and soon.

# 17

_Washington, DC_

The cloudy DC skies were no match for Sebastian's temperament. He stood quietly while being addressed by Kimberla Bacon, who was the SAC, Special Agent in Charge of his division. Affectionately called Chameleon by some in the agency because of the unique abilities and skills she showed as an undercover agent, Kimberla was a tall, black woman whose short-cropped hair made her look more like a dyke to him than the strong, dominant woman she was repped to be. Why she would be so interested in his cases he had no idea, but as far as he was concerned, as far as women went, being an SAC just wasn't their goddamn place.

"How can you possibly explain this situation, Sebastian?" Kimberla said, looking at Sebastian accusingly as she awaited his reply.

Sebastian sighed. "I already told you that. . . ."

"No, what you told me was that you had called Agent Cooper off the Jackson case, so why is she not back?"

Sebastian checked himself before speaking. He could feel his blood starting to boil. He scratched the back of his neck uncomfortably, then looked up at his SAC. "When my agent assured me that things were coming together again, I rethought the situation and figured we could still get Jackson," he finally said.

"And you didn't think to inform me?" Kimberla asked. She put her hand up then and said, "Don't bother answering that, I already know the answer." She sighed. "But tell me this, because I have wondered this from the very start assuming you would have known better. How come you don't have anyone else working with Agent Cooper to make sure she doesn't get in any trouble in LA?"

"I've kept a careful watch over Agent Cooper, Kimberla. I have always felt confident that she could handle things on her own, and she has. After she got out of the hosp—" Sebastian bit his lip before the words even came out, knowing that he let the shit slip out.

"Hold up!" Kimberla Bacon said, catching his slip of the tongue right away. "What do you mean after she got out of the hospital? Why was she in the hospital?"

"She had an accident while in LA." Sebastian swallowed.

"What kind of accident, Sebastian?"

Sebastian thought to think up a quick lie, but knowing Kimberla as he did, he knew she would check up on what he said. He figured, though, that he could at least twist the truth some. "There was an attempted robbery at Jackson's Malibu home. Agent Cooper was caught in the crossfire."

"An attempted robbery or some thug attack on Jackson?" Kimberla asked pointedly. "You should have sent her back here immediately!"

"Of course, and that is one of the reasons I asked her to come back after she was released," he explained.

Kimberla's eyes shot daggers into his. "Asked her? Just who is in charge here, Sebastian, you or her? You shouldn't have had to ask her, you should have *made* her come back. Especially being down there by herself!"

"Kimberla," Sebastian whispered, "you don't have to tell me what I should have done. I had to go on my gut feeling with this and that's exactly what I did."

Kimberla sat forward in her chair, looking at Sebastian angrily. "And your gut feeling was wrong. You and Agent Cooper have bypassed and broken every rule and regulation of the bureau, and I want her back here ASAP. Do you understand me? The way it's looking, both of you can be brought up on disciplinary charges. You get her back here or that is exactly what will happen, and I mean that, Sebastian."

"And what about Jackson!"

"There are far more important cases than Jackson's!" Kimberla Bacon exclaimed. "Although you seem to have forgotten that. This obsession that you have with him has not gone unnoticed by me."

"I am not obsessed," Sebastian insisted, "I'm simply trying to do my job!"

"Your job is whatever I tell you it is. Now you need to get control of yourself, and stop allowing your ego to run things, because there is no place in this division for any ego larger than my own. Is *that* understood?"

Kimberla Bacon crossed her legs, frowning as Sebastian ignored her, then picked up a lighter and started looking for his cigarettes. "Please don't smoke," she said. "It's quite gagging. And are you listening to me, Sebastian?"

At her words, Sebastian paused, nodded, and put the lighter down. "Of course; I'll be flying out as soon as possible. . . ."

Kimberla said, "Good. I don't want any mishaps with our agents. Getting T.J. Jackson comes second place to that. With a career criminal such as him, there will always be another opportunity and you know that, so you close this case and keep me clued in on things." She stood up to go. "Let me know when your plane leaves."

As the door to his office closed, an intense desire to slam it on the back of Agent Bacon's head went through Sebastian. He never could stand her and her high mindedness. Feeling a nervous itch, he wrestled through the rubble inside his desk, renewing his search for a smoke. He felt relieved when he found what he was looking for. Taking a long draw, he inhaled deeply. Just as the tobacco permeated through him, the phone rang.

Sebastian hesitated before answering. So much had been going on lately that wasn't what he deemed positive; at least not where he was concerned, it wasn't. After the third ring, he relented, and picked up the receiver.

"Sebastian Rogers here."

"What's rockin' in DC, my man?" came the cocky voice of Al Majors.

"Not much, seeing that not much has been happening on the West Coast, right?" Sebastian stated, eyebrows raised.

Al laughed. "More than you know, Special Agent Rogers. Your girl has been doing a lot of shit talking down this way, I've heard."

"Shit talking?"

"Yup. She's been trying to coerce T.J. out of doing the Met job, and she's using a most effective method from what I understand."

Sebastian hated when someone talked in riddles the way Majors did rather than being straight up, and riddles and games seemed to be the dude's forte all the time.

"Come on now, just spill it. Believe me, I don't have the time or patience for this shit today," Sebastian sighed.

"Okay, okay." Majors laughed. "Just thought you'd like to know that your little Hennessy is parting them thighs and giving up pie, you get my drift?" Sebastian gasped. "Anyhow, not that it matters much. I mean if I were T.J., I'd hit it, too, if she offered, but whatever happened to your dedicated FBI agent?"

"How do you know all this? *How?*" Sebastian spat out angrily.

"Now didn't your mama ever tell you that shouting gets you nowhere? What, do you have a thing for this chick or something?"

*No wonder she was so adamant about staying on this job,* Sebastian thought to himself. *She wanted to make sure that I didn't put another agent on it and then her precious Tristan James Jackson would be lost to her. Fuck! Fuck! Multi fuck!* Sebastian's mind screamed. There was no way, after all this hard work to get Jackson where he wanted him, no way he was going to let him get off just because Agent Hennessy Cooper couldn't control her fuckin' emotions and hormonal urges.

"Rogers?" Al called out to him.

Sebastian took a deep breath, fighting to anchor and compose himself. "Listen, right now there is less than a week before the scheduled date in New York. And we really don't have any time left, especially now with my SAC riding my balls. Once T.J. lands in LA, you just make sure that Rolez is dead. I'll take care of the rest."

"Why don't we just get the slate and then get rid of T.J.?" asked Al.

"Because, like I told you before, that would be too easy on him. A man like Jackson doesn't care about death. He's been facing that all his life, but the way he is now? All used to luxurious living and shit? To lose that would kill him for sure. Now as for Hennessy, she's obviously chosen sides. It's time to draw the battle plans."

Al Majors smiled wickedly. "My sentiments exactly."


*Santa Fe, New Mexico . . . Tristan*

My mind was filled with two different melodies. One was the duet by Prince and Angie Stone, "You Are My Sunshine," straight-up hypnotizing me with their words and rhythm. I'm a big fan of both artists, so this combo had me jonesing from the moment I first heard it. Also, the words sounded like my feelings for one special lady; enter the second melody on my mind, Hennessy . . .

I'm not a soft, wimpy man, yet my heart was gone, no longer belonging to the cool, calm brotha from Compton hood, Tristan Jackson. I was so deeply in love with Hennessy, just her name brought my heart to hammering. I closed my eyes as I relaxed in my comfortable Lazyboy chair in the den, picturing her smile, the gorgeous dimples that sprang up like a badge of beauty whenever she called them. Her big almond-shaped eyes, and mostly, her soft voice moaning out how much she loved me, how good I was making her feel, or just moaning out my name period. I shuddered, my body hardening in reaction to my daydreams. I took a gulp of the red wine that we had had at dinner, still filled to the brim in its glass. Although I had wanted to go for an after-dinner ride with Parry and James Bond, Hennessy had begged off, saying she was tired and wanted to retire early. I had had an itching to ask her if I could be tired with her and retire early, too, but thought better of it. I didn't need her thinking I was a raving, lovesick maniac who couldn't leave her alone for five minutes, even though to be honest I felt like that sometimes.

My face must've been looking rather clownish, because when I opened my eyes, Hawk and Mateo were both staring at me, looking rather clownish themselves in a mock sort of way.

"What's on your mind, hombre?" Mateo grinned.

"Oh, you know what's on his mind," Hawk said. "He's sitting here all by himself, moaning over something, smiling, and listening to love songs. It's sickening, ain't it, Mateo?" He looked toward Mateo, who laughed as he nodded his head in agreement.

"Pitiful, man. So what do we do with such a lowly piece of work?" Mateo said salaciously.

"Fuck both of y'all, you hear?" I laughed.

"Such language, *mi amigo,* in such a warm atmosphere of love." Mateo faked as though in shock. Both he and Hawk laughed, Hawk flopping down on the navy blue leather couch, lighting up a cigar.

"Now I just know you have another one of those," I probed.

Hawk reached into his front shirt pocket, pulling out his fat, gold cigar case. He offered Mateo one, who declined, and then me, which I accepted with a wink. One thing about my Italian brother was that he had the best cigars this side of the Atlantic, and wasn't hesitant to share them.

We all chilled quietly for a while, Hawk and I with our smokes, and Mateo with a Bacardi. I decided that now was as good a time as any to spit out what had been on my mind ever since my picnic lunch with Hennessy the day before.

"Guys, I wanted to run this past you two. Reynolds, too, but since he's not around right now, I'll see what y'all think first."

"What's that?" Hawk asked. Mateo also looked at me expectedly.

"Well." I swallowed. "You two know me, and when something is not going smoothly, or I get a bad vibe about something, especially a job as big as this one we are planning, I take note."

"And you feel that something is wrong?" asked Mateo.

"Not just feel it, I *know* something ain't right. I mean think about it, first Earl is killed, and then Hennessy is attacked. And as of now, we still don't know what any of that was all about, or who is responsible."

Hawk nodded, drawing on his cigar slowly. "I had a feeling this was coming," he said quietly.

I looked toward Hawk, knowing that even with his quiet response, he wasn't at all happy about what I had just said.

"Hawk, I know we've talked about this before, and I know you need the money, but can't you understand my hesitancy here? Even a little?"

Laughing, Hawk said, "Afraid not; see, from where I'm standing you haven't said much. Oh, except that something ain't *right*. But tell me this, T.J., since when have you lost your guts to the point of chickening out on something? What's happened to you?"

"Nothing has happened to me, Hawk. But let's get real here, okay? Do you want to jump into a situation that don't feel right, smell right? Did you enjoy your stay in prison? Are you in a hurry to get back there or something?"

"You know, man, T.J. may be right," Mateo said slowly.

Hawk jumped up and started pacing back and forth across the floor. "So this has all been a waste! Everything, all the plans we've had?"

"I'm not making this decision for you guys. It's up to all of us, not just me." I sighed. "I know I've committed to you guys to do this job, and I know we're talking about a lot of money here. So if you feel that I'm being unfair, and if the majority wants to stay with our plans, then we can go ahead with things, but I have to say I'm not feeling it anymore, and I think it would be a mistake. But it's the majority rule so . . . you two just say the word."

Both Mateo and Hawk were quiet as they thought things through.

"So you think we could pull this off if we did it at a later date?" Mateo finally asked.

"Of course not," Hawk said, jumping in. "It's now or never." He sighed. "Dayum, T.J., why do you have to put a damper on things like this?"

"But he's right," Mateo noted grudgingly. "Don't you think the feds may be looking at us now?" He looked from Hawk to me. "They're mighty quiet about Earl's murder and all, but for sure they could be watching us now, don't you think?"

"That's what I'm talking about," I pressed, "it's dangerous, guys, *too* dangerous." I paused briefly. "I've been thinking a lot about retiring. Just moving here to Jackson's permanently, maybe even selling my beach house. I think I'm getting too old for Bonnie and Clyde," I joked. Both guys looked at me a bit surprised.

I looked over at Hawk, trying to read his feelings on everything. I didn't want the guys to think that I was being a traitor or trying to dump out on them at the last minute, although realistically that was what I was doing.

"Hawk?"

"What can I say, T.J.? Seems like this is the way you and Mateo want to go. I'm outnumbered so, whatever," he whispered.

"It's not like that," I insisted. "How you feel is very important to me, man."

"And me, too," Mateo agreed.

"And what about Hennessy, and Reynolds, what will they say?"

I sat forward, feeling a bit stressed and running my hand over my face before saying, "We'll have to talk to them both, but I'm pretty sure Hennessy will totally agree."

"And Reynolds?"

"He may not," I acknowledged, "but he won't have much to say if the majority of us want out."

"Damn! What am I supposed to do about all the money I owe out?" Hawk stormed.

"Stop gambling, fool." Mateo laughed. Hawk gave him the evil eye.

"Listen, Hawk, I know you still have those stocks and CDs you can cash in, and you know I'll help you out the best I can. I'm not gonna desert you like that, and you know it!"

"Oh, so now I have to sell my stock. . . . That was my old-age pension, you know."

"Then it's time for your old ass to pinch pennies." Mateo grinned wickedly.

"Cut it out, Mateo." I stifled a laugh, but straightened my face as I looked at Hawk. "So, what's your vote?"

"Yea, I guess. . . ."

"Yea," Mateo echoed after him.

"And yea for me, too. And so like I mentioned, we'll talk to the other two, and we can all decide where we will go from here. But, I did want to mention that I'll be flying back to LA for Mother's Day. We can have a meeting about all this and any future plans we may have after I get back, if that's cool with you guys."

Hawk looked at me openmouthed.

"What?" I laughed.

"Nothing," Hawk said, shaking his head. "It's just that this is the first time I've ever heard you mention doing something for Mother's Day."

I finished my wine, looking into the empty glass before speaking. I knew that I had given a lot of revelations for the evening, and maybe my wanting to spend time with my mama was the biggest one. But Hennessy had helped me see some other things also, like maybe I hadn't always given my mom a chance, maybe I never stopped accusing her long enough to see *why* she did things, or said things, or had acted the way she had all of my life. I supposed the person who was going to be the most shocked to see me come Sunday would be Jillian Jackson. I only hoped that it would be a good surprise, and not an *I need some money, I'm busy, come back later, you think you're better than I am* surprise.

I sighed at the thought, looking toward the guys for my explanation. "Well, you're right. It's been ages since I've wanted to make plans with my mom. But," I said with a forced breeziness, "better late than never, right?"

"Yep, you right about that," Hawk said, "and . . . I think I'll go with you, not to your mom's, but I haven't seen my woman in a long time. I think I'll make a run over to her place."

"Old man, when you gonna stop messing with that dried-up hoe?" Mateo joked.

Hawk stood up, swatting at Mateo's ass. "I will when you start giving me that bootie you keep promising, *papi.*"

I laughed, taking a deep breath and shaking my head at Hawk and Mateo. Just as Hawk said he wanted to take a short run, I stopped him, putting my hand on his shoulder. "Are you sure we're okay, Hawk?" I asked. "You're important to me, man. . . ."

Hawk looked at me and gave a reluctant, lopsided grin. "Oh, course we are; we're partners, remember? Always have been, always will be."


*Hennessy*


I knew that Tristan was in the den talking to Hawk and Mateo, and was oh so tempted to creep in and eavesdrop, so tempted that it took me all of ten minutes to get up, slip on my robe and yellow satin slippers, and quietly tiptoe out of the princess room. I took a big breath and turned the corner toward the den, walking right smack into . . . Reynolds.

"Oops! Sorry," I said, backing up a bit.

"Where you sneaking off to?"

"No . . . nowhere. I just thought I would get some warm

milk to help me sleep; I have a touch of a headache, just thought that would help."

Reynolds put his arm across the doorway, then leaned up against its border, looking at me oddly. "Well then, maybe what you need is some Tylenol, not warm milk."

I laughed uncomfortably, trying not to seem nervous. For some reason, Reynolds was not letting me past. "Thanks, but really I prefer warm milk. My mother would always give me that as a headache remedy and I guess I've just sort of stuck with it."

"Ah," he sang, still blocking my way, "and where are you from again?"

"Yonkers."

"Yonkers . . . and you found out about us how?"

"What is this? Are you having me checked out again or something?" I asked. Finally he moved his arm.

"Naw, boo, just interested in knowing more about you. We never really had a chance to hook up, you know what I'm sayin'?" He reached out just then, running his finger down the front of my partly open robe, right at the swell of my breast. I jerked back. "Hmm," he moaned, "you're a beautiful woman, Hennessy Lewis. It is *Lewis*, right?" The Negro had the audacity to reach out and try to touch me again, but this time brushing his fingers across my concealed nipple.

Can I just say I was getting pissed? I fought hard not to drop-kick his cocky, insulting ass. Instead, I slapped his hand away. "Reynolds, if you ever touch me like that again I will kick your ass," I said, my hands clenching and unclenching rhythmically at my side.

He dropped his fingers slowly, still smiling at me. "Oh, you gon' *kick my ass* now? Dayum, girl, you one of them bad bitches, ain'cha? One of them Amazon bitches," he said, grinning broadly.

"If you don't let me past you're gonna see what an Amazon bitch I really can be," I whispered, feeling my heart beating rapidly.

Reynolds looked at me for a second, noting the fire in my eyes, then laughed as he floated his hand in front of himself as if giving me the green light to leave.

Glad to have a reprieve, I quickly walked past him, deciding that after this I really did need that milk.

"I guess you've just reserved that privilege for T.J., huh? Or have you just been enjoying a bit too much of *his* warm milk?"

"Excuse me?" I spat, indignantly.

He laughed, and then winked at me mischievously. "Nuttin', baby, I just said enjoy your warm milk."

# 18

*The next day . . . Hennessy*

I hadn't slept well the night before. Somehow Reynolds's big face kept creeping up into the camera of my mind. Not even so much his face, but his words. His words were enough to make anyone uncomfortable. I was trying, however, not to feel paranoid. I'm the type of person that usually goes on facts, not paranoia, but his asking, or rather his hinting as to where I was from, my name, where I had heard about them, all things that he had known about since the beginning, yet pretending as if he had no idea of them, registered to me that maybe he suspected something.

I sat on the end of my bed, quickly slipping on my Nikes. I had promised Aurora that I would help her with breakfast for the guys—I really just wanted to show Tristan that I could cook. I secretly hoped that Reynolds wouldn't be anywhere near the kitchen or dining room, and that wherever he always made off to after we had rehearsed for the job, he would have skipped off to this morning also.

I made my way into the kitchen. The smell of fresh-brewed coffee and banana bread filled the room. Aurora smiled brightly when I walked in.

"*Buenos dias,* Señorita Hennessy!"

"*Buenos dias,* Aurora." I smiled. "You have it smelling good in here."

Aurora walked over to me with a fresh, home-baked Danish in hand. "This is pecan; taste." I took a big chunky bite.

"Mmm . . . delicious. You gonna make these guys fat if you keep feeding 'em like this," I quipped, reaching out for the remaining pecan Danish in her hand.

"*Sí,* but happy, too, no?"

I laughed. "With a good cook like you, Aurora, they can't be anything but happy." I stuffed some more buttery Danish into my mouth. "Okay," I said, remembering my reason for being in the kitchen, a reason that didn't include eating a pecan Danish, "so what do you need me to do?"

"You can fry the eggs, but remember Señor Tristan likes his over easy, the others you can make medium."

I'd be all too happy to fix my baby's over easy eggs, I almost said, giggling a little to myself. I went to the fridge and pulled out the carton of eggs, figuring I'd do the others first; then I could concentrate on making Tristan's eggs just so. I had to laugh at my silliness, but then love made ya silly sometimes, and I *loved* Tristan Jackson, or like my grandma used to say, I loved his dirty drawls.

"You're smiling all happy; need I guess why?" Aurora grinned.

"Oh . . . I was just thinking about a certain *somebody,* and how special he is to me," I admitted.

Aurora put her pot holders on the counter and wiped her hands off on her apron. "So maybe now you can give him peace. . . ."

"You worry about Tristan, don't you?"

"Señorita, I want to see him happy; he's a good person. Many may not see that because of what he does. But I have always seen it, and I also saw the pain he went through after his Natalie's death." She paused briefly, as if trying to decide if she should continue on with this conversation. I hoped she did. Tristan would never tell me much about Natalie, only that she had died, and I got the feeling that he felt somewhat responsible.

"He loved her dearly, but after she was killed, he withdrew into himself. There was an investigation of course. Natalie's uncle, who is a policeman on the East Coast, he pushed hard to try to somehow pin the tragedy on Señor Tristan. Not that he didn't already feel guilty enough over what happened."

"What exactly happened to her, Aurora?" I asked, wanting to know, yet at the same time afraid of what I'd hear.

"It was a job that they all were working on. She was working with them on this particular one. From what I understand she and Señor were running for the getaway van, but he made it and she did not. They were being chased by the police, and did not know it. When Señor Tristan turned around, he saw Natalie shot, killed, but had to leave her there lest they all be caught." Aurora sighed deeply. "It was awful. Señor Tristan blamed himself and still does. And her uncle put out a campaign to destroy Tristan. He has been relentless."

"That's awful," I whispered, feeling my throat tightening. I leaned back against the counter, catching my breath as her words registered through me. It wasn't that I was not aware, hadn't always been aware of just what Tristan did for a living, but the realness of it, and the devastating effects that it caused, not only for him, but for Natalie, was shattering to me.

Again I had to look inside myself, and ask myself what I had gotten into. I was not someone who was unaware of how the system worked. I was raised a cop, and now here I was violating everything I had ever held sacred. What was I going to do once all of this came to a head? What if Tristan didn't want to be with me, marry me? What if he wouldn't give up the criminal lifestyle once we did marry? Could I live with that, or with a man who would not change?

"Señorita, don't think harshly of him because of what happened to Natalie," Aurora said, almost as if she had been reading my mind. "It was not his fault, and now he is a different person. Especially with you he is."

"How so?" I asked.

"I believe you are not really in this type of lifestyle. I believe that you were sent here to help him see that he doesn't need to be either. Mateo has told me that everyone is having second thoughts about the job you all have planned now, and I know deep inside that you had a lot to do with that."

Hearing her words I was oh so wishing that I could talk to her fully, really have her know me and my secret person of the heart. She seemed to know so much already, almost as if she were psychic.

"Well," I said cheerfully, wanting to lighten the mood, "we'd better get finished with this brekkie, or we'll have some mean, hungry fellas on our hands."

I was finishing my second cup of coffee when I felt Tristan squeezing lightly at the base of my neck at the breakfast table. I looked over at him and smiled. Mateo, noticing our intimate exchange, made a hooting noise.

"Don't do that at the table, Mateo," Aurora reprimanded as she refilled Hawk's coffee cup.

"Yes, *Madre,*" Mateo sang. Aurora gave him an evil eye, then scurried back off into the kitchen.

I laughed at them both, then turned my attention toward Tristan. "So, where is Reynolds this morning?"

"Who knows? I thought I heard him come in last night, but he wasn't in his room this morning when I peeped in."

"I think he's found some new coochie to hit." Mateo laughed, stopping abruptly at my aghast stare. "Sorry, Hennessy."

"No problem, hon." I smiled, shaking my head.

"Anyhow," Tristan continued, "I want to talk to him, so hopefully I can catch up with him tonight. I know he wouldn't miss a party."

"What party?"

"Señor Tristan is nice enough to host a Mother's Day dinner for *mi madre,*" Aurora explained, as she walked back in from the kitchen. I stood up and started helping her gather the used dishes. "Isn't he beautiful?" she added.

"He most certainly is," I whispered dreamingly. Tristan blushed at our praise.

"Maaaan, that's gay," Mateo teased.

"Shut up, Mateo!" Aurora and I said in unison.

Hawk laughed, still busy stuffing his face, and my eyes met Tristan's. Yes, he was beautiful; now if only he was free from what he had allowed society to make him, then we would be all right. . . .

*Washington, DC . . . Hennessy*

"Hello, darling . . ."

"Well, I'm shocked to hear you calling me without me having to harass you. It's a first since you've been on the West Coast."

Hennessy laughed. "Come on, Sebastian. I haven't been that bad; it's just that you've been so persistently nosy with everything. *Unusually* so."

"Nothing about this case has been usual, Hennessy. . . ."

"True," she said quietly. "I know that for a fact."

*Yeah, I just bet you do,* Sebastian thought to himself. He wanted to confront her on her two-timing, traitorous ways, but common sense stopped him. If he told her now that he knew what she had been doing, who knew what would happen? Right now, at least things were still on, regardless of what she was trying to prevent. Sebastian guessed that T.J. was too greedy to let her wiles prevent him from stealing forty million dollars, the same as Natalie's wiles didn't prevent him from doing anything. He only wrapped her up real tight, and pulled her into the hellfire with him. Only when the fire was heated up, he'd left her there to roast.

"So, what's going on now?" Sebastian asked Hennessy.

"Okay, tonight there's a dinner for Aurora's mother. Aurora's the housekeeper here, and then we are supposed to fly back out to LA."

"Oh, really?"

"Yep, Tristan wants to spend Mother's Day with his mom. That's sweet, huh?" she cooed.

Sebastian laughed, "Yeah, real sweet, Hennessy. Jackson is just as sweet as they come."

"Okay, okay, I know you don't mean that; I was just saying . . ." Her voice trailed off. "Anyhow, we should be back Monday afternoon to pack for New York."

"And then you'll be bringing it where?" Sebastian asked. "Did you find out who T.J.'s buyer is yet?"

"I didn't know you wanted me to. Is that important if we are supposed to confiscate the slate palette at the airport?"

She thought too much, Sebastian said to himself. Actually, her intelligence was one thing he had always liked about Hennessy Cooper, but in this case, she was thinking a bit too much, and interfering even more so. He felt this intense anger surfacing at the thought of her lying to him. He couldn't wait to face her with it, and see the stupid look on her face once she realized she had been found out.

"Just call it morbid curiosity, okay?" Sebastian finally said.

"Hmm . . . okay." She laughed. "Anyhow, he never really told us who he was selling it to; I remember either Hawk or Reynolds asking him though."

"Well, ask. Humor me, okay? Just for curiosity's sake like I told you. Anyhow"—Sebastian looked down at his watch—"I need to go. All of this should be over by Tuesday night or Wednesday and you can come back to beautiful DC. Sound good?"

"Uh-huh, I hear ya. Bye." She laughed, hanging up.

Sebastian took a deep breath after hanging up with Hennessy, and picked up the receiver again.

"It's all set for Tuesday night," he announced. "But get this, they are leaving for LA midnight tonight because T.J. wants to be with his mother for Mother's Day."

"Good." Al Majors smiled. "Perfect!"

"Are you thinking what I'm thinking?"

"Yup. Rolez is all mine. Now are you sure, positively sure that T.J. will be in LA?"

"Yes, I'm positive. Hennessy just finished cooing over how sweet he is to want to be with Mommy."

Al laughed. "Okay, then it's all set. Just be sure that Tuesday night when he gets back here from New York, there are LAPD waiting at his beach house to arrest him. Now what about your agent, is she gonna be with us or against us?"

Sebastian thought for a moment, knowing that despite the fondness he had always had for Hennessy, she was not on his side, and would do all she could to clear T.J. and give him an alibi for Rolez's murder. "No, she's not with us," he stated flatly.

"Then you know what I have to do, right?" Not waiting for Sebastian's response, Al went on. "We cannot have any witnesses for his defense. That includes your special agent. You take care of things over that way, and I'll take care of the dirty work." Laughing he said, "I know you feds don't like to get your hands dirty."

"Just do what you're supposed to do and I'll take care of things on my end," Sebastian said testily.

"Okay, Captain." Al smirked.

Just before hanging up, Sebastian thought for a minute and said, "Hey, about Hennessy, don't have her suffer—"

"Ah, a crooked agent with a soft spot?"

"Go to hell."

Al laughed again. "Don't worry, no blood, no pain, no suffering. Al knows how to treat a lady."


*Saturday evening in Santa Fe . . . Hennessy*

My conversation with Sebastian left me uneasy for some reason. I could hardly wait until this was all over, because I knew without a shadow of a doubt that he was going to have my head on a platter once he realized what I was doing. Tristan hadn't told me himself that the Met job was off, but I was feeling pretty sure that he was going to announce it. My heart beat faster at the thought. So many of my dreams for Tristan and me rested on his letting this go; It was the only hope I had.

As I finished dressing for dinner, I sprayed a touch of Cool Water perfume behind each ear, then walked over to the small table by the bed to grab my hand lotion. It was missing from where I had placed it. I pulled the drawer open, thinking it may have fallen inside accidentally. As I felt around in the drawer, a picture frame lying facedown caught my eye. I picked it up. It was a woman, a very beautiful woman who I recognized instantly. It was a copy of the same photograph that sat on Sebastian's desk in his office, of his wife's godchild. He had never told me her name, but he didn't need to. I knew right away that his wife's godchild was also Natalie, Tristan's Natalie. I caught my breath. Natalie must have used this room before, too. I swallowed the small bit of jealousy that ran through me at that thought. But so much was starting to make sense now. Sebastian's preoccupation with Tristan; the intense hatred he seemed to hold for him; his extreme concern over this case. But the question of why he had held this fact away from me was still left unanswered. A question that I intended to call him on as soon as I got an opportunity to talk to him.

Hearing a knock at my door, I quickly replaced the photo and closed the drawer.

"Hey." Tristan smiled seductively. I smiled back as he walked in and slipped his arms around me. "You look and smell good enough to eat."

I blushed, as I placed my arms around his neck. He also looked good enough to eat. "Hey, yourself," I whispered seductively. I was about to comment on how tasty he was looking, when he squashed my words with his lips, mashing his lips with mine. I moaned into his mouth, kissing him back deeply.

"Wait, Tristan," I said suddenly, pushing gently at his chest. I could feel his hands working up my inner thighs, pulling at my panties.

"Baby, I want you," he moaned. "We haven't had any time alone together for the past few days."

"I know and I want you, too, but tell me please, it's off, right? We aren't going for the palette?"

Tristan just smiled. "So if I say yeah, it's off, then I get some booty?"

I smacked his arm. "Stop it," I scolded, laughing.

"I love you," Tristan whispered. "And yes, New York is off. We only have to talk to Reynolds later on tonight on the way to LA. I talked to him earlier and he said he was coming, and I told him we were having a group meeting on the flight."

Can I just say that after Tristan's announcement, I was feeling very, very amorous? I almost purred out loud, looking into his beautiful eyes and feeling like maybe, just maybe I had a future with this complex and exciting man. Was I only dreaming? I didn't think so. At least I hoped not. In this case, I didn't care what he did, or had done in the past. And on a secret note, shamefully so, his bad-boy image even excited me a little. I pouted as he washed my neck with warm kisses. I should be ashamed of myself, I thought, as I led Tristan like a piper to my bed.

He stood in front of me at the bed, taking off all of his clothes and watching me with a heated look in his eyes. I undressed as quickly as he, feeling a wetness gathering between my legs. Tristan had a body that would turn any woman's legs to lava. His manhood stuck out strong and dark. I gulped back my desire as I looked up into his eyes, seeing his pleading look to make love to him.

"I love you, Hennessy," he whispered again.

"I love you, too," I whispered back. I then got on my knees in front of him as he lay back on my white rose spread and he moaned as I kissed his love, then I took him in my mouth.

We were late for dinner. . . .

# 19

---

*Santa Fe, New Mexico . . . Tristan*

Hennessy and I made sure not to come out to the dining room together, although it didn't matter much. We still got the knowing grins and chuckles from Hawk, Reynolds, and especially Mateo. She came out after I did, with flushed cheeks and looking straight-up radiant as far as I was concerned.

"Dinner is getting cold waiting on you," Mateo said to Hennessy. "Did you take a late siesta and oversleep, *chiquita?*" he joked.

"No, I did not," Hennessy retorted, clearing her throat. I noticed she wouldn't look at me though. I stared her down until she was forced to, then motioned for her to come sit down beside me. After we were all seated, I stood up to propose a toast.

"Okay, this is a toast to more than just Aurora's love for her mother." I looked toward Aurora's mom, a beautiful, graceful Mexican lady whom I had never gotten to know as well as I had wanted to, but who always treated me like a son. She and Aurora were part of the reason that my goal had always been to make Jackson's my permanent home, and the place that I would someday raise my own children. "This is a toast to friendship," I continued. "There's a scripture in the Bible, not that I'm a Bible scholar or anything," I joked, drawing everyone's laughter. "But, um . . . I have some love for the Word, and I do remember a passage that reads, *There is a friend that is sticking closer than a brother,* and I believe that that is what we have here tonight, that kind of bond, and friendship." Raising my wineglass again, I toasted, "So here's to love, friendship, and bonding."

"Love, friendship, and bonding," everyone echoed after me.

After my toast, we all dug in. We hadn't wanted Aurora to be busy serving us while she was celebrating with her mother, so we all pitched in. Hennessy was like a lil' hostess. She fit so perfectly in my life, I wanted to make her a permanent part of it, and that realization took me by surprise. I caught myself smiling at her throughout the evening, with her smiling back at me like we were sharing big secrets, and I realized that I was happy, a feeling I had never felt much in my life.

Reynolds was unusually quiet though. I felt bad that I hadn't explained what was going on to him, but he had been hard to pin down the past few days. I was starting to think that Mateo was right, that Reynolds had found him some pretty *chica* in the city that had him pretty much whipped. I decided to ask him.

"Hey, Reynolds," I called out, nodding my head toward the porch. He followed me out.

"Wassup, dawg?"

I gave him daps, then took a sip of my drink, and leaned back against the porch rail. "You're flying out with us tonight, right?"

"Yeah, I told you I would be."

"Oh, I know, it's just that we haven't had much time to talk lately, and you're always in the city. What? Have you found some cute Lolita out there or something?" I joked, punching him on the arm.

"Well, you know all of us can't be as lucky as you, right?

You and that sexy Hennessy." He shook his head, looking over at her through the porch screen. "Man, you struck gold with that. Tell me something . . ." Reynolds leaned closer to me. "What she like? I mean, is she a hot piece in the sack or what?"

I don't know why, the guys and I had always joked and talked about the women we got up with, but for some reason I didn't want to talk to Reynolds about Hennessy, and I felt kinda pissed at him asking if she was a *hot* piece.

"You know I don't see her like that," I said uncomfortably.

"What?" Reynolds looked at me as if surprised. "Oh, so it's like that, huh?"

"Naw, it's not like that, Reynolds. It's just . . . I just don't look at Hennessy as a hot piece, you know? She's kinda special, man."

"Uh-huh, well, you know what I always say: a hoe is a hoe is a hoe." Reynolds hocked up and spat out a big glob of phlegm.

"Shit, man, you nasty!" I exclaimed. "Don't be spitting in my yard. And look, I don't know about them trick hoes you be seeing, but Hennessy ain't one of them. She's a lady. Speak of her as such."

"A'ight, nicca, whateva." Reynolds laughed. "I'm just saying I got yo back, boy. You done got a lil' weak in your perception since our Compton days."

"Perception?" I asked, obviously not getting the point of the conversation. But then again Reynolds had been acting weird as hell lately.

"That's right, 'cuz see, there used to be a time when you knew as well as I knew, you can't trust nobody." Reynolds's eyes glanced over at Hennessy, who was looking in our direction. "Now here you are, trusting some woman, of all people, a woman. And one you don't even know—"

"Stop right there, Reynolds, okay?" I interrupted. "What's this all of a sudden downing on Hennessy coming from? I wanted to talk to you about something else, not her, and we haven't even had a chance to because you'll so hell-bent . . ." I paused, sighing deeply. "Listen, forget all that, okay? But just for the record, I *do* know her."

Reynolds laughed humorlessly, and started walking toward the doors to go back inside.

"Reynolds?"

Circling back around to look at me, Reynolds said, "Listen, remember this?" he made the sign of crip love. "One thing we always knew, before we got caught up in this world of diamonds and glitter, is that you can only trust yourself and your boys."

"But we're not boys anymore, Reynolds. We're men, and this ain't Compton. Our whole world does not consist of hookers, thugs, and hoes."

"A'ight, man, whateva," he said, walking into the house and letting the porch door slam loudly.


*Midnight rendezvous . . . Hennessy*


The evening had been so beautiful, I was sad to see it end. Mrs. Rivera was just as sweet and warm as Aurora, and funny, too. After dinner, dessert, and a couple of hours of cocktails, however, Tristan informed us that it was time to get ready for our late night flight to LA. I finished packing my bags, kissed Aurora good-bye, and smilingly made my way to the plane with Tristan, Hawk, and Mateo.

"Tim!" Tristan called out. "How's it going, man?"

"It's been a long day, too long in fact." Tim Redmond sighed.

I walked over to the plane entrance, pulling my bag along with me. It was pretty heavy being that I usually overpacked.

"Let me help you with that." I looked up to see Tim Redmond's smiling face, his blue eyes twinkling at me.

"Thanks, Tim," I said.

"I would've helped you," Tristan said slowly.

"What'd I tell you about that jealous trait, man?" Mateo laughed.

I smiled at them both, actually feeling pretty good that Tristan showed any jealousy toward me. I looked at him.

"Um, can you help me with my vanity case, Sir Tristan?"

Tristan smiled, playing along with my game. "Anything for you, milady," he said, with a fake English accent.

Everyone was happy and ready to go. The only person who appeared to be missing was Reynolds. I looked around uneasily. Ever since our exchange the night before in the hallway, I felt apprehensive around him, or whenever he was mentioned. I had been right when I had told Sebastian that we were underestimating these guys a lot. Tristan and Mateo seem to be the only ones who totally believed and trusted in me. I guess I was most surprised at Tristan, or maybe surprised was not the right word. Thankful maybe that he trusted me, meaning his feelings were sincere, but sad in that if he ever found out I wasn't who I had said I was, would he believe that I really loved him?

"I guess Reynolds changed his mind about joining us," Tristan said, sitting beside me on the plane.

"Good," I spat out without thinking. Tristan laughed, looking at me with surprise.

"Hey, what's up with that? I thought you liked Reynolds."

"Well, I really don't know him enough to like him or dislike him," I explained. "He's just so ghetto." I shrugged. "I don't know."

"Well, you know that I'm ghetto, too, right?" Tristan teased.

"No, you aren't. I know maybe you were raised that way, but you are a very distinguished, handsome, articulate man."

Tristan looked thoughtful, and then nodded his head in agreement. "This is true what you say, milady; this is true."

"You're crazy!" I giggled. My laughter was stilled when Reynolds's head popped through the plane's entrance. *Great . . . I* thought.

"What, y'all trying to leave me behind or something?" Reynolds said. Throwing his small suitcase over his head, he flopped down in the seat right in front of us. He looked odd, kind of high like. I inched a bit closer to Tristan.

"You knew what time we were leaving; where did you run off to?" Tristan asked him.

"Just needed to take care of something," he said evasively.

Hawk and Mateo settled in, Tristan and I cuddled closely, I was feeling pretty relaxed. Tim Redmond had us in the air and on our way out of Santa Fe within the next five minutes. The view was as beautiful as ever, especially as we coasted over the mountainous regions of the Santa Fe ski basin. This was truly a beautiful place, and only the lights from the plane lent the mountains light, giving them an odd, smoky appearance.

I sighed, laying my head against Tristan's shoulder. Just as I was about to drift off to sleep, he tapped me on my arm. "Listen, guys, we need to talk about some things," he said. I sat up abruptly.

"Reynolds, I wanted to holla with you earlier about this. I've already talked with Hawk and Mateo, and of course, Hennessy."

"Talked about what?" Reynolds asked, flipping around in his chair.

"Well, we've all kinda decided to forgo the Met job for right now. That is, with Earl's murder, and the little oddities and—"

"*What the fuck.*" Reynolds shouted.

*Uh-oh*, I thought to myself. My heart started beating rapidly.

Tristan looked at Reynolds as if he had lost his mind. "Man, don't raise your voice at me. Have you flipped the hell out or something?"

"No, nicca, you have! How you think you s'pose to just cancel shit, with no notice, nothing? How you figure that?"

"If you'd shut up for a minute, I was trying to explain," Tristan hummed out between clenched teeth. "This is not the first time we've had to cancel a job, Reynolds. So why you trippin'?"

"Yeah, Reynolds," Mateo agreed. "Remember we had to cancel that joint in London that time. You didn't have a problem with it then."

Reynolds looked over at Mateo. He had a crazed look in his eyes that I didn't like at all. I tightened my arm around Tristan's.

"Shut the hell up, you fuckin' spic!" Reynolds stood up, looking around at everyone, his eyes moving rapidly. I could almost swear he was on something. In fact I was certain of it. He had the typical look of a heroin addict, or maybe crack.

"Fuck you, Reynolds!" Mateo stood up, staring him down angrily. Reynolds lurched forward, grabbing Mateo by the collar.

"Cut it out!" Tristan exclaimed, pushing Reynolds roughly away from Mateo, causing Reynolds to fall clumsily to the floor. "What's gotten into you, man!"

Reynolds got up, still looking wild and out of control. "Me? What done got into me? What the hell you think, T.J.? You, *my brotha;* you're the one, you who's supposed to have my back, but instead you sell out, and I'm the one kept in the dark, when I'm the one who's been there for you from day one. *I'm the one!"*

"Reynolds, you need to sit on down and calm down. You're definitely overreacting," Hawk said quietly, trying to calm him down. "We all are together in this; ain't nobody been trying to cut you out of nothing."

Tristan, looking upset, took a deep breath and tried explaining himself again. "I'm sorry if you think I've been trying to keep things from you, or haven't had your back, Reynolds. You know that's not true. We've been cool with each other since high school. Don't do this now. . . ."

Reynolds obviously wasn't hearing reason. Suddenly, he looked in my direction. "And look at you," he said to me, his voice slurred. "You stuck-up bitch! This is all your fault. You think I don't know what you've been up to? You think I don't know who you are? *Beotcch!"*

*Oh no! He knows; he knows!* My training as an agent kicked in, and I had an instant desire to flee, find a way out. But I was on a plane, thirty, forty thousand feet in the air, with nowhere to run. My cover was about to be blown, and I was trapped.

Tristan jumped instantly to my defense. "Man, sit your high ass down, and don't you ever, *ever* talk to Hennessy like that again!"

"Oh, so now you taking sides against me again? Siding with the bitch?" *No, not here, not now . . .* "Look at her, man, look at her!" *Please don't let him say it . . .* "She ain't no professional thief from New York," *No . . .* my mind buzzed . . . "She's five-O, T.J. Naw, she's worse; she's the feds, you hear me? She's fuckin' FBI is what she is, your precious Hennessy don' got your stupid ass!"

*Oh my God . . . I'm dead.*

# 20

*Somewhere over the Santa Fe mountains . . . Tristan*

Reynolds's words didn't register with me right away, but once they did, I knew I had to be hearing things, or he was higher than I had originally thought he was. Everyone got quiet immediately, everyone, that is, but Reynolds.

"That's right, she fooled everybody, everybody but me, that is," Reynolds yelled out.

"Hennessy? It's not true, *hermana*, is it?"

Hawk looked toward Mateo, who had just spoken, his eyes narrowed. "I knew it," he whispered. And me, I was frozen, afraid even to look at Hennessy lest I saw something in her eyes I didn't want to see.

Finally, I did turn to face her. Her face was a blotched haven of pain, and fear. . . . Her mouth opened, then closed again. Finally as I was looking into her eyes, the truth hit me like a ton of bricks. A sick, heated wave of nausea hit my stomach, almost doubling me over.

*"Are you a federal agent?"* I had asked her weeks back.

*"Do I look like a federal agent, Tristan?"* she had responded.

"You didn't say no, did you?"

"What . . . what?" Hennessy quipped, looking like a trapped bird.

"When I had asked you, that first lunch we had together, if you were an agent. It just hit me that you never really said no." I laughed, realizing my own stupidity. "My God, you're good!"

"I was doing my job," she said weakly, her eyes brimming with tears. Probably fake tears, I thought to myself.

Pain raced through my body like lightning. "Your job? *This* was your job? Well, unless the job description for FBI agents has suddenly changed, then you sure do a lot of overtime and extracurricular activities with your *job,* Hennessy."

"Tristan, don't; it wasn't like that with us and you know it." Her tears were flowing freely now, and they angered me, angered me because I was the one who was fooled, and not just by a federal agent, but by a woman whom I had given my heart to.

"What do you want to do with her, T.J.?" Hawk asked.

"*Do* with me?"

"Shut up, okay?" Hawk sneered. He looked toward me again. "Man, she knows a lot; do we just let her walk?"

"Tristan, I love you; I didn't pretend with that," she whispered.

Her words made me snap, causing me to raise my hand up involuntarily to slap her. All I saw was red mental stains and the pain of being duped. "Don't you say that to me; don't you fuckin' *dare* say those words to me!" Hennessy drew back, throwing her hands up to her face in defense.

"I tell you what we do with her," Reynolds cut in, "I say we cancel the bitch right here." He then grabbed Hennessy by the hair, pulling her back against his chest and sticking his .22 at her head. "And then throw her ass off the plane."

My heart lurched. My desire to strike her myself was replaced by fear. I was afraid to excite Reynolds lest he shoot her. Hennessy's eyes grew huge. "Tristan, please don't let him . . ." Reynolds tightened his arm around her neck. She cried out, trembling.

"Let her go, Reynolds!" Mateo screamed, just as I was about to demand the same thing.

"Reynolds, we ain't killing nobody; not today. So get that gun out of her face and let her go, now," I whispered in a low tone. I didn't care who or what Hennessy was, I was not going to sit and watch Reynolds hurt her. I didn't even want to think about the fact that I was in love with the little lying . . . *I had been such a fool!*

Reynolds cocked his gun as if about to fire. *No!* my mind screamed. I automatically reached out to grab Hennessy from him. He looked at me threateningly and held Hennessy tighter.

"Let . . . her . . . go," I warned again.

"Even now, huh? Even now all you think about is this bitch!"

I tried reasoning. "Reynolds, if you kill her, they will get all of us on capital murder. That's the death penalty, man, and I don't know about you, but I'm not feeling like dying no time soon."

"He's right, Reynolds," Hawk agreed. "Let her go right now, and let's think this thing out."

"Don't you guys see?" Reynolds explained crazily. "If we let her get away, she's gonna put all of us away, even if she has to lie to do it." I shook my head no, as Reynolds slowly started dragging Hennessy toward the entrance.

Just then, Tim Redmond came in from the cockpit, having put the plane on auto. "What the hell is going on back here!" he exclaimed. When Reynolds turned his head around then to face Tim, I saw a chance to get Hennessy and the gun away from him. Mateo, seeing what I was about to do, lurched at him at the same time. I grabbed Hennessy, yanking her from Reynolds's arms. He right away retaliated, screaming out like a madman.

"No!" he shouted, raising the gun toward Hennessy. "I'm killing this bitch! She's ruined everything!" Mateo reached him just in time to knock his arm in the opposite direction, causing Reynolds instead to fire at the plane.

"Oh, shit!" Tim Redmond screamed.

Reynolds worked himself around, still fighting to shoot Hennessy. I had her down in the seat, using my body as a shield to hers. Mateo again pushed, almost disarming him. They flipped and rolled, twisting around the bucket seat.

Almost in slow motion Reynolds raised the .22 once again. Beating Mateo out in strength, he aimed wildly, but this time away from Hennessy and me, and fired toward the front of the plane. Hennessy screamed, and we all jumped at the loud pop sound. "Damn!" I heard Hawk cry out. Focusing my eyes, I was able to see what he was screaming about, Tim Redmond's eyes stared straight ahead as he fell back in a sitting position, blood slowly trailing down the right corner of his mouth. He gurgled once, twice, looking down at his stomach, his shirt bloodied. Hennessy screamed again.

"Shit!" I exclaimed.

"*La puta madre!*" Mateo shouted out. "*Bastardo!* Look what you've done!"

"Look what you made me do!" Reynolds looked toward Hennessy again, and was just raising his gun again toward her when out of nowhere, Hawk charged, punching him so hard he was instantly knocked unconscious.

We were all quiet, only hearing each other's rapid breathing for a second. Then remembering Tim, I looked toward the front. Tim, who was, up until that point, sitting up, fell back weakly, his head banging against the pilot gears. The plane jerked suddenly, going in a downward position.

"What's that?" Hennessy asked, still trembling.

Hawk and I raced up toward Tim. "Shit!" Hawk shouted. "We're going down!" But I was noticing something else also as I looked down at Tim Redmond, two lifeless eyes, peering up at me, unblinking.

*Dulles Airport, Washington, DC*

It was hard for Sebastian to get a midnight flight to LA. He huffed and puffed at the incredible amount that he had to pay in order to get the last-minute first-class seat. One thing about Sebastian, he never ever traveled anything but first class. Even with his not so rich pay as a special agent, he was able to weasel his way in. It never took more than a flash of his agent ID to the attendants to get them hurrying to oblige him. This time, though, things were a little different, in that even though they were able to get him in first class, it cost him big, but he wanted to be in LA and settled in time to see the look on T.J. Jackson's face when things came to a head. He smiled, thinking about the money flow he was going to have once he returned from LA. It wouldn't matter whether he flashed his agent ID or not then, and although the dollars were not the main reason he was heading to LA, it sure was nice icing on the cake after nailing T.J.'s ass.

"Flight 497 to Minneapolis/St. Paul now boarding at gate seven."

That was his flight. Sebastian made his way quickly to the gate, not wanting to be the last person boarding, then having to deal with some simple-ass fool mistakingly taking his seat. He was finally settled in. The smiling faces of the stewardesses beamed as they walked around to get a careful eyeful of their distinguished first-class passengers. Within fifteen minutes, they were up in the air.

"Can I get you something, sir?" asked a tall blonde.

"I'll have a bourbon, straight please."

"Would you like a midnight snack, sir?" she pressed.

"Um, no, just the bourbon, please," Sebastian said pointedly. The stewardess smiled, hurrying off for his drink. Sometimes they tried too much to please, Sebastian thought impatiently.

He settled back, and opened his bag to pull out his notebook computer, figuring he would get in a little solitaire to pass the time. Just as he had booted up, his cell phone dinged.

"Hello," Sebastian said.

"They're in the air; Reynolds contacted me right before they flew out; that was about twenty minutes ago," the voice on the other end announced.

"So, when are you going to do it?"

Al laughed. "You're in a hurry, aren'cha?"

"You're goddamn right I am. This shit has been too long in coming," Sebastian said angrily.

"Well, how 'bout this? Come tomorrow morning you'll have your body. I got big plans for Manuel tonight, big ones."

"Here's your drink, sir." Sebastian looked up at the big brown eyes of the flight attendant.

"Thanks," he retorted. He waited till she had moved on with her little tray to another passenger, then turned his attention back toward Majors. "Well, here's to dead bodies, hmm?" Sebastian hummed, giving a toast in the air.

"And here's to dead presidents," Al chuckled, and hung up.


*Santa Fe mountains . . . Hennessy*


"Oh, God, we're gonna crash!" I shouted. I felt hysterics coming over me, fear hitting me in waves. I always knew that flying was gonna be the death of me. Tristan and Hawk moved Tim Redmond's body away from the cockpit, Hawk jumping into the pilot chair.

"Can you land it!" Tristan exclaimed. Hawk was quiet, focusing on the gears. "Can you?" Tristan shouted again.

"Man, I'm trying, okay?"

I didn't want to move but was afraid to sit tight lest my chair be my casket. I looked at Mateo. His face registered the same fear as mine, although he tried to conceal it. The plane raced faster and faster in a downward spiral. I closed my eyes and gave a silent prayer to God that if He would just save us I would be sure to take communion every Sunday. And I wasn't even Catholic. Just as I was saying amen, the aircraft lurched. I screamed out again, holding on tight to the back of the chair in front of me. When I opened my eyes, Tristan's were locked with mine. I couldn't read them, but I did see something, concern? I knew his concern couldn't be for me, not with what he now knew about me, but he comforted me nevertheless.

"Don't worry, people; he's gonna land this," Tristan assured us. I nodded as though he were directing his words to me. Our crashing wasn't my only worry either. As we rocked and bumped and rolled downward, Reynolds moaned slightly, as if he was about to come to any moment now. I sighed, closing my eyes again. If this wasn't the worst day in my life I couldn't imagine one worse.

Another lurch. I screamed inside, hardly able to stop it from flowing out of my mouth. The plane howled, jerked, then hit with a thump. I opened my eyes again. Tristan sat back in the chair right behind the cockpit, holding on tightly the way I had been doing.

"Hold on, everyone!" Hawk shouted. As far as I was concerned Hawk would be the next best thing to Jesus if he landed this plane with all of us in one piece. "Holy shit! Hold on!" he shouted again.

We were then rolling, but not in the normal way a plane lands; we were rolling sideways, skidding across the ground.

"Come on, baby, come on! You can do it. *You can do this!*" Hawk screamed, talking to Tim Redmond's plane as though it were human and following his strict orders. And I only hoped that in this case, she would follow his directions. I looked out of the window. There were trees spinning all around us. Just as I thought we were surely going to run right into one, we came to a screeching stop.

"Oh!" My head jerked forward, then backward, basically rattling my brains to death. I heard Mateo praying quietly in Spanish, and imagined that Tristan and Hawk had to have been praying, too. I closed my eyes in thanks. When I opened them again Tristan was standing over me.

"Are you okay?" he asked.

I nodded. "Ye . . . yes, I'm fine." I went to get up, but got dizzy and fell back against the seat. Tristan caught my arm.

"Are you sure you're okay?"

I felt this joy rush through me. He cared! His concern was for me! I looked at him; all the love I felt inside had to be shining on my face. I reached out to touch his cheek. "Yes, darling, I'm okay," I whispered.

Tristan jerked back, the concern in his eyes clouded over to be replaced by . . . *hurt?* Then indifference. He pushed my hand away.

"Fine. Come on off the plane."

# 21

*Santa Fe Mountains . . . Tristan*

One thing for sure, my plans for Mother's Day were not working out. After Hawk, Hennessy, Mateo, and I got off the plane, all I could do was look around me. The beauty that was to be seen in the mountains was still there, but this was one time I was not happy to see it. We left Reynolds in the plane, along with Tim's body. I didn't want to look at Hennessy. Even when I helped her down from the plane I couldn't bring myself to really look her in the face. Only minutes before I had found myself getting soft inside, and as far as I was concerned that soft shit had been my downfall. I could not believe I had let her get me all wrapped up, and I mean *all* wrapped up where I was forgetting who I was, and what I was, thinking that maybe I could be someone different, the person she was convincing me I could be. And all this time, she was just waiting for me to slip so she could pull out her credentials and pat herself on the back for a job well done.

"What do we do now, T.J.?"

I turned around to Mateo's concerned voice. "Well, we figure out where the hell we are, and we try to get this plane back in the air, I guess," I said. Hennessy cleared her throat. I looked toward her. "Yeah?"

"Well." She looked around at me, Mateo and Hawk. "Do any of you know how to fly that thing?"

"Of course I know," Hawk said sarcastically. "I just landed it, didn't I?"

Hennessy's face reddened. "Yes, I know you did. You did a wonderful job, by the way. . . ."

Hawk looked at her. "So since I saved you, would I get off on good behavior?"

"I don't have anything on you guys." Hennessy sighed. "You can believe what you want about me, and I know all of this looks bad, but I am not trying to hurt any of you. And like I said, I don't have anything to arrest you for."

"And we're supposed to believe you?" I joined in.

"Yes, you should, Tristan. I have nothing to gain from lying to you." She moved her hands around pointing toward the plane and trees. "Look around us; what do I have to gain?"

I laughed, sneering a little. "Maybe your life?"

"Oh, so do you want to kill me now, Tristan?" she asked quietly, as though we were alone. I finally met her eyes. She looked scared, nervous, but also determined that I see something, understand something although I could not grasp what it was. I looked away, deciding that I didn't feel like playing mind games with Hennessy. Right now, the biggest thing was figuring out how we were going to get out of here, and back to either Jackson's or LA, and with the way Reynolds had been acting, we needed to make it back to LA and fast.

"Believe it or not, you're not that important, Hennessy," I said blankly. "Who you should be worrying about is Reynolds; he's desperate to kill your ass."

"And what about him?" she demanded. "He killed that man. What are you going to do about that?"

I was about to make another remark before Hawk jumped in. "Listen, you two need to stop squaring off with each other and worry more about how we're gonna get outta here!"

He was right, I knew. I felt myself breathing fast, as if in a race. Swallowing my feelings, I finally looked over at Hennessy. "You're right, Hawk. This is not even worth it." I turned my eyes away from her, wanting to give her the feeling of no importance. "We need to find out how much damage is done to the plane and see about getting it fixed. Do you think you can do it?" I inquired.

Hawk sighed. "I don't know, but we have to try."

I had noticed that Mateo was extra quiet, and was about to check on him, when I saw him and Hennessy wrapped up in conversation. Unbelievable . . . I thought. Even now, she was using her wiles to her advantage. I felt hot feelings washing over me, but didn't want to pin down exactly what they were. I couldn't. Hawk had already walked toward the back of the plane to view the damage. I, too, had damage, and decided I didn't like being ignored, so I joined Hennessy's and Mateo's conversation.

". . . and I honestly didn't expect to like you as much as I do, Mateo; that's the truth . . ." she was saying.

"That's what I don't understand, *hermana*. You seemed so sincere; how can you be a cop?"

"Because she's a professional actress; it's as simple as that, Mateo," I cut in flatly.

"Have you stopped throwing darts at me long enough to ask me anything, Tristan?" Hennessy shouted.

"Okay, let me ask you this, why'd you fuck me, huh?"

Her eyes got big and watery. "Oh that is so low, so vulgar . . . so low of you. . . ."

"Come on, guys . . ." Mateo said uncomfortably.

"Naw, baby, it's a real question. I really wanna know, why? Can you tell me that? What's your real name, by the way? Where are you *really* from?"

Hennessy exhaled deeply, and wrapped her hands around her arms. "My real name is Hennessy, but Cooper, not Lewis, and everything else I told you is the truth, I really am from Yonkers." She looked at me, eyes pleading, and then looked over to Mateo. "And honestly, once I got to know you guys, I really wanted to stop you from doing the Met job, because I feel that you are good people and I knew that you would be arrested as soon as your plane landed in LA from New York. Yes, at first my job was to find out what was going on, and to set you all up. It's my *job*. But that doesn't make me a bad person, just like I don't feel that doing what you do makes you all bad people. It's just time to stop because you will get caught; it's only a matter of time. And, Tristan"—this time she looked solely toward me—"I wanted to be with you; I still want to be with you," she whispered.

Her eyes looked so open, pleading, as if she was being real with me, but it was so hard to believe someone when everything I knew about her had been based on a lie. As if on cue, Mateo looked at us both, then told us he was going in to check on Reynolds.

"You two need to talk," he said, before going inside the plane.

Things were extremely quiet after that.

"I'm gonna go see if I can help Hawk out somehow," I whispered.

"Tristan," she interjected, "please believe that I do love you. I've risked everything to be with you, my job, my reputation. My God, even my life."

"How did you risk your life?" I laughed bitterly. "You know I'd never hurt you, even if you are a lying, deceiving bitch. You did a good job on me, you know that? How did you get so good at this, huh?" I moved a bit closer to her, almost breathing the same air as her. It was hard to believe that just hours earlier we had been wrapped up in love, and I had been so convinced that she was the one for me, had been so sure that I wanted to spend my life with her. And now, now I could only imagine how she must have been laughing, every time I said I love you, laughing, every time I touched her, or kissed her, laughing inside, at me?

"I know what you're thinking, baby, and it's just not so . . ." Hennessy put her hands on my face. Her aura was drawing me like a magnet, even in the New Mexican wilds, even with my knowing she was an agent, even with us being parked on a cliff and unsure where we would be going from here. My eyes were drawn to hers, uncertainty and mistrust in mine, I'm sure, an unclear emotion in hers, or at least it wasn't clear to me.

"Well," Hawk's voice broke in suddenly, "I see what's wrong, I'm gonna have to fix the rotors. Looks like when Reynolds decided to lose his fuckin' mind, he shot a hole right through them."

"Do you have the parts for that?" I asked.

"No." Hawk sighed. "The best I can do is a patch-up job, and hope and pray it will get us to LA without our having to stop for anything. It will take me at least three to four hours to do this."

Four hours . . . I looked at Hennessy, who was still holding an expectant look in her eyes. These were four hours that I hoped I would be able to stay far, far away . . . from her.

*Beverly Hills, California*

The plans for the night were set as far as Al Majors was concerned. He had one thought on his mind: payback. Tonight it was Manuel Rolez's turn. He sat quietly in front of Manuel's house, hardly able to contain the excitement inside himself; hardly able to calm the instinct just to roll inside and hand-deliver his deadly present to his old friend. But he knew he had to be patient. Just a little bit longer . . .

"Okay," Al finally said. "It's time."

"I think we should wait, Al. We don't even know for sure that he's in there alone. You wanna take that chance, yo?"

Al was silent for a moment, looking over at the well-manicured lawn, bordered by freshly cut shrubbery. He and his two flunkies, as he liked to call them, had been scoping out Manuel Rolez's place for well over an hour. Even though Rogers had wanted him to call him before they moved on the hit, he wasn't about to take orders from that nervous pig. On checking things out, Al had found out that Rolez had plans to fly out to Pouce, Puerto Rico, but he wasn't sure what time in the morning, or even if it would be morning, that Rolez would fly out, and Al didn't want to take the chance of missing him. Patience was not one of his strong points, but then again, Al thought, laughing, a lot of admirable qualities were not his strong points. But right now he didn't really give a damn about that; he wanted to taste blood, Rolez's blood.

"If he's not alone, we take care of him and whoever else he has with him," Al announced. Marley, who had just spoken, gave Al an uncomfortable stare. "What the fuck is wrong with you, boy? You fuckin' chicken shit or something?"

"Naw, man, I was just thinking that—"

"Am I paying you to think, muthafucka?" Al spat viciously, looking over at the two teens. Marley and Wayne were exact opposites in the looks department. Marley looked his part, a street-hustling thug with the typical wild bush hairdo, gold teeth and tattoos to boot. But Wayne could have been someone like Bill Cosby's son. Clean cut, short fade, the young black man that most middle-class black fathers would smile at if he showed up at the door to date their daughter. "Just shut up and sit and do as I tell ya," Al whispered out to the two of them.

Marley looked toward Wayne, who sat quietly in the back-seat of the silver Lexus Al Majors had gotten them to pick up earlier from some guy's beach house. Neither of them, Marley nor Wayne, knew this Al guy too well. They only knew he had offered big dollars for them to help him smoke some Mexican dude, and since murder wasn't something either of them was new to, it would be a piece of cake. Or so they had thought. Marley was starting to realize that this would be a lot different than just pulling a few drive-by hits on opposing gangs.

"Let's go," Al said, opening the driver's door of T.J. Jackson's stolen Lexus.

Rolez had music playing, and loudly. Al smirked, thinking that anyone would think Rolez was setting up his own murder, as if he knew he was about to die, and like them sad-ass fools on the Titanic boat, wanted to die to the sounds of music, but instead of it being sappy orchestra music, he was dying to Shaggy's "It Wasn't Me."

Al put his finger up to *shh* Marley and Wayne, although they could have told him it wasn't needed. Marley didn't know about his boy Wayne, but he was scared as hell. This shit was a bit too much like *Scarface,* as if they were trying to smoke Al Pacino or something.

"Wayne, you go stand by that door over there; Marley, you come with me," Al whispered his instructions. Both guys obeyed immediately. Pulling out his semiautomatic, Al held it close to his face. He smiled, closed his eyes and walked quietly onto the deck to Manuel's pool, where Manuel was chillin' in his hot tub.

"Wassup, *papi*?" Al crooned.

"Huh!" Rolez sat up, looking shocked to see his old comrade and now enemy standing over him with a semiautomatic pistol. He jumped up instantly to reach for his own weapon, which normally he would keep on him, but tonight having had company, much needed company to help relieve some of the sexual tension that was buzzing through his body, the only thing he had on him now was a flaccid dick that only moments before had been hard and raring to go. He had almost made it to his bathrobe before bullets penetrated his body. He flipped around, screaming, "*Bitch!* Uhh!" Al and Marley dispensed more rounds into Manuel Rolez's body, Al laughing all the while.

Marley couldn't believe what was happening. This dude was more than dead, yet Al Majors was still pumping him with lead. The water in the hot tub that had seconds before been blue with white bubbles now bubbled with blood. The sounds of Shaggy still played on. Marley looked over to where Wayne had gone. Wayne's eyes had the same look of shock that he was sure mirrored his own.

"Oh my God!" a female voice screamed out. A young black woman, who obviously had been Manuel's booty call for the night, dropped the tray of iced tea she had been holding. Clad in bikini panties and top-naked, she looked from Manuel's bloodied body to Al, to Marley, to Wayne.

Al's face took on a dark, satanic glow. He gestured toward her. She took off to run, with Marley right behind her, grabbing her from behind and dragging her toward Al. "Wayne, take care of that, we can't leave no baggage behind," Al stated.

Wayne looked shocked, pointing toward himself. "Who? Me? Man, naw, man, I don't be killing no females, yo!"

Al's eyes widened at the open defiance. "Oh, you don't, huh?" He reached out his hand for Wayne's piece. Wayne looked at him in puzzlement. "Give me that, you don't need it if you scared to use it."

The girl twisted, and squealed in Marley's arms. Al held Wayne's gun and looked at it, as if it were a foreign object. "Yeah, if you scared to use it, no use it being in the wrong hands . . . not a nice piece like this." He looked in the hole of the pistol. "But I tell you what . . . I'm not afraid to use it." With those words, Al brought the gun swiftly up to Wayne's face, and fired. The girl screamed.

"Oh, shit!" Marley exclaimed, holding the girl tighter as he watched the wide-open, lifeless eyes of his homeboy, blood pooling into one of them. He looked at Al, the madman, afraid even to speak.

"I hate a hardheaded kid," Al said, shaking his head. "He should have listened. Now"—he looked Marley in the eye— "kill her."

Marley threw the young girl down on the deck pavement. "No! Please God, no!" she screamed. Her screams were finally muffled, when without hesitation, he shot three slugs into her, quieting her voice.

# 22

*Deep in the Santa Fe mountains*

Reynolds tried to open his eyes, meeting pain in his right jaw. On recollection, he remembered that either Hawk or Mateo had given him the right hook that had sent him sprawling into another world. It was probably Hawk, with his cut-up ass, Reynolds thought. He finally sat up; looking around, he saw Mateo looking at him with a grim expression.

"Where are we, Mateo?" he asked.

"We're wrecked, thanks to you," Mateo said testily.

"What? How?"

Mateo nodded his hand toward the covered body of Tim Redmond. "Who is that?" Reynolds asked.

"That's your handiwork. You're gonna tell me you don't re-member?"

Reynolds sighed, closed his eyes, and remembered back to what had happened, Then he remembered something else, Hennessy. He jumped up. "So where is she now? Where is our special agent?"

"Sit your ass down, Reynolds! And don't think I've forgot-ten about you calling me no spic either; I don't appreciate that shit."

Reynolds sighed, looking into the darkened eyes of Mateo. He had really fucked things up. He and Mateo had always gotten along good. Everyone liked Mateo. But Reynolds knew that sometimes he couldn't control the things that came out of his mouth when he was high; that's why he needed so badly to get himself together, which took money. His mind suddenly shifted to T.J.

"I know I fucked up, man," he tried explaining to Mateo, who had sat down, gun in hand, looking at him cautiously. "I know I fucked up, but you know that T.J. isn't thinking straight either. I mean he let that broad in on us; he let her know all our business, fucked up our money and everything."

Mateo was shaking his head even as Reynolds spoke. "You're wrong, Reynolds. If Hennessy hadn't been the one that was sent to infiltrate us, then the feds would have sent someone else, someone who would not have warned us the way she did about the setup. She could have kept to her job and not given a fuck about us, amigo. Then we would be in jail come Tuesday night. Think about it, amigo."

Reynolds was ignoring all of Mateo's sane reasoning. His hands were moving of their own volition.

"And T.J., he betrayed us, all of us, including Tim over there." He pointed to Tim's body. "He is dead and it's T.J. that really killed him, T.J., not me!"

"Listen, Reynolds, the only one who's betrayed us here is *you!*" Mateo said, pointing to Reynolds. "We wouldn't be stuck out here and Tim wouldn't be dead, if you hadn't lost it like you did. So stop trying to blame everyone else for what you yourself did, because I'm not buying it, *comprende?*"

Both guys got quiet, looking at each other with wary eyes.

"It's gonna be okay, hombre, believe me, it will be," Mateo continued. Reynolds nodded in the affirmative, although he seemed unconvinced. Mateo backed toward the door of the small plane. "I'm gonna go take a leak; don't try to leave the plane, you hear me? Just stay put, and I'll be right back."

Mateo stared Reynolds down, making sure he understood

what he had said. After Reynolds nodded at him, Mateo made his way out of the plane. He at first thought he would let Hawk and T.J. know he was taking a bathroom break, but then decided that since he would only be a minute or so, and wouldn't be going far, he would let them keep working on getting them back in the air.

Hennessy was nowhere to be seen, but still Mateo didn't wanna take any chance of her getting a whiff of his manhood. She might just take a liking to his big burrito, he thought, laughing to himself.

He found a comfy spot by a wooded cliff nearby, and had just finished his turn with nature when he heard an odd sound. It was hard to see in the darkness and with the trees around, but just as he was zipping his pants and about to have a look around he felt a sharp pain at his left temple, then darkness. . . .

*Tristan*

I had to work hard to fight the urge to go see what Hennessy was up to. The last thing I needed was for her to think she still had a grip on my heart. Did she? I knew the answer, but time would take care of that, I figured.

"Hold the light steady, T.J.; just a little bit more and I should have this bolt in; then you can take a break," Hawk promised.

"Okay, sorry," I said.

Hawk drilled for a second, then stopped, looking at me. "Listen, man, why don't you go take a cigar break now? I'll be okay." Hawk handed me one of his famous smokes. I looked at it, smiling.

"Okay, I'll take a break under one condition."

"What's that?" he asked.

"If you take one with me." I smiled. Hawk winked, and gave me a light.

"You have a deal," he said.

*Hennessy*

I was sick and tired of throwing rocks over this bottomless pit called a mountain. I didn't dare go over to where Hawk and Tristan were working, lest I get more of Tristan's snide remarks. And I didn't want to go to Mateo, who was watching Reynolds, because . . . well, because that's pretty obvious.

I sighed, throwing another rock over the steep, dark mountain. I stood up and brushed my hands off on my jeans. We had been grounded for about an hour. I don't know what I expected, but other than Mateo, I felt pretty much hated. Good ol' Mateo; I smiled to myself. He was the real deal, and it's rare that you find genuinely nice men like him. It's just a shame that he allowed himself to get caught up in crime the way that he had. We hadn't had much time to talk about that, but I did know that he didn't hate me, and kind of understood my position. I decided I would scope him out, maybe get him to come off of the plane and talk to me a little. Maybe he knew of a way I could get Tristan to open up to me, to listen to what I had to say, because regardless, I was not going to give up on the man I loved. I was glad I had done what I did, because if I hadn't, things would have turned out badly for him. So regardless, I had *no* regrets. If anyone could help me get Tristan to see reason, it was Mateo.

I made my way back toward the plane. Prickly branches swiped my skin as I walked along the basin. I had just walked past a flowered steep, when I heard a groaning sound. I looked over to where the sound was coming from. I couldn't make it out perfectly, but I could see a body lying on the ground. On a closer look, I could see it was Mateo!

"Mateo! Oh, my God, what happened to you?" I ran over.

Leaning down, I reached to feel his pulse; it wasn't strong, but it was there. "Sweetie, I'll get Tristan and Hawk; don't you worry, it will be okay," I said unnecessarily. Although he was moaning, Mateo was out cold. I looked down as I felt a slick wetness when feeling for his pulse. It was blood. "Oh, gosh, you're really hurt!"

"Trying to be a Good Samaritan, I see." My head jerked up at the sound of the familiar voice, Reynolds's voice.

I blinked away tears, trying to make out his face. "You . . . you did this?" I croaked.

Reynolds pulled me up from Mateo, circling his hands around my waist.

"Reynolds, he's hurt really bad. I know you couldn't have done this on purpose, but we have to get Tristan and Hawk; we have to get Mateo some medical attention, please. . . ."

"Please?" he said teasingly. "I want to be pleased, too, Agent Hennessy." Reynolds ran his hand over the top of my breasts the way he had in the hallway that night. I jerked away, swatting at his hand. "Oh yeah, I remembered you said before how you would what? Kick my ass?" He laughed. "Whatcha gonna do now, you badass Amazon chick? You want to get some help for Mateo, don't you? Just how bad do you want it?"

There was no way I was gonna stand here and let him pull this crap on me, but looking around, I realized I had no one to help me anywhere near, and even if Tristan or Hawk was nearby, would they help? I knew that Reynolds was unstable, and even though he was all up in my face and was giving me the gags, I decided that it would be smart to play him a bit, rather than rile him.

"Listen," I said, smiling coyly, "you're right; we never did get to know each other as we should have." I put both my hands on his chest, rubbing it up and down. "I always did have my eye on you, why, with you being so *diesel* and all."

Reynolds grinned, and pulled me closer to him. "I knew it; I knew all along you wanted some of this. Fucking around with honky eyes when you could've had a real black man all along." He put his hands to my shoulders and started pushing downward. "Why don't you get down on your knees and show me what you do best."

I panicked. No, he did not want me to give him oral sex. . . . He pushed me down with more force. I felt my eyes filling up, knowing there was no way in the world I could play act that well, to put my mouth on this pig. I resisted.

"Unzip me," he demanded.

"No, please . . . I—"

"I said unzip me, and if you bite . . ." He yanked my hair viciously, causing me to cry out in pain. "If you bite, I'm gonna put a hole in your head right here, *and* in Mateo's, understand?" I looked up at him. My eyes were swimming. I nodded yes. My hands were shaking as I unzipped his pants. I could feel the cold metal against my face. His stank growth protruded toward my mouth for a second before he put his hand on my jaw and squeezed, forcing me to open. I thought quickly.

"Wait, wait," I said seductively. I could feel the urge to panic, but fought to calm myself. "We have a minute, boo, let's not rush things, okay?" I reached beneath his manhood, and stroked his testicles. He moaned deeply, then finally loosened his grip on my jawbone.

"Oh, yeah, you do that so good. . . ."

I continued to caress him, forcing a tempting smile on my face. "You like that, don't you, baby?" I whispered.

"Oh, fuck yeah; you sweet bitch. Now suck it; put it in your mouth," he panted out.

"Like hell!" I said, powering up my strength and punching him as hard as I could in his testicles.

"*Ohhh!*" Reynolds screamed out. As he curled over in pain, fighting to catch his breath, I punched him there again for good measure, and ran. I didn't run fast enough though. I don't know what the animal was made of, but my attack to his manhood didn't stall him long enough to give me even a foot of freedom. I felt his big hands yanking at the back of my hair, throwing me to the ground.

"You hoe-ass bitch!" he screamed, slapping me roughly across the face. Before I could even recover from that sting, his big body covered mine. "I'm gonna fuck the shit outta you; then I'm gonna kill you, whore!"

I felt the buttons to my blouse rip off, then my bra, leaving my breasts openly exposed to him. He moved his face down to them, biting my nipple, *hard.*

"Awww!" I screamed out in pain. He bit down again, then

ripped my jeans open, fighting to yank them down my hips. I then kneed him hard in the stomach, causing him to grunt. As I struggled to get up he grabbed my hair again, then slammed my head down against a rock. My eyes went blurry.

"You ain't bad enough, bitch! You hear me? You ain't bad enough!" Reynolds screamed out, as he grabbed my throat, holding it in a choke hold. "Now you calm da fuck down while I give you the fuckin' you deserve."

Although I was not a tiny, weak woman, Reynolds was so big, I couldn't even budge to defend myself, I could only lie there helplessly, knowing what was about to happen to me.


*Tristan*

Hawk and I worked quietly, or rather, he worked. Outside of being good at thievery, Hawk was a trained aircraft pilot and mechanic, having served for five years in the air force reserves. But as he had been reminding me for the past few hours, his tenure with the good ol' USA military had been brief, and he had to work hard to remember his training in a field he had lived another life ago.

"So, where is Hennessy?" Hawk asked, as he was tightening one of the spare breaks we had found in storage.

"Hell if I know," I said, yawning carelessly.

Hawk laughed. "Man, why you wanna sit there and act like she don't faze you?"

"Because she doesn't," I insisted. "You guys sure don't act like she faze you much either. I mean seeing that she's an implanted snitch, neither you nor Mateo seem as angry about it as I would have thought."

"It's not that I'm not angry. But remember I always did have my doubts about her, so I don't feel as betrayed as you do. But one thing about her has also not escaped my notice; if it wasn't her, and if she hadn't fallen in love with you, we would soon be doing some serious time. The feds were on to us, man, from the start." Hawk wiped the sweat from his forehead, leaving an oil streak, then said, "She talked you out of our doing that job for a reason."

"She's not in love with me," I said flatly, as I handed him a handkerchief.

Hawk shook his head slowly. "Like I said, she talked you out of our doing the New York gig for a reason. If that woman was not in love with you, why would she have done that? Looks to me like she's taken a big risk, for you."

I tightened my heart. It was surprising that Hawk, of all people, would be speaking up for Hennessy, I had always known he didn't care much for her. Either way, to believe what he was saying would mean to open myself up again and be her toy. I had always prided myself on being smart. Maybe the fact that she duped me, and had done it so well, made it hard for me to believe anything good about her.

"Listen, I'm gonna go see what Mateo is up to, and how things are going with Reynolds. He probably has come to by now."

"Okay," Hawk said. "I'll work on this rotor a bit more. We don't wanna be out here all night."

When I got to the plane I noticed two things. One, Hennessy was nowhere around, and two, on entry, neither Reynolds nor Mateo was inside the plane, only Tim Redmond's covered body. I felt an uneasy feeling grip me. *Where was Hennessy?*

"Mateo! Hennessy! Where are you guys? Reynolds?"

I looked around me; still no sight of them. The longer I looked, the faster my heart seemed to be beating. I decided to walk about the mountain trail. After walking for two or three minutes, I heard a sudden scream. I ran toward it. I saw Reynolds atop Hennessy with his hand covering her throat, his pants down, trying to hold her naked legs open with his free hand, his bare, black ass pumping. I instantly saw red.

"Get the fuck off her!" I screamed, kicking him hard in the back. Reynolds grunted, falling away from Hennessy. I noticed her fighting to cover herself, adjusting her clothing before I saw Reynolds charging at me.

I ducked at the first onslaught, before Reynolds came charging again. He swung, I swung, landing fist to bone and skin again and again. I could taste blood in my mouth where Reynolds had hit. Let's face it, Reynolds was a huge brotha. But I was relentless, still picturing him attacking Hennessy. Reynolds hauled himself atop me, knocking the wind out of me. I felt myself fall back, and just as I was catching my bearings, my feet slipped, and I was hanging on the edge of a cliff, a cliff I hadn't even had any idea was behind me. Looking down, all I saw was blackness, but I knew if I fell into that blackness, it would mean my death.

As I struggled to pull myself up, I suddenly felt a sharp pain in my fingers. I looked up to see Reynolds, staring down at me, as he lifted a rock again to slam down on my hand.

*Hennessy*

I felt dizzy, shaky from trying to fight Reynolds off of me. The buttons were gone from my blouse; there was no use in trying to close that up. But I was able to slip my bra on, covering myself a bit. I pulled up my jeans, closing them as my hands shook. Tristan and Reynolds continued to fight, and Reynolds appeared to be getting the better of Tristan after a while. I looked around, trying to see if there was anything that I could use to help Tristan. Then I heard Mateo moaning again. I wobbled over to him.

"It's going to be okay," I said shakingly, as I cradled his head in my lap. My head jerked up as I heard Tristan cry out; then I saw him fall over the cliff. "Omigod!" I screamed. Laying Mateo's wounded head comfortably on the grass, I rushed toward Tristan. I stopped as my foot kicked something in the grass.

Looking down, I saw that it was the pistol Reynolds had had. I grabbed it up quickly.

When I got nearer to Tristan and Reynolds, I saw Reynolds banging Tristan's hands, trying to make him fall.

"Reynolds!" I called out. He looked up at me, spotting the gun in my hand.

"So what you gonna do, bitch, shoot me?"

I looked over to where Tristan was still struggling to keep himself from falling; my heart sank as I realized that he wouldn't be able to hold on much longer.

"Move away from the cliff, or yes, I will shoot," I said, threatening Reynolds by aiming the pistol more steadily at him.

"Give me that gun, *now!*" he screamed. Suddenly, he raced toward me, and my fingers squeezed, again and again and again . . .

# 23

_____

*Santa Fe mountains . . . Hennessy*

I fell to my knees almost at the same time as Reynolds. The look on his face when the bullets went through him was a look I would never ever forget. It wasn't that I had never shot anyone before, but I had never killed anyone, that's for sure. Reynolds fell backward, like a fallen tree, his eyes never leaving mine. I put my hand on my chest, feeling momentarily frozen.

"Hennessy, help me!" I suddenly heard Tristan cry out. I got up quickly, and ran over to him.

I reached out my hand. "Grab my hand, hurry!" I exclaimed.

"No, Hennessy, I'm far too heavy for you. Get Hawk, now!" he screamed back.

"Please, trust me. Grab my hand, Tristan!"

"What's going on here?" Hawk's voice called out from behind me. He looked around himself. "Good Lord, T.J., Reynolds, what the *hell* is going on around here!"

"Hawk you have to help me pull Tristan, he can't hold on much longer!"

Hawk stepped over Reynolds, and quickly gripped Tristan's hand. Just as Hawk took his left hand, Tristan's foot slipped on a rock that he was obviously using to hold himself up with. I screamed. He was barely there. The only thing he had to hold on to was Hawk's hand. Both men were shaking in their attempt to pull him up over the edge of the cliff. I closed my eyes, giving a prayer to God to please save him. One thing I truly believed was what my mother had always told me, that God does not let the good perish with the wicked, and even with Tristan's past, the fact that he was willing to put all of that aside, and pursue the good, showed that he had a good heart. God would not be so cruel as to let me lose him now, not now . . .

I opened my eyes from my prayer just as Hawk miraculously pulled him up, both men falling into a sweaty heap on the ground.

"Oh, thank God!" I cried, falling into Tristan's arms. I didn't even worry about him pushing me away. I had him back, safe and sound, and nothing else mattered but that. Thankfully he didn't push me away; he held me just as tightly as I held him, finally pulling away to look into my eyes.

"Did he . . . did Reynolds?" I knew what he was asking, and I gladly shook my head no.

"You got here just in time, but he hit Mateo with something; he's in bad shape."

Hawk had already gone over to where a moaning Mateo lay, checking his vitals as I had done.

"I don't know what the hell he hit him with, but we have to get him out of here, and fast. I'm almost done with the repairs. Let's get Mateo back to the plane, and we should be able to pull off in twenty minutes or so," Hawk said.

Tristan got up slowly; he had a cut on his lip, and a huge bruise under his left eye, but considering everything, he was looking pretty good.

"You look like you've been through hell," he said to me.

"I was just thinking the same thing about you."

Tristan smiled hesitantly. "Come on, let's get Mateo up and out of here." He and Hawk picked up Mateo together. Mateo wasn't big, but dead weight was always extra heavy. I looked over and down at Reynolds.

"Guys, what . . . what about Reynolds?"

Tristan looked sad, as did Hawk. "I can't believe it . . . I just can't," he whispered.

"I'll come back and get him after we get Mateo to the plane. You're in no shape to carry his weight."

Tristan looked at Hawk, thankfully.

Following behind as they carried Mateo, I couldn't help turning around one last time. I looked mournfully at Reynolds's body.

"I'm sorry," I whispered, "so very sorry. . . ."

*Tristan*

Later while on the plane, Hennessy was playing nursemaid to both Mateo and me. She had cleaned his head wound the best she could, and had him resting quietly on the backseat. Now she had turned her attention to me.

"Aww!" I flinched as she touched a deep wound on my forehead.

"I'm sorry." She sighed. She reached out at my forehead again. I jerked back. "Look, this is a pretty bad cut and you got dirt in it. Just let me put some peroxide on it, okay?" I hesitated. "Come on." She smiled slightly. "Don't be such a big baby."

"All right," I relented, "just don't go overboard with the meds."

She assured me that she wouldn't, and went on with her handiwork. Afterward, she sat down quietly beside me. We had a moment of tense silence.

"A lot has happened, hasn't it?" Hennessy said in a whisper.

"Yeah, it has," I agreed.

I heard her take a deep breath; then she reached out and touched my arm.

"Tristan . . . I love you so much," she said intensely.

I didn't want to speak at first, but her silence demanded I respond. I looked into her brown eyes, and looked away, focusing instead on her chin.

"Nothing is as I thought it was, Hennessy."

She seemed to pause for a moment before responding to me. "I know that, baby, and I totally understand why you would doubt me. But . . . but can you honestly look at the situation and say you don't know how much I love you?"

I swallowed, still not quite looking at her. "This is not the time for this. . . ."

"Then when will be the right time?" she pressed. "I love you; I was trying to protect you. The only mistake I made is not holding on tight to my heart when it came to you. My being an agent is not a crime, Tristan. I was trained to do this, but falling in love was not on my agenda. It just happened, and I'm not sorry, not one tiny bit."

"So what do you plan to do now, give up your job to be with me? Because you sure as hell can't be an FBI agent if we're together. Did you figure that all out? How were you figuring things, Hennessy?" I asked in frustration. Her face held a wild array of emotions, finally settling on resignation.

"Would you give up your work to be with me?" she finally asked plainly.

"You don't even need to ask that. I proved I would when I gave up that palette . . . knowing it was what you wanted and thinking that you and I were gonna be together."

Hennessy's eyes got hopeful. "See, so it's not too late; we can fix this." At my quietness she asked, "Tristan, what bothers you the most? The fact that I'm an agent, or that you lost control over your heart? Because I know you love me; I *know* you do."

"All set and ready to roll," Hawk cut in.

I breathed a sigh of relief. I don't know why. Maybe Hennessy was getting a bit too close for my comfort, but God help me I still loved her. Maybe, just maybe there was the slight chance we could fix this, as she said. But so much had happened, and we had a hell of a mess on our hands. Could I trust her? I looked into her brown eyes, which were still focused on me. I saw love, hope, and determination in them, all qualities that I admired, but at the same time, could I really trust her?

"Let's get out of here, people," I finally said, looking at Hennessy but speaking to both her and Hawk. "We need to get Mateo to a hospital."

*Los Angeles, California . . . Hennessy*

I felt so tense on the way to LA. Tristan was right. So much had happened. It was mentally, emotionally, and physically taxing. I didn't try to talk to him about anything that had to do with our relationship anymore on the flight back. He had moved to sit closer to the front anyhow and I wanted to tend to Mateo, so I sat by where he lay. I had to give it to both Tristan and Hawk. They were so concerned about Mateo that not once did they voice any feeling or doubt about having an ambulance waiting. I knew there were unspoken questions, though, questions like, was I going to do anything to hurt them, and what would I say about Tim Redmond and Reynolds? Simply put, though, I would tell the truth.

When we finally landed, Tristan walked to the back of the plane to Mateo and me.

"So are you going to tell your superiors about what's happened?" he asked.

"I'll tell them the truth," I said, mimicking what my thoughts had been.

"You mean *everything?*"

I sighed. This was really getting to be too much. "Tristan, no, I don't want to tell them *everything*. I stepped over major lines with you, and I could get into a lot of trouble and you know it, so I would rather they not know about all of that. Of course, if it would make you feel better telling them, then you do what you have to do."

Tristan gave me a knowing look. "You know I wouldn't say anything to hurt you, so don't worry about it."

I smiled inside. That was one point in my favor at least, but when I looked at Tristan again, he wasn't smiling. Hmm . . . minus one point, I supposed.

"Well, I better call the SAC here in LA. I haven't talked to anyone from the bureau in a while," I stated. Tristan looked very uncomfortable.

"So, what are they going to say about what's happened?" he asked.

"I suppose they won't be too happy; after all their job is to bring down criminals."

Tristan raised an eyebrow. "And I'm the big bad wolf, right?"

I swallowed uncomfortably, but looked at him with focused intensity. "Not to me you aren't. . . ."


*Tristan*


If it wasn't for the fact that Hawk was doing the same thing, I would think that I was dreaming, or at least was crazy, sitting around waiting for an ambulance for Mateo, and for the FBI and police, who were good buddies with the woman that I was still very much in love with. There, the truth was finally out, in my mind at least if not anywhere else. There really wasn't any reason to keep lying to myself, but letting her know was another story.

The ambulance roared into the small landing field, followed quickly by unmarked vehicles that I knew had to have FBI agents inside.

"Wow . . . what are we gonna do now, T.J.?" Hawk asked, walking up behind me.

I sighed. "I don't know. I mean we haven't broken any laws, but I guess now it really is time to retire, huh?" I laughed weakly.

"What about her?" He nodded toward Hennessy, who was walking over to meet the paramedics.

I swallowed, averting my eyes from Hawk's. "It's over between us, I guess . . . and I guess we also really should thank her, huh? Like you said before, she kept our asses out of prison."

"Yeah."

We both took a deep breath at the same time, and went to join Hennessy, who was directing the paramedics inside the plane to Mateo. For some reason, neither of us mentioned Reynolds to each other. Things had fallen apart so badly, the shit was unbelievable; and Reynolds and Tim being dead was even more unbelievable.

An extremely tall dark-skinned brotha approached us just as we were following Hennessy and the medics back into the plane.

"I'm Agent Jacob White. I understand there's been a murder aboard this plane?"

I looked him up and down, feeling him out. "Not a murder, an accident. Follow me and I'll show you."

"Where is Agent Cooper?" he asked.

I let out a short laugh. "Didn't you just see her? She's in the plane, too. Now if you'll follow me, I'll show you Tim Redmond's body and explain exactly what happened."

The plane was small and tight, especially with the medics inside, working on Mateo. I peeped over toward them, stopping briefly. "Is he gonna be okay?"

The paramedics had started strapping him to a stretcher. One of them nodded to me, meaning yes, I guess; then they had him out of the plane within seconds. Hennessy's eyes found mine.

"It's gonna be all right," she whispered to me.

"Yeah," I whispered back, unconvinced. I felt so fuckin' powerless, a feeling I hated more than anything. She silently mouthed, *I love you* with her lips, then slipped out of the plane.

When I got over to Hawk and Agent White, standing over Tim's body and talking, Agent White looked at me suspiciously.

"So if neither of you did this, where is the guy who shot him?" he asked.

Hawk and I looked at each other, each waiting for the other to respond first.

"What, was that a hard question or something?" the agent asked sarcastically. Just as I was about to answer, his cell phone went off. "White here," he said. "Yeah? Okay, Agent Cooper is somewhere around here. I'll let her know. Right, no problem." He hung up his phone, eyeing Hawk and me again. I answered before he could re-ask his question.

"Reynolds, Reynolds Moore is who shot him," I said. He had this look on his face that I had figured was coming anyhow, a *yeah, right* look.

"So where is this, this Reynolds, hmm?"

"He's dead, Jacob, and I shot him. His body is also on the plane."

Agent White, Hawk, and I all turned in the direction of Hennessy's voice. Her face had a determined look. She appeared totally different from the soft, beautiful creature that I had made love to at the spring. She looked . . . like a federal agent.

"You want to explain exactly what's been going on here, Hennessy?" Agent White said impatiently. He and Hennessy were on first-name terms, I noticed. Didn't know why that irked the hell out of me; maybe it was just tangible proof of who she was.

"We have a dead body here, and two notorious"—White looked both Hawk and me up and down—"people here. Now you're telling me that *you* shot Reynolds Moore?"

Hennessy sat down, sighing, as if extra tired. Figured she would be. I was exhausted myself. It had been a long night, probably one of the longest nights of my life, and a lot of shit had happened. Hennessy looked up at White.

"It's a long-ass story, Jacob. . . ." She then proceeded to tell her story as we stood over the corpse of Tim Redmond.


*Minneapolis/St. Paul International Airport*

Sebastian felt as if he wanted to explode. He had been laid over at MSP, the Twin City's airport, for over an hour. Here he thought he was doing something by getting the midnight flight out, thinking he would arrive in LA in enough time to get tucked away in his hotel, and get a front-row seat for the fireworks that were sure to stir up when Manuel Rolez's body was discovered, with T.J. Jackson's guilt written all over it, and instead, here he sat in this dingy-ass airport.

He sighed, looking around. He wasn't the only exasperated-looking person in this godforsaken place. Just as he decided he would get a coffee to help relax himself, his cell phone rang. It was Special Agent in Charge Bacon in DC.

"Sebastian, how long till you get to LA?" she asked.

"Well, there's a layover in St. Paul; hopefully we'll be back in the air in about another hour," Sebastian replied.

"Well, you may as well hear this from me. There's a bunch of BS going on in LA. I no longer have to wait for you to pull Agent Cooper off of the Jackson case. Her cover has been blown. The Jackson sting is over . . ."

# 24

―――

The ticking clock seemed to be drowned out by the sound of my heartbeat as I sat at the round table at the divisional office of the Federal Bureau of Investigation in Los Angeles.

I fidgeted, feeling nervous. Somehow I knew this day of confrontation would come. Even though I had explained the events from the time we had left Jackson's till Tim's death, our semicrash land, all the way to Reynolds's crazy attempted rape, all the way to the attempted murder on Tristan, it still wasn't enough. Everyone still wanted a personal explanation on how my cover was blown. The special agent in charge, Milton Walsh, stared at me with unblinking eyes.

"So, what happened, Agent Cooper?"

"I really can't say what happened exactly," I answered. "Everything was still in motion, I had just hours before talked to Agent Rogers from DC, and we were on our way here to LA."

"And who are we?" Milton Walsh queried.

"Well . . . well, I'm referring to Tristan Jackson, Mateo Milan, Reynolds Moore, and Frank Mattucci. We were on our way here, at midnight, when Reynolds had a breakdown of sorts."

Agent Walsh looked at me, as if he didn't believe me. "What kind of breakdown?"

I wasn't sure how to explain the whole scene of events without giving away the fact that Tristan had decided to cancel the Met robbery, and I knew that once Agent Walsh knew about that, he would also want to know why I hadn't contacted Sebastian to let him know what was going on.

I cleared my throat, feeling an aching stress bolt flashing through me. I really was tired of pretense. I had done it so long with Tristan and the guys, and now if I kept quiet on what had really gone down, I would be starting another pretense campaign that I really wasn't prepared to deal with.

"Reynolds Moore was upset about something that Tristan Jackson had told us about the plans for the New York robbery. Basically they were canceled, and Reynolds didn't like that," I said.

Agent Walsh took a deep breath. He was a white man, with a dark complexion, and looked as if he were about to explode right then. "You mean to tell me that you were aware of Jackson's plans to cancel and you didn't inform anyone?"

I swallowed. "No, I didn't. It was a judgment call."

"A judgment call? Who the fuck are you to be making any judgment calls?" he lamented.

I closed my eyes before speaking. I really didn't know any of the people who worked for the West Coast bureau, except for Jacob White, who had worked in DC with me on many cases. But it didn't take a person with a Ph.D. to know that this Walsh fella had a problem with women, and from the way he was snarling at me, it was a serious problem. I opened my eyes again, having rested them for a second.

"Well?" he screamed. "Answer me, damn it!"

Before I could answer, the door to Agent Walsh's office opened and in marched Sebastian. I couldn't even think of what he could possibly be doing in LA, before he, too, looked at me with a livid expression, but when he spoke, his words were low and measured.

"Good afternoon, Hennessy."

"Sebastian . . . what, what are you doing in LA?"

Sebastian smiled slightly. A smile that I wasn't at all sure was very sincere. "Came to check on how my favorite special agent was doing."

I sighed, half expecting Agent Walsh to bust in with the news about the case being over. When he didn't, but instead looked at me with a snarl, I knew that I would have to break the news to Sebastian myself.

"Things are rather . . . confusing right now, Sebastian," I said quietly.

"Oh, yeah, I heard about your cover being blown. And, um . . . I suppose there was nothing you could have done to prevent this, right?"

"No, there wasn't. As I was telling Agent Walsh, Reynolds Moore, who as you know worked with Tristan Jackson, exposed me to him. How he knew about me is something I just cannot figure out."

"And I suppose you feel that your involvement with T.J. Jackson had nothing to do with it?" Sebastian asked. I was actually shocked. How did he know I was involved with Tristan, and just how much did he know? "I tell you what," he continued on, "don't answer that, okay? I already know."

"How?" I asked.

"How what? How do I know that you were sexually involved with one of the most notorious—"

"Sebastian, stop it please," I cut in, taking a deep breath. Things were quiet for a moment. Agent Walsh was still observing, obviously waiting to see how Sebastian was going to put his agent in check. I felt trapped.

Emotional exhaustion overtook me and I flopped back into the chair that was behind me.

"Okay, Hennessy," Sebastian finally said, "I won't say another word. But I will say this much." He leaned his hands on the armrest of my chair, bringing his face almost nose to nose with me. "You have destroyed a major case that we have worked years to organize. And maybe it's not much to you, but I can guarantee you this much. I'm gonna have your badge for this shit. Bet on it!"

*Malibu Beach . . . Tristan*

Even though I've been through some major drama in my life, I have to say that the last hours or so had to be the wackiest. Maybe some things were out of my control, but yet, if someone other than Hennessy had fooled me as she had and I had come to know about it, I would have made sure they weren't physically fit for life. What made it different with her was that I loved her, and there was no way I could get around the reality of it.

After the feds were finished with us, Hawk and I grabbed a cab to take us to LA General where Mateo had been taken. He had a severe concussion but luckily would be okay, the doctors said, which we were happy to hear. It was bad enough with Tim being dead, and Reynolds, too. Just thinking about him made me sick to my stomach. Reynolds and I used to be so close, so I should have guessed when things were going sour, when he wasn't feeling the closeness of our friendship anymore. And I guess he was feeling mad jealousy over Hawk, too, which was odd since the four of us, Reynolds, Hawk, Mateo, and I, had worked together for years without disturbance. Whatever had caused his change of feelings and brotherhood, it really didn't matter now, he was dead and nothing could change that fact. Now it was time for me to organize my life and figure out what I wanted to do with the rest of it. But whatever I did do with it, I wasn't sure if it could include the woman I loved, who I now knew to be Special Agent Hennessy Cooper.

After bidding Hawk good-bye, I had the cabby drive me to my place, which was a ride and a half, cost me thirty dollars one way. I shook my head at the ridiculous amount, paid the fare, and started for the door. I had to snicker at the look on the dude's face when he realized I had only left him five extra as a tip, but with the long turns he took, deliberately increasing the meter time, which of course increased his pay, I really felt he had earned exactly what I gave him. He grumbled, mumbling to me, "Hurry up, I have other passengers to pick up." I winked at him as he drove away in a huff.

My Lexus sat quietly in my driveway. I swear I missed my silver baby. I left my bags on the gravel and gave Miss Lexus a rub along her tail end. She was still shining through slightly dusty paint. Something caught my attention though, something inside my vehicle. I walked around and peeked inside the window. The first thing I noticed was the streaks of blood that covered my backseat.

"What the hell?" I spoke aloud to myself. I opened the back door. Along with the blood was clothing. I also picked up what looked like a shoe poking out from the bottom of the front seat, inching toward the back. When I pulled it out it ended up being not a shoe, but the butt end of a semiautomatic pistol that appeared to have been broken in half. Right away I felt this odd premonition come over me. Some bogus shit had been going on lately so this should not have been a surprise to me. I got out of the car, wiping the spots of blood off of my hands onto my jeans, grabbed my bags, and rushed into my house. I knew that the first thing I needed to do was to call Hawk, and see if he had seen anything weird at his place.

I walked inside, took a breath, and set my luggage down by the door. My place didn't appear to be broken into. That at least was a good thing. I had half expected to find another dead body lying around. The last time I had come home, that's exactly what I had found, and no matter how busy I had been with Hennessy and the training for the heist, when the lights were out at night, I still saw Earl, lying in a pool of blood on my couch. I looked over to what was now a new couch, being that I had had my old leather one removed and had purchased a new navy blue suede one as a replacement. There wasn't a body there this time, but there was a black bag that I knew wasn't mine and had not been there when Hennessy and I had left a few weeks ago. I walked over to the bag, looked around as though I were being spied on, and then opened it.

On my opening the bag, green peeked out as big as day, money green, which filled the bag to the brim. Along with what had to be about ten thousand dollars in unmarked fifty-dollar bills was also jewelry. I pulled out some of it, looking closely at it and wondering who the hell it could belong to. Wondered, that is, until I saw it, the big *R*, my old partner's signature that he had on anything and everything that belonged to him and that could be branded.

Just as I was puzzling over who, what, and why, the doorbell rang. I got up and rushed over to answer it. There stood Hennessy with her eyes big and questioning.

"Tristan, your car has blood all over it. Did something happen?" she asked, before looking down at the blood that was still on my hands and now also on my shirt and jeans. "Oh, my God, what happened?"

I moved aside from the door, giving her access inside. "I don't know, I got here a few minutes ago and this is what I found."

"But you're not hurt, are you?" came her concerned cry.

"No, no, I'm fine." I walked quickly over to the black bag. "I'm fine but look what else I found."

She picked up the lumps of money as I had, shaking her head in wonderment. "Tristan, did you take this money?"

"What?" I asked in surprise. I had almost forgotten about her police status, not even thinking twice about showing her everything that I had found, but I supposed she hadn't come here to see how I was doing. Just like everything else about her, this was simply part of her job. Why did I let myself forget, or think that she could be here now for any other reason? "Oh, I guess you're here on official business, Agent Cooper." My eyebrow rose sarcastically.

"No," she cried, "I'm here because I miss you and wanted to see how you were. Why are you making it out like I'm your enemy, Tristan? You know I love you. . . ."

I knew she loved me? Did I really? I felt the sudden anger that had surfaced over me leave as quickly as it had come. We were both quiet for a moment. Mixed emotions rolled through me. I suppose Hennessy could see that confusion on my face. She reached out her hand, caressing me on my cheek.

"Let's call this in, okay?" she asked.

That woke me up fast. "Call what in?"

"We really need to have the LAPD come check all this out. I mean the blood had to have come from somewhere," she stated.

I started shaking my head even before she finished speaking. No way did I want the cops running around my place asking a bunch of fuckin' questions. "Hennessy, I don't want their asses up in here. Nope, forget that!" I shouted.

"But we have to." Hennessy brought my face around to hers, looking deep into my eyes. "Everyone is wanting and expecting you to slip up, but if you do everything according to the law, you win, not them. Trust me, please?" she asked again.

Before I could respond to her, the phone rang.

"Hello."

"T.J., you won't believe what I just saw on the news." It was Hawk.

"What's that?" I asked.

"Manuel. They found his body and the body of some young girl in his poolhouse."

"Manuel Rolez!" I almost shouted.

"Yep. Thought you would be interested in that."

He was right, of course, but *interested* couldn't even touch what I was feeling, thinking. Rolez was dead, blood was in my car. Something had gone on at my beach house, or at least things had been set up to look as though it had.

"Thanks for calling, man," I said to him. I turned around after hanging up and looked at Hennessy. She had a solemn, yet expectant look on her face.

"Okay," I whispered to her, "call your people. I'll trust you. . . ."

# 25

*Los Angeles Police Department*

Marley sat quietly as he was questioned again and again about the murder of Manuel Rolez and Alicia Matthews, who had been their victim's booty call that night. The thing is, when they had told him her name, it hadn't even fazed him. The hardness of the streets left Marley unmoved with just about everything. That same street hardness allowed him to plant a look of total chill on his face, even with the harsh interrogation he was under.

"Do you wanna spend the rest of your life in prison? Is that what you want?" Agent Jacob White was asking him. "You wanna play house in the Cali pen with your, um . . . *boys?* Because I'll tell you this, lil' man, your boys, your so-called *dawgs,* they don't give a fuck about you. Just like Al Majors doesn't give a fuck, so why are you protecting him!"

Marley snickered a bit, then looked toward Chad Williams, another agent who sat quietly beside Jacob White, smoking a Merit. He nodded at him. "Wanna share one of them smokes with me, dawg?" Marley asked him.

Chad Williams looked at him pointedly. "First of all, I'm not your dawg, understand?" He passed him a cigarette, then a light. Marley nodded his thanks, still smiling as he lit up and took a long draw.

"Are you planning on answering me or not?" Agent White pressed.

"What exactly are you asking me, yo?" Marley said, looking away from the two agents as though bored.

"*What* did you do with Al Majors? And do you know his whereabouts right now?"

"Shit . . . I don't know that nicca, I'm not his keeper; I didn't do shit with him, and that's all I can tell you, yo."

Jacob White was fighting to control his temper, which had never been easy for him. Especially when it came to dealing with street punks like this piece of shit that sat in front of him. He had been eager to pick up Mark Richardson, better known as Marley, when the news from the streets had gotten back to them about his big mouth and his brags on how he had helped Al Majors in a murder. And now this ignorant, cocky thug was sitting here, acting as if he were a goddamn choirboy. The bloodied body of Alicia Matthews belied that myth. As for Manuel Rolez, as far as Jacob was concerned, Rolez's carcass could rot in hell. He had pulled that poor young girl into his fucked-up world and had gotten her murdered.

"Then how about this, *yo?*" he mocked to Marley. "How about the fact that Al Majors is free and how about the fact that he probably knows we are talking to you right now? How about the fact that if we wanted to, we could let you walk a free man and that Al would then make sure that you were free for all eternity, when he blasts your ass and sends it straight to hell where it belongs?" Jacob White could see the conflict flickering across Mark Richardson's face. He hoped that it meant that some of what he was saying was getting through to the wayward teen.

"So what are you saying, if I talk, then you let me out of here?" Marley asked.

Jacob looked at Chad Williams, laughed a little, then looked back toward Marley. "Hell naw! What I'm saying is we will keep you alive, and believe me, considering all the shit you've been up to, not only with Majors . . ." Marley looked surprised. "That's right." Jacob White laughed. "I know about all your little street hits and activities."

"So then if you can't do shit for me, why the fuck am I in here?"

Jacob leaned over the table, inching his face closer to Marley. "Because you want to do the right thing, right? And tell me all you can about Majors. And also, because I just might be able to pull a few strings for you, and get you more leniency considering your age."

"And what would that mean for me?" he asked again.

"It means the difference between life in prison, and that's a long-ass life being that you are only eighteen, and perhaps instead getting about forty years, with the possibility of parole in, say, fifteen years? You still would be young enough to have some kind of life. Think about it."

Marley chewed over what had been said. He thought back to what had happened that night, and saw the look of surprise, then death on his boy Wayne's face. Even now he could still feel the same fear he had felt at how vicious Al Majors was. Not that he was some kind of punk, but he could tell that his life wouldn't mean any more to Al Majors than Wayne's had. He figured it was now time to play it smart.

"A'ight," he said. "A'ight, I'll tell you what I know. . . ."

Jacob White felt instant relief, then pressed the button of the tape recorder that sat on the table between them.

"Okay, first of all, why did Al Majors want Manuel Rolez dead?"

"Hell if I know. All I know is that he offered me and Wayne two grand each if we helped him out with it," Marley said. "First he got us to go to this dude's house over in Malibu Beach. We hotwired his Lexus, and that's what we used to do the job."

"And who did the Lexus belong to?"

"Some mofo name Jackson," Marley explained. "He didn't tell us everything, just to get the car, get back to him, and then we made our way over to the Rican dude's crib." Marley stopped, waiting for Agent White's go-ahead. When he got none, he continued his story. "So, we got there. We all had our piece, semi-automatics. So like we went up in there, you know what I'm saying? And, man, that Majors? Whoa! That white nicca is a crazy muthafucka."

"White nigger?" Chad Williams finally spoke.

Marley gave him an incredulous look, as if he had flown in from Mars or some distant land. "You don't know what a white nicca is? An Eminem mofo, you know, white peeps who try to act black? Anyhow, that's how this mofo was. So like we get up into this crib, the bitch is laid out to the max, yo. So we get up in there and we go in the back, the pool and this Jacuzzi and shit is there. And inside the Jacuzzi is the Rican dude."

"Manuel Rolez?" Agent White asked.

"Right. So I was like laid-back, I was like chillin', you know? Next thing I know it was like a muthfuckin' *Scarface* flick up in that muthafucka."

"So you trying to say you fired no rounds?"

"Fuck, naw! I just watched, yo. He the one that did all the killing, and Wayne."

"So how did Wayne end up lying among the dead?" Jacob White asked.

"Well, Al got mad 'cuz Wayne wouldn't waste that bitch."

Jacob's eyebrows rose at Marley's derogatory speech. "You mean Alicia Matthews?"

"Yeah, whatever her name was. So like he told him to cancel her and Wayne got all scurred and shit, and so like he got shot, like *bang!* Just took my boy out just like that. I told you, man, that Al a crazy muthafucka."

"So who killed Alicia Matthews?"

Marley stammered. "Al . . . Al did it, I swear I didn't shoot no damn body. I was just there, yo. I was chillin'."

Jacob and Chad Williams looked at each other, both of them shaking their heads at the ludicrous words of Marley that he actually had no physical part in the murders.

"Okay, homeboy, thanks for your cooperation," Jacob White said.

"So what's gonna happen to me?" Marley asked anxiously.

"Well, for now, until we get more facts, you're gonna be booked for accessory to murder one."

After Marley was booked, he was walked casually up to the night lockup. The cell was full, crowded with everything from violent drug dealers to cold-blooded murderers, murderers who really weren't any different than he was, seeing that only he and Al Majors knew that he had been just as involved in Manuel Rolez's murder as Al had been. And had actually been the one to shoot Alicia Matthews. But he'd be damned if he would spend the rest of his life in jail over that shit. If he hadn't shot her, then he would be where Wayne was, six feet under.

He hardened his expression again as he sat down amongst the other cellmates looking straight ahead of himself, that is, until he noticed one of his boys from the East Side sitting over in a corner by himself. He hadn't seen him since they used to hang out at them white boy raves in Chico back in da day. He smiled, feeling a bit relieved to see a familiar face. What he didn't see was the tall, slim brother coming up behind him.

"Hey," the guy whispered. Marley turned around curiously.

"Yeah, wassup?"

The guy looked around, then leaned in and whispered in Marley's ear. "I got a message for you, from a friend."

"Huh? What the hell you talkin' about, nicca?" Marley then felt a sharp pain coursing through his stomach, as the guy stabbed deep, then pulled down, ripping through vital organs. He looked up, staring in shocked surprise into the eyes of the guy who had stabbed him.

"Al wanted you to know, you need to learn to keep your fuckin' mouth shut. . . ."

*Somewhere in LA*

Al laid his head back, slowly sucking on a Popsicle as he waited for the other end of the phone to pick up. It took about three rings.

"Yeah."

"Is he dead?" Al asked.

"Of course he is. I told you not to worry about it."

Al grunted, unconvinced. "Oh, fuck what you told me; you also told me that those agents would never get a chance to talk to him. Now there's no telling what that piece of shit don' spit outta his mouth."

"Well, he can't spill anything else now, can he?"

"Uh-huh, and what about those two agents?"

"Shit, man, do you expect me to have two federal officers killed just like that?"

"I don't give a rat's ass what you do!" Al shouted. "But I tell you this, Special Agent Sebastian Rogers. If I go down, you go down."

"I've told you before about threatening me," Sebastian warned. "Thing is, if you had kept that drug addict fool Reynolds Moore in check, this would never have happened. You couldn't have picked a more reliable sidekick?"

Al laughed wickedly. "Oh, hell no, you ain't gonna put this fuckup on me. It was your agent that did all this, her and her beckoning pussy that snagged T.J., and it was your decision to have her as your undercover agent for this."

"Okay, okay, there's no use in throwing darts as to who's to blame. Right now, we just have to be concerned about getting out of this mess," Sebastian reasoned.

"There is no *us*, my man. There is a you, and there's a me. You have not lived up to your part, meaning ain't a damn dime in my pocket from all this. Yet I did everything I was supposed to do. I kept with my part of the bargain."

"And so did I," Sebastian broke in.

"Except for the fact that I'm wanted right now, and no one has a clue about your crooked ass. . . ."

"Listen, Majors, I really don't think Marley Richardson gave them anything that would seriously incriminate you, and even if he did, he's dead now; therefore he cannot testify, so if you were picked up, then the evidence they have against you wouldn't even hold. Also, they questioned him without a lawyer present. Believe me, you have nothing to worry about."

"You mean we have nothing to worry about," Al emphasized. "Like I told you, if I go down, you go down. Remember that, Agent Rogers."

Sebastian hung up from Al Majors, feeling the same feeling that had been in his mind since he discovered the mishap of their plans. He couldn't allow some lowlife to ruin his reputation or even have him looking over his shoulder for the rest of his life. He would have to find a way to get rid of him.

## Malibu Beach . . . Hennessy

It felt so good to see a bit of trust in Tristan's eyes. At least I hoped it was trust. He was quiet when I called my old friend Jacob White to come to the beach house. When I called Jacob, I was told that he was in a meeting, meaning he was probably interrogating some poor soul. I had known Jacob White long enough to know that he could be a trip when it came to his trying to get questions answered. But still, he was one of the most intelligent agents I had ever known, and was completely devoted to his job. A six-five, chocolate-complexioned powerhouse of a man, he had given up a golden opportunity to play pro football with the NFL after college, and had instead decided to join the bureau. Thinking about him, I could truly see now that I was in the wrong line of work. I really didn't have his spirit and I especially didn't have his inequitable devotion to the job. Even though I felt I could be a good agent, and that I was smart and always considered myself a devoted woman, I obviously didn't have the same drive as he did, or even as my father did with the NYPD. I knew that if my dad were in my shoes, he would have handled things entirely differently. I was a good agent, but I was more like my mother in one respect. I especially saw that now. Because even with her words of how desperate and traitorous it could be, she would have done exactly as I had; she would have followed her heart. So I couldn't feel any regrets. The only regret I would feel was if things didn't work out where I could be with the man I loved for the rest of my life. The only regret I felt at the moment was that he no longer loved me back.

We both sat quietly, waiting for Jacob to arrive, me sipping on a Cherry 7-Up and Tristan looking rather dry mouthed. I lifted my soda bottle up to him.

"Want a sip?" I asked.

"No, thanks," he replied. "What I do want is for this Agent White to hurry up and get here so I can take a shower and go to bed. It's been a long-ass day."

"Yeah, it has been," I agreed. I thought for a moment, breathing in deeply before I spoke again. Although I knew I had to have answers from him, I was hesitant. "Tristan, when all of this is over, what's going to happen with us?" What felt like long moments passed.

His face was undecided, but after a moment, he finally spoke and said, "I don't know. I guess we'll have to take it one day at a time."

"But you still love me, don't you?"

"Do you still love me?" he asked in return.

I didn't answer; instead, I walked over to him and sat in his lap face forward. While he didn't encourage me in any way, he didn't push me away either. I put my hands on either side of his face, then brought my lips to his forehead, planting soft kisses everywhere. He moaned a little, then slipped his hands around my waist, pressing me down against his hardness. The doorbell rang. We looked at each other, both of us breathing hard.

"We better answer that," Tristan whispered, slowing removing me from his lap. We both stood up, still eyeing each other heatedly. He finally moved over to the door and opened it. It was Agent White.

"Hello, again," he said to Tristan, and then looked over to me. "Good evening, Hennessy."

"Hello, Jacob." I rushed over and gave him a welcoming hug.

"Did you look inside my car?" Tristan asked him.

"Yes, I did, and I'm not at all surprised at what I saw."

"Why is that?" I asked, surprised. Even though I knew Jacob to be a fair man, the blood and materials inside Tristan's Lexus were very incriminating.

"Because," Jacob continued, "today we picked up a young man, Marley Richardson, who basically admitted to hotwiring your car, and using it in the Manuel Rolez murder."

"Are you serious?" Tristan jumped, looking mildly shocked. "Who was this kid? Why would he want to kill Manuel? And why did he steal my car to do it?"

"Well, I can't reveal too much at this moment. The case is still very sensitive, and besides that, we haven't found Alfred Majors yet. He's the ringleader in all this, according to Marley Richardson."

"Whoa!" Tristan exclaimed. "Why am I not surprised?" He walked over to his large picture window, which faced the beautiful red sands I had admired since the first day I had come here. "That pimple-faced faggot tried to stick me."

"So you know him?" I asked, trying to get a gist of what was going on.

"Yeah, I know him." He turned around to face Jacob and me. "We used to be partners, years ago."

"Along with Manuel Rolez, of course," Jacob said. "All of this is documented. What we don't understand as of yet is why Majors would want to set you up." Just then, Jacob's cell phone rang. "Hello?" he answered. "What? Damn! I'll be right there!" He then hung up.

"What's wrong?" I asked.

"I need to get to the jail. Marley Richardson has been murdered."

# 26

*Malibu Beach . . . Tristan*

The door closed. I looked at Hennessy, and she looked at me. Neither one of us knew quite what to say really. Hennessy spoke first.

"So tell me about Alfred Majors, what kind of work did you do with him?"

"What kind of work do you think?" I said defensively. "You know what I am, Hennessy, I never put on a pretense for you."

"What you *were*," she said emphatically.

"Yeah, whateva. Anyhow, I need to shower. Maybe it's time for you to get back to your hotel room."

She looked a bit rattled. "You're right."

"Unless you want to spend the night here," I said slowly. She looked surprised. "I don't know . . ."

I laughed. "You don't know? Is it that hard a decision? You either want to or you don't."

"No, I mean . . . I guess I shouldn't. I guess it wouldn't look very good."

I gave a tight smile. "Yeah, kinda thought you would say that."

Hennessy started gathering her purse and jacket. She stared

at me for a moment, then said, "I swear you go from hot to cold. The reason I'm saying that it wouldn't be a good idea is the investigation that's going on right now. Staying with you . . . my staying the night would not go unnoticed."

I knew I was behaving childishly, but when it came to her I just somehow couldn't see reason. I hadn't held on to my sense of reason from the moment I first met her, and things sure weren't about to change now. I wanted to believe she was being real with me about what she was feeling, but when someone had been unreal with you from the beginning it wasn't easy to suddenly have this trust thing.

She finally said her good-byes, kissed me softly on the lips, and waltzed out. I locked the door behind her and made my way to my room. This house just didn't have the same home feeling that it had had before. Although it never did give me the comfortable and free feeling of Jackson's, it was still mine. Now I felt as if it had been invaded. Growing up, I had seen so many people go through having their homes lose the flavor by the gang shootings that would occur, or children who would be shot sitting quietly at the dinner table, taking away the home sweet home from the family. Now my home sweet home was gone also. It left when I saw my adopted father in forever sleep, and even though I tried not to think about it too much, it was hard not to when I was here, feeling the force of what had happened to him touching me all over.

Maybe that was why I wanted Hennessy to stay with me here tonight, although I would never tell her that, have me looking like some whining punk. Instead of worrying about things like that, I needed to be thinking about Al Majors. He was a real character. I had met Al through Manuel Rolez years ago, and even though I had always had my misgivings about him, when Manuel insisted that he was trustworthy I had agreed to do a couple of local jobs with him. Al was a control freak, always wanting to make the final decision on things, but since I was the one footing most of the money for necessities, and since my ideas were what brought us together, I wasn't about to let him lead me by the ass. After our last outing, I decided that we weren't compatible and parted ways with both him and Manuel. Manuel became somewhat like an arch competitor throughout the years, and as for Al Majors, I supposed he felt slighted when he came to me that last time asking for a loan. Since I didn't feel I could trust him when we were working together, I sure didn't feel I could trust him when we were not. After I turned him down by not responding to him, I just hadn't heard from him anymore. That is, until now.

I showered, shaved, and then slipped on a pair of cotton loungers before relaxing on my bed. I was about to get myself a beer, figuring that maybe it would help me sleep better, when the phone rang. Hennessy's musical hello sung out to me.

"I just wanted to let you know I got in okay," she said.

"I'm glad you called," I replied. "I was just thinking about you."

"You were?" she asked in surprise. "I'm surprised you even care."

I sighed. "Of course I care if you're okay, Hennessy. You know I do. Everything that's happened has just been hard to take, is all."

She was quiet for a minute, doing the same thing I was doing, I suppose, thinking about the past, the present, the future, and how we as a couple might or might not fit into that.

"So, what are you doing?" I finally asked her.

"Nothing, just relaxing. But I wanted to call and say good night. I need to get to sleep. Tomorrow I have a meeting with the grievance board. You know, internal affairs."

"And why do they want to meet with you?"

"Because, Tristan . . ." She sighed. "I broke the code of ethics when I got involved with you; you said that yourself. They want to talk to me about what happened. I could be fired."

It hadn't hit me until then how much she did put on the line in order to save me. The realization of it warmed me, more than I cared to admit.

"I'm sorry, babe," I whispered.

"I'm not. No matter what happens, Tristan, I could never be

sorry for meeting you. I could never be sorry for working as hard as I could to make sure you didn't make the mistake of your life. And that's all I want to say about it now. A little birdie may be listening."

I knew she meant that my phone was probably bugged. Most likely that's how the feds found out about Hennessy and me.

"Okay, so will you call me tomorrow and let me know how things go?"

"I'll call you as soon as I get out of my meeting, okay? And, Tristan?"

"Yeah?"

She paused for a minute. "Promise me you'll be careful. Don't go after Alfred Majors, or do anything that would give anyone a reason to arrest you."

"I won't," I promised.

"No," she pleaded, "I mean it. We have a chance, a real chance. Give it time?"

"Baby, I promise, I'll be good as gold," I said, smiling.

"Okay." She sighed. "I'm gonna go now. Good night, my love. . . ."

"Good night."

Later I was lying in bed, finally able to get some sleep after countless hours of thinking too damn much. I was in a deep slumber when the phone rang. At the third beckon I was able to muster up the energy to reach my arm over and grab the receiver.

"Hello?"

"'Sup, T.J., remember me?" a deep voice asked. On recognition, I woke up completely. Al Majors had an unforgettable voice.

"Are you responsible for all this shit that's been going on?" I asked him. "What are you trying to do, Al, and most important, why?"

"Why?" Al laughed wildly. "Why do you think, you dumb-ass fuck? I wanted the same thing you wanted. I wanted that forty million, and you fuckin' owe me, too."

"Owe you? How you figure that?"

"I was never good enough when we were working together, was I? You had to have more upscale partners, like yourself, right?" Al said sarcastically.

I couldn't believe that after all this time this crazy character was still tripping about our canceled partnership. But then again, he always did want to be in control. His controlling ways made me not wanna deal with his ass in the first place.

"Al, you need to look at yourself as to why we stopped dealing, man. You want everything your way, and with me, that just wasn't gonna happen. I'm sorry you couldn't deal with that."

Al laughed again. "Fuck you with ya sorry ass, T.J., and that stank bitch, too. Where she at anyhow?"

I answered him very slowly. "What do you know about Hennessy? She ain't got nothing to do with you."

Al just about barked in my ear. "She's the reason behind all of this! I know what was going on up at your ranch. She played you for a fool, man. And I know she smoked Reynolds, too." He sniffed. "Yeah, that bitch has a lot to answer for, a lot!"

Reynolds? Slowly the missing pieces were starting to make sense, starting to fit. Al had to have an informant that was close to me, and it was none other than my ol' homeboy Reynolds. I must have whispered Reynolds's name out loud because Al was laughing like a loony.

"That's right, Reynolds it was. Surprised?" he spat. "Don't be, man, there's a lot of shit you don't know; that's 'cuz you're a stupid-ass bitch. Watch your back, T.J., or else you may end up like that raggedy old Jew you knew."

I didn't have a response for Al, not that I had much of a chance to give one. He had hung up immediately after *his watch your back* comment. The desire for revenge weighed heavy on my mind. I couldn't seek revenge from Reynolds, but Al . . . His words made one thing clear. He was responsible for Earl's death. Yeah, I had promised Hennessy I would lie low. But I had lain low once before when Earl was first killed, and now I was at the point of being a sitting duck. There was every reason to believe that Al would come after me, and Hennessy, too. Most crazies didn't reason much, and to him, we were the reason he was in the position he was in.

I jumped up as these thoughts flew through my head. I knew that no matter what she said, I needed to be with Hennessy. Because regardless of who she was, what she was, and what she did, I loved her. I wasn't gonna let another woman I loved get hurt or killed because of me.

Hennessy had given me her hotel room number. I quickly slipped it into my pocket and made for the door, but not before I slipped my .38 in my back belt hook. I wasn't taking any chances.


*Hennessy*


I heard a soft tapping at my door, but my body would just not move. *Tap, tap,* again. I groaned, and sat up. "Who in the world could that be?" I said to myself. I got up and flung the door open without even looking out the peephole.

"Don't you ever, *ever* do that again!"

I looked at Tristan with an astonished expression. "Excuse me, but what are you doing here?" I asked him smartly. He pushed his way into my hotel room, and locked the door behind him.

"I'm here to protect you, since it's clear you can't do it yourself," he said hotly. "Damn it, Hennessy, that could have been Al Majors at your door."

"Huh?" I shook my head as if it were covered with cobwebs. "Why would he be at my door?"

Tristan sort of ignored me at first, then walked over to my queen-size bed, sat down, and took his shoes off. My guess was he planned to stay. Hmmm . . .

"Sweetie, um . . . what are you doing?" I asked him, nodding my head toward his feet. He ignored my nod.

"Al called me tonight, Hennessy, and he all but admitted that he killed Earl."

"He told you that he did it?" I asked in surprise. "Did he tell you why?" I could hear the pain that was still in Tristan's voice at the mention of his murdered mentor.

"Nope, but I didn't ask. I was too surprised at the revelation. And that's not all. Basically he also knows *everything* about you. I mean I wouldn't be surprised if he had someone from amongst your people working with him."

"No way, I know all the guys I work with; they are all dedicated to their jobs." Tristan sort of grunted in disbelief. I shook my head at him. "My goodness, he does have you spooked."

I walked over and sat down beside him on the bed. I noticed him looking down at my ample cleavage that was visible with my low-cut nightgown. I felt my nipples harden as he stared.

"I just know how he operates. Anyhow Al called me about thirty minutes ago, bitching and whining about past problems he and I had." Tristan sighed suddenly. "And he told me something else, too."

"What's that?" I asked.

"Reynolds, Reynolds was working with him, with Al Majors."

I stared at him, my mouth agape.

"That's a trip, huh? I would never have thought my childhood homie would double-cross me, or any of the guys really. I guess that just goes to show you that you can never really know people. I was once told by a very wise man that one should always be careful to watch out for the serpents in your corner, people who you think you can trust, but who are really just positioning themselves for an opportunity to screw you over. I guess I should have listened."

We were both quiet for a moment. His words were deep, but I really hoped he wasn't thinking that I was that serpent in his corner, although he would be right in that feeling, I supposed.

"I'm sorry, Tristan. I know how much friendship means to you," I said solemnly.

"Yeah," he said slowly. "Anyway, I don't want anything to

happen to you. I'm not gonna allow Majors to come in here and try to hurt you."

"And you think he will?"

Tristan shook his head. "I don't know, but just in case . . ." He started removing his jeans and shirt. "Just in case, I'm bodyguarding you tonight." I opened my mouth to protest.

"Yeah, I know what you're thinking," he said, cutting in. "But we'll worry about what people think tomorrow. Tonight, I just want to hold you and protect you, and that's exactly what I'm gonna do."

At those words, Tristan crawled under my bedcovers and then reached out his arms. What else could I do? I fell into them.

# 27

Since Hennessy had her meeting with the grievance board, I thought I would finally do what I had come to LA to do in the first place, visit Jillian Jackson. I knew she would be surprised to see me. I supposed I never really paid enough attention to my mom. It was time for a change.

"Well, what are you doing here, stranger?" my mom asked as she opened the door.

"I've been in LA since Sunday, Mom. I was planning on coming by then to see you."

My mom sniffed, looking at me sideways. "So what happened to your plans? Got sidetracked?"

"Kinda, yeah," I said slowly. I looked around the house. Surprisingly it was clean, and my mom appeared to be sober, too. "So how've you been?" I asked her, turning around and giving her a crooked smile. She had her hands wrapped on either side of her arms. She looked *tired*.

"Are you okay, Mama?" I asked her. I could see moisture in her eyes, which shocked me. My mom never cried about anything, ever.

"Yeah, I'm fine," she said faintly. "What did you need, T.J.?"

What did *I* need? Damn, that was a change. Usually it was her telling me what *she* needed. Something was definitely wrong here. "I don't need anything. I just wanted to come see you, that's all."

"Well, like I said before, that's a big-ass surprise," she hooted, then spat out, "You want sumpin' to eat? I fixed some bacon and oatmeal."

I was about to say no, but the look on her face, something in her expression made me nod yes.

"There's something different about you, Mom," I said, as she poured hot, steaming coffee in a mug for me.

"Oh, yeah? Different how?"

"I don't know, can't quite put my finger on it yet." I stopped, counted to ten before speaking again, then asked, "Are you, um . . . off of the—"

"Drugs?" she cut in.

I flushed uncomfortably.

"Don't let the cat hold your tongue, boy; just say whatever you're feeling. And to answer the question you never asked, yes, I am trying to drop the habit, and it's not easy either. But," she said solemnly, "nothing in this life has ever been easy for me, so it's no surprise."

I took a bite out of one of the huge, hot biscuits my mom put on my plate. I wanted to measure my words carefully before I spoke. Funny thing is, I had never known just how to talk to her. Even though I was an only child, we had never gotten to the bonded type of relationship that most sons had with their mothers. Thing is, she simply was never quite there, not emotionally, to reach out to.

After swallowing some of the biscuit, I gulped down some more coffee. Then finally I spoke. "Why have you always held back from me, Mama?"

"Held what back, chile?"

"You know what I mean," I insisted.

"No, I don't! Boy, you just blame me for everything, don't

you?" She sighed. "You were always in the streets too much for me to get a chance to be close to you. So don't you dare blame me now!"

"I'm not blaming you," I whispered.

"Oh, you ain't, huh? Witcha self-righteous ass. You just a fancy gansta, T.J. You ain't no better than me! You ain't no betta than none of these people round here," she said, swinging her hands. "None of us!"

I felt a big-ass lump forming in my throat. *Naw, I ain't dealing with this,* I thought to myself. I stood up quickly to take my leave.

"Yeah, that's right," my mom screamed, "go on and go, like always, everybody always running from me; you ain't no different. No different!"

"Okay," I whispered again. I walked quickly toward the door. "Thanks for the breakfast, Mama."

Something stopped me from walking out the door, I don't know what it was, but suddenly I looked back. My mom was pressed up against the wall by the kitchen door, her head in her hands, crying silent, but uncontrollable, jerky, hiccupping sobs. I ran over to her.

"What is it? What is it, Ma?" I cried.

"You . . . you think I'm happy the way things are with us? You think I don't think about you every day, and the mistakes I made with you?" my mom cried, looking at me with tear-clouded eyes.

"I wish things were different, too," I stated, hardly being able to hold back my own tears. "I've *always* wanted to be close to you."

"It's the drugs, T.J. The drugs they been talking to me, calling me. And I want to get away from it so bad, so bad." She sniffed. "I want to make up for not being there for you, but I ca . . . can't . . ."

"Then I'll help you. I'll help you, okay?"

My mom cried even harder. I was hesitant since she had never hugged me, at least not any time that I could remember in my thirty-two years. But I wanted to hug her, wanted to let her see that I did love her and I did care. When I pulled her head to my shoulder I wasn't sure if she was gonna push me away or not, but she didn't. Instead, she cried harder still as if she were letting out all the old bad feelings we had carried with each other since forever.

"It's gonna be all right, Mama, I love you."

## Los Angeles, California . . . Hennessy

The air in the room was humid, stifling, still. It seemed to me as if all eyes were directed on me. Internal affairs had sent over two of their top officials who were interrogating cases in the West Coast.

"Agent Cooper, can you tell us exactly what you feel went wrong on this assignment?" asked Officer Cecil Mickle.

I took a deep breath, and then I spoke. "Well, for one, I don't think we were completely up on what was happening outside of Tristan Jackson's camp. There were other people involved, and other things going on. Alfred Majors for one." I looked over toward Sebastian, who sat across from me. "We needed to have all our Ts crossed and Is dotted and we didn't." Sebastian smirked at me, knowingly. Cecil Mickle addressed me again.

"So you don't feel that your relationship with Jackson had anything to do with your cover being blown?"

"My relationship with Jackson?" I said, swallowing.

Officer Mickle leaned over to the other internal affairs officer to his left, whispering, then turned his attention back toward me. "Let's end this line of questioning for now," he said. "Tell us exactly what happened on the plane ride from Santa Fe, New Mexico."

"Well, we were heading for LA. Tristan Jackson and the other men, Mateo and Hawk, wanted to visit their mothers and lady friends for Mother's Day. So we were on our way. During this time, Reynolds Moore showed up, late, and apparently high. Tristan informed him that there was a change of plans for the heist in New York, and that's when Reynolds lost it."

"What change of plans?"

"Tristan had decided that, um . . . that he would cancel," I said.

"And why don't you tell them why he decided to cancel, Hennessy?" Sebastian pressed.

"Special Agent Rogers, we're asking the questions here, okay?" Cecil Mickle said forcefully, reprimanding Sebastian. If I weren't so nervous I would have poked my tongue out at him. Sebastian apologized for his outburst, and then looked at me, quietly, intently.

"But that is a good question, Agent Cooper. Do you know why he decided to cancel? And did you know about it before he informed Reynolds Moore?"

"I found out that night, before we were on the plane," I answered.

"And did you inform your superior of this change of plans?"

"No, I did not."

Officer Mickle raised an eyebrow. "You didn't? Can you tell us why?"

"It was a judgment call," Sebastian coughed out, laughing. I looked at him, astonished at the bitter tone of his voice. Sebastian was surprising me more and more here lately. Although I understood and knew how important his cases were to him, he was taking this one personally, and I now knew why: Natalie. And I definitely planned to call him on it when I got a chance.

"Again, Agent Rogers, if you can not control yourself, I'm going to have to ask you to leave!" Officer Mickle said. Sebastian looked at me with narrowed eyes, gave a sigh, then sat back, looking away from me.

"Agent Cooper, go on."

"I don't know why I didn't call and tell Sebastian," I started saying.

"But according to our records, you *did* call him." The officer sitting beside Officer Mickle finally spoke up. He fiddled through some papers that were in his hand. "You called him around six that evening." He looked from Sebastian to me. "Am I right?"

"Yes, you are correct," I finally said. "I did call him earlier, but I didn't know for sure at that time that the New York robbery plans were canceled."

"Hennessy, how the *fuck* didn't you know?" Sebastian shouted. "It was only hours later that all hell broke loose on that plane! You know goddamn well you knew. You were screwing him, weren't you? So I'm sure he told you during your pillow talk; you *knew!*"

"Get the hell out, now," Officer Mickle said. Sebastian got up roughly, knocking over his chair in the process, and slammed out the door.

I took another needed breath and ran my shaking hands over my face. When I looked up again, both internal affairs officers were looking at me.

"I'm gonna ask you some questions point-blank, you understand?" Officer Mickle asked. I nodded yes.

"Do you feel that your actions in this case in any way undermined the success of its operation?"

"Yes," I answered. "But—"

"No buts, just answers," he said. "Next question. Did you at any time become physically involved with Tristan James Jackson?"

"Yes, I did."

"Did you engage in sexual intimacies with him?"

I paused for long moments, closing my eyes before speaking.

"Did you engage in sexual intimacies with Tristan Jackson?" Officer Mickle asked again.

"I made *love* with him," I said finally. "There is a difference, Officer Mickle."

"Oh, really?" he asked, sarcastically.

"Really."

"And you don't feel that you dishonored yourself as a federal agent by getting sexually involved with a suspect?"

"I know I did. I don't have any defense to that, but—"

"You don't feel that you broke the Code of Ethics?" he cut in.

"I *know* I broke the Code of Ethics, and it's for that reason that I feel that I should resign immediately as a U.S. federal agent."

A look of shock shined on both officers' faces. "What? You're just going to resign? Just like that?"

I stood up slowly, feeling a tear tracing down my cheek.

"I love my job, I have always loved being with the agency. But to me, the purpose of our work has been somehow twisted. We have an obligation to stop crimes and criminals, not make sure that the crimes take place so that we can add more criminals to our already crowded penitentiaries." I paused, wiping the wetness from my face, then continued. "If I did something wrong by stopping a crime, then shoot me, but I don't feel guilty about that. Yes, I knew that Tristan Jackson was thinking about canceling his robbery plans even before he announced it to the other guys, and yes, I encouraged him to give up that life. I did it, and you know what? I'm not sorry. I'm glad. And I'll tell you something else I'm not sorry about. I'm *not* sorry that I fell in love with him. I'm not sorry that I showed him that love. The only thing I'm sorry about is that by my stopping a crime from taking place, I am no longer qualified to be a federal agent."

The reaction to my words was silence, and to break the silence, I reached into my purse, took out my FBI badge and my gun, laid both on the table, and walked out.

Once I was outside the doors, I leaned against the wall, holding my stomach tightly and taking deep breaths. I looked up to see Sebastian standing in front of me.

"Never get a woman to do a man's job," he said.

"I did my job, Sebastian. Problem with you is, maybe you didn't do yours. Besides that, why didn't you tell me that your goddaughter had been involved with Tristan? Why were you hiding it from me?"

Sebastian laughed. "You've been doing your homework, I see. It was none of your damn business, Hennessy. Jackson killed Natalie, just as surely as if he had aimed the gun and pulled the trigger himself. He *will* pay. . . ."

I shook my head at Sebastian in disbelief; it was as if I was seeing a totally different person from the one I had known and admired all of these years. "You shouldn't even be with the bureau, Sebastian . . . you shouldn't, you—"

"And what about you?" he cut in, "Are you so honorable? You've been a disgrace to your badge, and you truly make me sick for what you've done. But don't worry, I'll get your loverboy sometime or another. Believe me, my job is not finished. But you are." His eyes peered deeply into mine before he walked away, and I saw something in them I had never seen before.

Hatred.

# 28

*Los Angeles, California . . . Hennessy*

When I got out to my car, I felt so relieved, so indescribably relieved. Even though I was still shaking from my confrontation with Sebastian; even though I had just lost my job, I was free, free from the chain that was holding me back from fully expressing my love to Tristan. I wanted to see him, celebrate that freedom with him as soon as possible. I picked up my cell phone to call him and let him know that I was on my way.

"Hello," he answered.

"Hey," I whispered. "I was hoping that you were home."

"Where are you?"

"I'm on my way to Malibu Beach," I said.

"So . . . what happened?"

"You know, it's funny, because I lost my badge, but oddly enough I don't care."

"Oh, no," Tristan said. "I'm sorry, Hennessy. I know you were worrying about this happening." He sighed with regret.

"Tristan, did you hear what I just said? I don't even care. I mean, they were going to cite me for breaking the so-called Code of Ethics, and ask me for my resignation anyhow, so I just resigned."

Tristan was quiet. I felt a bit of alarm at his silence. Maybe he didn't want to be with me? Maybe he was still angry that I had fooled him. Maybe I was just a big fool. "You don't seem happy at my news," I choked out.

"I am happy. I just don't want you to be regretting things, Hennessy, or feeling like I ruined your life."

"But I don't! And I won't, and I can't wait to see you," I cried, feeling a bit choked up. "I'm on my way there now, okay? Give me ten more minutes." I hung up quickly before he had a chance to respond. I was not going to lose Tristan. There was no way I could stand losing two things that were important to me, all in one day.

After hanging up with Tristan, I relaxed back a bit, deciding to listen to some Sadé along the way. The soft sounds of *Lover's Rock* purred through the speakers, relaxing me. I needed to shake these negative thoughts about Tristan not wanting to be with me. He had been honest all along about his feelings for me. It had been me who wasn't honest. I knew he loved me.

Something broke into my train of thought, I wasn't sure at first, but it appeared that every time I would turn, a black Expedition would turn at the same time, slow down at the same time, and speed up at the same time. I was being followed. I sped up, but the faster I went, the faster the Expedition would go. When I got to a fast turn, the SUV turned right behind me, then slammed hard into the back of me, causing a scream to fly out of my mouth. I was scared for two reasons. One was that I didn't see any other cars on this road but mine and this big black vehicle that was trying to run me down, and two, I was driving a rental car, and I didn't have a job to pay for any damage, and hadn't put extra cover on it when I rented it. My hands were literally shaking as I tried to keep my wheel steady.

"You crazy bastard," I whispered, as I slammed in the opposite direction of the SUV. I looked in my mirror again. The Expedition had disappeared. "Thank you, God," I whispered.

My heart was beating fast all the way till I got to Tristan's sandy driveway. I jumped out and walked quickly toward his door, looking around me as I walked. I knocked loudly on the door. When the door opened up, with Tristan standing there smiling at me, I let out a deep breath and fell into his arms.


*Tristan*

Seeing Hennessy so worked up had me in shock. "What's wrong? What happened?" I asked her, dragging her into the house.

"Somebody . . . somebody . . ."

"What?" I pressed.

"Somebody was following me just now, trying to run me down," she cried.

Hennessy's eyes were red and puffy. And although her face was dry I could tell she was holding back tears. "Goddamnit!" I said angrily. "Did you see who it was? Was it Al? I'm going to see if they're still out there!"

"No!" she cried, wrapping her arms tight around me. She buried her face in my chest. My heart was beating fast at the thought of someone trying to hurt her. I was not gonna let that happen again. I couldn't! "Stay with me; I need you," Hennessy whispered. "I need you so much. . . ."

I looked down into her eyes. "Are you sure you're okay?"

She nodded. "Yes, it just shook me up a bit. Today was just too much, period. I should've rammed that idiot off the road instead of panicking like I did."

My eyebrows rose. "Well, I'm glad you didn't try anything foolish, Superwoman."

Hennessy sighed, drawing closer into my arms. "You're right, but let's just be together today, Tristan, let's just forget about all the madness that's been going on, and shut out the rest of world. All I need is you; you're all I need, darling."

"You're all I need, too, baby," I whispered back. I cradled her in my arms, and let her love soak through me.

We made a silent pact, to leave the outside world behind us. But even without swearing to ourselves to do that, it was hard, too hard. Still I tried to stomp any subject outside of us whenever I felt it coming on. I ran a hot bath for us, adding bath salts to ease away the day's stress. I turned the water to a soft bubble.

I let Hennessy relax a bit in the bath while I made a call to LA General to check on Mateo. I was a bit frustrated that he wasn't in his room; probably gone out for tests, or taking a shower, I thought. I called Hawk. He didn't answer either. Damn, I thought, ain't nobody contactable these days. The thing about Hawk was I knew he was all into his old lady, and needed this break to spend that time with her. I figured I'd hook up with him in the morning. For now, I could think of one lady that I wanted, needed to check up on.

I peeked inside the tub room where Hennessy was all laidback in the hot, scented, bubbling water.

"How's the water?" I asked her, smiling gently as I removed my own clothing.

"Mmmm . . . it's great," she cooed. "But, it could be nicer if I had company."

"I was just about to do that," I said, smiling. I slipped into the water and was grabbed by Hennessy before I was even completely inside. I laughed. "Check you out." I grinned.

She ran her fingers down the side of my face, biting her bottom lip as she stared into my eyes.

"What?" I laughed again, mostly because I didn't know what to say.

"You have beautiful eyes. You're just a beautiful man, Tristan, and you've reeled me in hook, line, and sinker."

"No regrets?" I asked her, looking at her intently. It was so important to me that she didn't regret getting involved with me, although I knew I had cost her greatly.

"None whatsoever," she said quickly.

I covered her lips with mine, kissing her deeply. I pulled her closer to me, molding my body with hers. When our kiss finally ended, I didn't know who was more stirred, she or I.

I washed her, very slowly, making sure to caress every part of her. She then did the same to me. By the time we were done, we could hardly get out of the tub quickly enough, or get dried fast enough. Oddly, once we were on my bed, I was stuck on what to say or do next. It was almost as if we were about to make love for the very first time. I curled my arms around her and rubbed her shoulders softly.

"I want to go back to Santa Fe," she said out of the blue.

"What . . . do you mean now?"

"No." She laughed softly. "But as soon as we can. Right now I want you to touch me, here," she pulled my hand to her breast. Her eyes were smoky with desire as I squeezed.

"What else do you want me to do?" I whispered.

"I want you to lie back and let Hennessy *Cooper* make love to her man."

"Oh," I said hoarsely. I lay back per her request, not sure how to react to this new Hennessy, this open and real Hennessy. I closed my eyes for a second as she rose up and turned on some music. She grumbled for a minute that I had too much rap for her taste, but then sighed contentedly when she found an oldies-but-goodies radio station. She smiled and swiveled back over to me, doing a little nude dance before climbing atop my legs.

"You're gonna make me pull you over here, girl," I said jokingly. She laughed a little, then lay down over me, kissing and licking me softly at the crook of my neck. I sighed at her touch and brought my hands to her back to press her to me.

"Uh-uh," she protested, then moved my hands to either side of my head. "Let me savor you. You just lie here, okay?" She kissed down my chest flicking and biting at a nipple. I groaned.

"But I want, I need to touch you, too," I whispered to her. I hushed when I felt her warm lips licking down my stomach, kissing my abs, then playing with the silky hairs that ran down from my navel and beyond. My breath quickened when she moved down lower and blew warm air up and down the length of me, finally replacing the air with her hot tongue. I brought my hands to my face, gasping aloud as she took me fully between her lips and began sucking slowly. Her long hair blocked my sight from what she was doing, but then I didn't need to see. I *felt* it all, all over my body in tingles and shock waves of pleasure. I sat up on my elbows, touching and caressing her hair as she worked her magic. Just as the strength in my arms was about to give out, she looked up, kissing just the tip of me and mouthing to me, *I love you.*

"I love you, too," I whispered out to her. I was about to say something else when she took me fully in her mouth again, slowly suckling me up and down. I moaned loudly. My head fell to the bed as all my energy was spent, but for the uncontrollable thrusting I was doing despite her efforts to hold me down as she worked me, sucking, licking, loving me.

"Hennessy! I can't . . . I can't . . . oh, baby!" I moaned. I was lost in delirium, rolling my head back and forth from side to side. Just when I felt I could take no more, she stopped. My blurred vision tried to focus in on her. I felt her sliding down onto me, and I moaned again as her warm wetness enveloped me.

"Oh, Tristan . . ." she moaned, swiveling her hips up and down then in a circular motion.

"Yes, yes . . ." I whispered. I pushed her hips downward as I thrust upward inside her. She lay down fully atop me, then found my lips and slipped her tongue inside my mouth. I grabbed the opportunity and flipped her completely over, hooked her fingers with mine as I began to rock, in and out, slowly, faster, rolling, grinding my hipbone against her clitoris in the old lover's dance. I felt her muscles grabbing me in a clutch. I cried out as she gripped and released me rhythmically inside, rolling her hips at the same time. I heard myself crying out each time she squeezed till finally with one last thrust into her, her little squeezes were not of her own accord, but were the spasms of the orgasm racking her body. Her release pulled mine out of me, and I exploded, spilling myself inside her.

"Did I pass out?" I choked out moments later, once our breathing had almost returned to normal.

"No." She laughed huskily. "But I would wake you up if you had. I want your complete attention, Mr. Jackson."

"And you have it. . . ."

"I love you, Tristan," she said with intensity.

"And I love you, baby," I whispered back, "more than you'll ever know. . . ."


## Somewhere in LA

Al was fidgety. He was pissed and irritated at having to hide out in this dirty, crappy hotel room. He knew that the manhunt was on. Every shitty cop in LA was probably looking for him. What got to him the most was that half of the muthafuckas were crooked. "Frontin' muthafuckas," he said aloud.

He got up and closed the suitcase he had packed.

"Yeah, it's time for me to get outta here," he said. "But first . . ." He took out a long pistol, blowing on the tip of the barrel. After loading it, he slipped it into his gun belt, grabbed his suitcase, and looked around.

"Good-bye, LA, time for a new adventure for Alfred Majors. But first, I have to say good-bye to a few friends."

Al had plans, plans of revenge. He got into his black Expedition, started it up, and pulled out of the parking lot.

The phone rang inside the hotel room registered in Al's name. On the other end of the line, Sebastian waited impatiently. He slammed the receiver down when there was no answer.

"He's not there?" Agent Jacob White asked him.

"Naw," Sebastian answered.

"Well, we should go over anyhow. See what we can come up with in the way of evidence."

Sebastian reluctantly agreed. He had wanted to go over to Al's hotel room also, but not to look for evidence. He wanted to confront Al Majors himself, and he wanted to be sure to legally blow him to hell, shutting his big mouth up forever.

# 29

*Los Angeles, California*

"Man, you look like you're preparing for World War Three over there," Jacob White commented as he drove into the hotel parking lot. He couldn't help but note the way Sebastian was loaded up with weapons. He had one small piece in his ankle belt, one at his waist, and was slipping a third in his side pocket.

"Can never be too careful," Sebastian responded.

"True, but Majors is not even at this hotel."

Sebastian looked at Jacob sideways, ignoring his comment. "Let's go," he said flatly, opening up the door on his side.

When they got to the hotel door, they found, of course, that it was locked. Jacob was just about to go around to the front in order to get a key to enter, when Sebastian had a better idea and kicked the door open with one hard thrust. Jacob looked at him in surprise.

"What can I say?" Sebastian smirked. "All those Tae Bo lessons had to come in handy sooner or later."

Jacob shook his head again as they entered. He didn't know a lot about Sebastian Rogers, but what he did know had him convinced that Rogers was a bit too aggressive for his own taste.

Once they were in, they quickly made rounds, checking all the drawers and under the bed and mattress for anything that would clue them in to the whereabouts of Al Majors. They came up with nothing.

"This is getting crazy," Sebastian hissed out. "Nobody can clean up this good."

"Well, he obviously can," Jacob noted. "Looks like he had a maid service clean his apartment, and it's not much different here either. Either that or he knew we would be searching and didn't want us to find anything."

"Damn it!"

Jacob looked toward Sebastian. He almost looked as if he were about to have a heart attack. "Calm down, Agent Rogers; it's not that important, you know. I mean we knew he wasn't here. I'm just as disappointed as you are that he left not a clue to his whereabouts, but to be honest with you, right now I'm just ready to go home. I've been on duty ever since Sunday."

"Okay, fine," Sebastian said, sighing. "I'll take you back to headquarters; then I'm gonna come back and look around a bit more myself."

"What? What are you looking for, Rogers?" Jacob asked in frustration.

"I don't know, okay?" Sebastian swung around, looking Jacob in the eye. "But I do know I'm not gonna be whining about how many hours I've worked. I don't quit until the job is done. Maybe that's one of the problems with you West Coast agents. You're too soft!"

"Okay, fine, I'll stay with you!" Jacob said, throwing his hands up. "I've worked and trained in DC just like you, so that comment doesn't apply to me. Anyhow, where else do you want to look?"

"Where else could he be?"

Jacob thought for a moment. "Hard to say. I would suppose he may be trying to leave town though. But that would be surprising since he was working so hard to set T.J. Jackson up. I'm sure he's still pissing a brick about him." Suddenly Jacob's eyes lit up as a thought hit him. "Hold up! You think maybe he'll head to—"

"Malibu Beach!" Sebastian shouted. He made quick headway to Jacob White's car, slamming the door behind him. "Hurry up," he called out to Jacob.

"Hold up," Jacob said, as he got into the car. He started it up and started backing out. "We should call for backup."

"We don't need no back up; I got my backup right here," Sebastian said, pointing to one of his guns.

"Whoa! Hold up now; I'm not into the supercop antics."

"Just go," Sebastian demanded. "We aren't even sure he's there. Go!"


*Malibu Beach . . . Tristan*

"Look, you need to chill, lil' boy," Hennessy joked. She was fighting hard to get her jeans zipped up and buttoned. I pinched her behind again, causing her to jump. "Oh! See, you're looking for a fight now," she warned, putting up her fist.

"Oh, you wanna box? Huh? Huh?" I teased. We rolled and tussled on the bed before I ended it with a soft, sensual kiss to her lips. When it ended, Hennessy's eyes were misty.

"So when can we leave?" she asked, lifting up from me. "For Santa Fe, that is. I was very serious earlier about going back there. It was so peaceful and beautiful, and it's where we were happy, isn't it?"

"I feel like that, too," I said. It meant a lot to me that she loved my home, and I couldn't wait to talk to her about making it her home, too, if she would have me. "But listen, why don't we talk about that during our walk? I promise I won't throw you in the water," I joked.

"You better not." She laughed back. "Let me go pull my hair back and I'll be right out."

I smiled at her as she bounced into the bathroom, shaking my head at her vanity. Her hair looked just fine to me; everything about her was just *fine*.

I walked out into the hallway, figuring I'd make up a basket of cheese, crackers, and wine for our late night stroll. I laughed, thinking that if I was romantic enough, maybe I'd get lucky again before the night was through. So wrapped up was I with my naughty thoughts that at first I didn't see the tall willowy figure standing casually beside the kitchen door with gun in hand. When I did, my eyes opened wide.

"Wassup, my man?"

"Al. How the hell did you get in here!" I exclaimed.

"You're asking *me* how I got into your house?" He laughed. "Shiiit . . . you really are losing it, pardna. When have I ever needed a key? It's one of the things you liked about me, remember?"

"Okay, so what do you want?" I asked. I felt around to my lower back for my gun, and almost moaned aloud when I realized that I'd forgotten to put it on. Al laughed when he realized what I was doing.

"Ahh, naw! What is this? The big, bad, green-eyed jigga ain't strapped?"

I felt my panic button being pushed, and looked around wildly, trying to think of something I could do. When I looked back over at Al, he fired. "Ahhh!" I cried out, as burning pain shot through my right arm. I fell back against my stereo, causing it to fall loudly to the floor.

"Tristan!" I heard Hennessy scream. She came running down the hall, looking from me to Al.

"Well, hello, Agent Cooper!" Al sung out. Hennessy ignored him, and reached out to me.

"Are you okay, baby?" she cried. I stood frozen against the wall, still trying to think of a way to get me and her out of this deadly situation, or at least, how to get her out of harm's way. I knew what a ruthless nut Al was.

"Of course he's okay. Look at him, Miss Lady. Don't he look okay?" Al looked half crazy, and I hoped that Hennessy could recognize the look in his eyes and act accordingly and not panic too much over me.

"Let her go," I said to Al. "She hasn't done anything to you, man. Just let her go, it's me you want."

"Oh, oh!" Al laughed. "So you still think you the big man, huh? Da boss man? You giving muthafuckin' orders around here?"

"Naw, you are, and I'm just telling you . . ." I cringed again as pain shot through my arm. "I'm just telling you that you don't have any reason to hurt her." Hennessy moved closer to me, wrapping her arms around my waist. Her face read fear, but in her eyes I could see her mind working, trying to figure our way out of this situation alive.

"All righty," Al said. "I have an order for you. Are you ready, boss man?" He mocked. "I want you to get on your knees, and I want you to beg me not to waste your bitch."

"Al . . ." I stammered out.

Al aimed his gun downward, shooting me in the shin. I fell to my knees, fighting hard not to cry out again in pain.

"Oh, my God!" Hennessy screamed, falling down beside me. "Oh, God, please don't, don't—"

"*I said crawl, muthafucka; beg, muthafucka!*"

"Please don't shoot her!" I screamed. "Goddamnit, what the hell do you want, Al? What do you want from me?"

Al laughed madly, proving yet again that he had snapped. "You just gave me what I wanted, and it feels sooo good." Almost in slow motion his gun rang out again; this time, his bullet was aimed at Hennessy.

"Nooooo!" I screamed, as she fell back against me. Her white blouse was stained with blood. Her eyes flickered a few times, and then closed.

"Oops, sowrry. Did I do dat?"

I didn't hear Al anymore though. I couldn't hear or see anything, but Hennessy, bundled up beside me. My mouth opened and closed in horror. "Not again," I moaned, "not again. . . ." I touched her face, streaking it with my own blood. I finally looked over at Al, narrowing my eyes.

"You faggot, coward-ass—"

"Oh, don't worry, T.J., you're gonna join her in a minute. In fact, you're gonna join her right now," Al said, laughing. His laugh was cut short, though, as rounds of bullets coursed through him. He staggered, his eyes wide in death, as he fell in a heavy heap to the floor. I looked over to the door where the shots had come from. There stood a tall, familiar-looking white man, with ice-blue eyes.

"Help her; he shot her," I cried out.

"Damn," he said, "Hennessy done got all wrapped up with the wrong people, again."

"Huh? Help her!" I demanded again. I could feel Hennessy stirring in my arms. That gave me relief to know at least she was still alive.

The man looked out the door, as if expecting someone else to walk through any minute.

"You don't remember me, do you, T.J.?" he asked, looking back toward me.

I looked at him again, still feeling something familiar about him, but unable to put my finger on it, or maybe it was the fiery pain in my arm and leg that was blocking my memory.

"No, I don't; should I? You're a cop, right?"

"Do you remember Natalie? You do remember Natalie, don't you, you no-good piece of shit!"

Recognition finally set in. His eyes were almost unforgettable. He was Nat's uncle, the same uncle who had sworn vengeance for her death a year ago.

"Yeah, see, now it's all coming to you, ain't it?" he spat. He pulled a handkerchief from his pocket, then walked over to Al Majors and picked up his gun.

"You're Natalie's uncle," I gasped out.

He laughed. "Wrong. She was the love of my life; she was *mine!* That is, until she got involved with the likes of you. And you killed her. . . ."

"I didn't . . . I didn't," I whispered, shaking my head slowly.

"Like hell you didn't! If Natalie hadn't gotten involved with you she would still be alive; she would still be with me. You killed her. . . ." The eyes of the man whom I had thought to be Natalie's uncle grew cloudy, as if he was in a daze. I looked around wildly, still trying to find a way out.

"Keep your ass still!" he said, aiming his gun at my head. I stilled immediately.

"You see, I hadn't planned on killing you, T.J. If you had gone on with your little museum robbery none of this would have happened. And look at Hennessy, bless her heart." He looked down at her, shaking his head. "She was innocence, just like Natalie. And look at her now; look at what you've done to another beautiful woman, one that was foolish enough to love you. And now, now it's come down to this."

I felt Hennessy stir again, then saw, from the corner of my eye, her reaching down to her ankle. I could hear the sounds of sirens getting closer and closer. And this crazed man in front of me, looking around at the sound of them.

"Whoa, time to end all of this," he said. "I'm gonna have to explain how Majors shot you good people, then how I hero-ically had to put him out of his misery. Hell, I should get a medal for this one." He laughed.

"You're not gonna get away with this," I said.

"Oh, but I will; I already have."

"Rogers, where are you?" someone called out. The man looked toward the door in surprise. I felt Hennessy moving again. When I looked down at her, her eyes were open, but weak. She had a small pistol, pointing toward him.

"Put the gun down, Sebastian," she whispered weakly.

"What?" he spat out. "My, how the mighty have fallen! You're gonna shoot me, Hennessy? Me who you admire so much? I don't think so. You just don't have the balls. . . ." He smiled, then looked down at her, pointing Al Major's gun in her direction. Hennessy fired. Rogers fell back, stumbling, looking down at his bloodied chest in shock. Hennessy fired again, this time hitting him square between the eyes.

"Hennessy!" a man's voice cried out from the door. Both she

and I looked up at Agent White, who had a shocked look of surprise on his face at the bloody mess before him. "What the hell?"

"It was Sebastian, Jacob," Hennessy whimpered. "It was Sebastian all along. . . ." Her body trembled convulsively, then went limp.

"Baby, don't die on me, don't!" I moaned to her. I looked up at the sight of Agent White. "Call an ambulance!"

# EPILOGUE

*Santa Fe, New Mexico (one month later) . . . Hennessy*

"Wake up, señorita, wake up."

I stirred at Aurora's soft voice. The feeling of warmth that floated into the princess room was almost like a healing to me.

"How are you feeling, Hennessy?" Aurora smiled.

"Pretty good," I said. "What do you have there?" I pointed toward the tray of goodies that I could smell tingling my nose with its tasty aroma.

"Crab cakes. Señor Tristan told me to make sure yours were well done, that you didn't like mushy fish. So, well done it is," she said, smiling.

I giggled, thinking back to when we had had our first lunch together, and crab cakes had been on the menu. "He's so thoughtful," I said to Aurora.

"Yes, he is. But I told you about that," she said, winking.

"About what?" came a voice from the door.

"Now see that, you're out there eavesdropping. You may hear the wrong thing one day." I giggled again. I had to put my hand on my stomach bandage though, still feeling the tenderness from my wound. Tristan hobbled in on his crutches.

"Oh, I won't ever hear anything but good coming from you, baby girl, I know you got nuttin' but love for me." He winked.

I flushed, looking at him warmly.

"Well," Aurora said, standing up, "I'm going to leave you two alone and get the lunch dishes cleaned up." She discreetly closed the door behind her, but not before giving me a knowing smile.

"Hi," I whispered.

"Hey," Tristan sang back. He hopped over to the bed, using his good arm to pull his hurt leg up beside me.

"We're just a mess, aren't we?" I laughed.

"A good mess though," he insisted. "I'm just glad you're okay. I was really worried there for a while."

"Oh, I'm a tough cookie, I bounce."

"Like Tigger?" Tristan joked.

"Yep," I said cockily. "So, did you talk to the guys? Are they flying in?"

"Yes, Hawk should be in tonight, and Mateo said he wouldn't be able to get a plane in till tomorrow morning."

"I can't wait to see them," I said, thinking about Mateo and his fun-loving, sweet self.

"I can't either," Tristan agreed.

After a moment of silence I said, "I still can't believe that Sebastian was so . . . so ruthless. I'm just glad that Jacob heard enough to validate our testimony as to what had happened." I sighed. "I still can't get over having shot him though."

"You had to do it, or else you and I would be dead instead of him."

"I know, but still, he and I used to be so close. It's hard to believe, to believe . . ." I sighed. "He planned to set you up all along, and he used me to help him do it. It's just so incredible that I could have been so wrong about someone I have known for so long."

"People are not always who we think they are, Hennessy," Tristan said sadly. "I feel the same way about Reynolds. *Boys* for life. I guess that don't mean much these days."

I knew he was talking about Reynolds. But just to be sure . . .

"Do you feel like you can trust me, even though I wasn't who you thought?" I asked.

"I *know* I can trust you," he said confidently.

I paused for a moment, still not sure things were completely okay with us. "And, um . . . you don't think that I'm a . . . a snake? Or like you called it, a serpent in your corner?"

Tristan laughed. "Well, if you are, then I want you to wrap yourself around me forever."

I sniffed, holding back happy tears. "Okay. I love you, Tristan James Jackson."

"I love you, too," he said, smiling softly. His hazel eyes shone brightly at me.

"And you know what? We were gonna be together any-how."

"Oh, yeah?" He laughed.

"Yep, Aurora told me."

"Told you what?" he asked.

"It's our *destino*. . . ."